The Days of Judy B

The
Days of
Judy B

ROSE HEINEY

First published in 2008 by
Short Books
3A Exmouth House
Pine Street
London EC1R 0JH

This massmarket paperback published in 2009
10 9 8 7 6 5 4 3 2 1

A CIP catalogue record for this book
is available from the British Library.

ISBN 978-1-906021-35-1

Printed in the UK by CPI Bookmarque, Croydon

Jacket design: James Nunn

To Mum, Dad and Nicholas

"...being a tardy, cold
Unprofitable chattel, fat and old,
Laden with belly, and hardly doth approach
His friends, but to break chairs, or crack a coach.
His weight is twenty stone, within two pound,
And that's made up as doth the purse abound."

BEN JONSON, THE UNDERWOOD

"Extra! Extra! Hey, look at the headline,
Historical news is being made.
Extra! Extra! They're drawing a red line
Around the biggest scoop of the decade.
A barrel of charm,
A fabulous thrill,
The biggest little headline in vaudeville!
Presenting,
In person,
That three foot six bundle of dynamite –
Baby June!"

GYPSY

The Days of Judy B

WOMEN, IT SEEMS, are making concerted efforts to take control of their lives. Last Tuesday's *Telegraph* reported that the average British woman – that fanciful skinny-jean-wearing, couscous-eating, *Grazia*-reading creature who lives precisely halfway between Islington and Salford – delights in spending her days cleaning, trimming and perfecting her house, her body, and her future. The ladies of this land, apparently, devote at least sixteen hours a week to "personal organisational activities". At the centre of this obsessive compulsive regime is "body sculpting", a practice focused largely around making oneself eminently photogenic and shaggable. A gym subscription is as much an accepted monthly outlay as a heating bill, a sports bra as necessary a garment as a pair of foxy Saturday night heels. We're all jogging and stretching and grinding our way down to sample size, with varying degrees of success.

A saturation in Pop Culture (Capitals Strictly Ironic, people), could be blamed. Or over-exposure to glossy magazines. Or the sitcoms and sketch shows where, to be mainstream-funny, one must also be acceptably svelte.

I, personally, blame September. September is the real start of the year, the time when the truest, most heartfelt resolutions are made and broken. Summer has wound down, the 4X4's cascade back into Fulham, and Octavia and Benedict are laced firmly into the new school shoes. The feeling everywhere is one of determined, perhaps irrational resolution. I will lose the weight by October, find the man of my dreams by November, meet his parents at Christmas and then start revving up for the big spring wedding. This process must, undoubtedly, begin with a few "organisational activities", and where better to start than with than one's own body.

I should, in true Judy B style, be discouraging you all. I should be saying "be happy, ladies, curves are sexy, who cares if it doesn't happen for you this year?" I should be telling you to relax, pour another glass of wine, wait for the right man to come to you. But unfortunately for you, I'm feeling rather driven at the moment. Maybe it's because my gym has just installed a new chocolate vending machine in the steam room, and suddenly I rather fancy going. Maybe it's the yummy browns and greens of the new Dune strappy sandals (the grown-ups' back-to-school shoes).

Or maybe it's because I turn twenty-four – almost halfway to thirty, a mere year off my quarter-century – in a few months, and I would like, for once, to have a real reason to celebrate, not just the annual excuse to get boozed up, shriek raucously at girlfriends, and drunkenly conjure the ghosts of boyfriends past. I want, for better or for worse, to welcome in a Brand New Me.

I don't know why I want this. But I can only say what I feel – go for it. Hit the gym. Clean that pigsty of a kitchen. Shake up your body and dust off your mind. If you want someone to love you, give them a reason to do so. And loath as I am to say it, Now Is The Time

Judy's Purchase of the Week: The new Mac fuchsia eyeshadow. Fabulous! Decadence itself, I can't wait to see who it'll lure into my web of sin…

JUDY BISHOP

1.

3rd September, 2006

Everything takes ten years longer when you're fat. Relationships must take their time to run the sordid gauntlet of bloat; confidence must jump, at length, through hoops of blubber and gunge. First impressions – for the physically becoming, a fast-track to acceptance – are your worst enemy. No-one will take a punt on a fat person. Romantically, professionally, conversationally, no-one will ever glance your way and think "Why Not?" They know precisely why not. You are adorned with splurging, quivering, shameful reasons for them to assume that you are lazy, greedy, embarrassing and bitter, dragging your deep-fried cross with you wherever you fatly try to go. It takes courage and grit for a large person to squeeze themselves into a niche that one of the great and mighty slender can, and will, occupy without a second thought. You have to run and fight, but not so much that you get sweaty and people laugh at you.

It's tough, but you get used to it. I have. I see myself, first and foremost, as a musical theatre performer. I have been an aspiring musical theatre professional for the last four years. Few people know this. Most (tens of thousands of coffee-swilling Sunday newspaper consumers, actually) know me as Judy B, everyone's third-favourite light-hearted columnist. For almost a year, I've churned out 500 jaunty words a week on a topic of my choice. I e-mail them to Olivia, the juvenile sub-editor who's absolutely thrilled to be the first recipient of Judy B's glorious weekly outpourings. She sees her own life reflected in my words – the parties, the escapades, the cheeky cocktails.

Olivia will phone me fifteen minutes after I file my copy and ask, with a polite chuckle in her voice, if I could add or cut thirty-five words, "just to make it fit". I charmingly oblige, in the knowledge that her weekly chat with me is probably one of the highlights of her fledgling professional life. Olivia has a delightful telephone manner, as do I. We stay firmly on the girly side of professional intercourse. I once saw her, from a distance, at the paper's Christmas party. She is small and taut-figured, poshly well-maintained, with smooth hair, bright eyes, and skin rendered almost translucent by the apparently regular sensual application of Eve Lom face cream. As I stood next to her at the party, I could feel my shoulders rounding, my skin getting rougher, my perfume getting cheaper and my gross, jelloid feet rolling still faster over the edges of my optimistically purchased shoes. We exchanged noises of female greeting that couldn't quite be described as words, and she expressed her pleasure at being offered the privilege of editing my column. She has now done so precisely forty-three times, the pleasure, apparently, never diminishing.

My finely polished and borderline-humorous shit will appear forty-eight hours later in the wanky little views-and-shoes "Lifestyle" section of a national newspaper. The column will generally relate, in some vague way, to the female condition, or at least to those aspects of it which I can deduce from a flick through this week's glossies, two hours in front of the telly, and a stroll along Oxford Street on a weekday afternoon. My "work" will appear under an expertly airbrushed byline photo (no jowls in the Lifestyle section, please), just above the contents list of this week's supplement – an interview with someone up-and-coming in some sexy field, a few seasonal recipes mostly involving figs and Italian ham, and six pages of photographs of moderately affordable shirt dresses, the models styled to look intelligent, sexy, and ever so slightly louche ("We want her to look like a hooker, but a hooker who's read Proust"). My writing is aimed at the desired consumer of this material, the twenty-something woman (or perhaps "gal") who flicks through the Lifestyle section while her boyfriend skims the Motoring pages, or the Sports monthly pull-out. In my editor's ideal world, they'll finish the paper, nip out for a latte, spend the afternoon watching the free DVD, share a spinach omelette, then creep upstairs to try out a cheeky little something they picked up in the page 19 sex column. The next morning they'll go off to their reasonably lucrative jobs, have a productive, sociable and stimulating urban week, then wake up next Sunday morning refreshed and ready to enjoy their next broadsheet-dictated day off.

For too long, I have contributed pleasantly to these imagined people's Sundays. I started submitting articles to the paper (always the same paper, the paper my parents bought and read, the paper I have grown up with and know as well as I would a dull and predictable husband) when I was at university. Cambridge, actually. I won't be coy about it; I got in because I did my homework, passed my A-Levels, and paid attention in my interview. I didn't charge into the university on a white horse, brandishing an ancestral shield and killing poor people. I just got in, ordinarily, from a good school, and then muddled through an English degree, and had a lovely time.

An absolutely lovely time. I expect I will devote the rest of my life to recapturing the frenetic, turbo-charged, gleeful productivity of university life. Those three years have grown only more vivid since I began to slump on into my twenties; I zoomed around the undergraduate community, acting, singing, performing comedy. I went to the Edinburgh festival twice, toured schools in Europe playing Mama Rose in the Musical Theatre Society's production of *Gypsy*, wrote and performed for the Footlights. I drank hideously and failed to hand in work, but I had a career, I had fans, and towards the end I had a position envied by ankle-biting first-years. All this in spite of being fat – properly fat; a beaming face perched atop a quivering, lipid hell, a pumpkin on a pile of tripe. Not that this stopped me from posing nude for the university "No-Diet Day" student calendar; sprawled over the counter in McDonalds with only a Big Mac box and a McFlurry to defend my modesty.

I've thought extensively about this over the last year, and I genuinely believe that I was fabulous; shining, ambitious, destined for great things. No rose-tinted spectacles are required; I was a thing of glory. No-one can take that away from me.

I supplemented my parental allowance with occasional journalistic earnings. It started in a very tiny way; in my first year I contributed three hundred words to a larger feature – for my current paper – on social events at high-powered universities. My chosen subject was the Cambridge Queerbop, a *Cage aux Folles*-themed triumph of amateurish kitsch. My take on it was one of keenly amused innocence – the chubby little bi-curious fag-hag and her big silly night out. The article was noticed; I was asked to write another. By my final year, I was publishing about two articles a term. Pocket money, nothing more. I joked with my student theatre friends about my "whoring", and how I might, possibly, keep it up later in order to supplement my "acting" wages. I was certain that there would be acting wages. I was a performer through and through, and that state had to – would – continue.

My articles were, for someone my age, witty, incisive and original enough to warrant a second glance from the editor of the LifeStyle Review section. I moved to London, lived with a flatmate – my then best friend Emma – and continued to submit my neatly structured burbling. After a year I was offered the Page 2 column; thrillingly young, pleasantly bright, eminently typical.

That's where I've been for the last year. Grinning out of my byline, exuding good cheer and casting positive thoughts over a confused and transitory world of fashion, relationships, jobs and the dreadful trials and obstacles of modern life, such as smeared make-up and the horrors of getting rocket stuck in one's teeth on a first date. I'm quite popular. I get fan mail. Not much, and often of the green ink and semen stains variety, but once a fortnight the paper passes on a few letters of praise or disagreement (not that I write much which could be disagreed with). I always reply, a charming one-liner thanking them for their interest. I sign my note "Judy Bishop", sometimes putting a little heart above the "i", instead of a dot.

It's piss-easy, the whole sordid business. Every Friday I haul myself out of bed and get into Judy B mode. My routine is sacrosanct; I drink two glasses of wine, eat a packet of Sainsbury's cupcakes, scratch my arse, put some pants on, sit at my computer, and scrabble around on the internet trying to find a news story or statistic insignificant enough to become a vehicle for whimsical feminine humour, ideally relating to the urban upper-middle classes. I write for an hour, e-mail it in to the office, then drink the rest of the wine while I wait for the polite phone call from Olivia. My chat with her always feels like a small victory; she may be slim, well-dressed, and achingly cool, but I – fat, drunk and, more often than not, naked – have just made five hundred pounds in the time it takes her to put on eyeliner.

The rest of the morning, the day, and the week, are then my own. After filing my copy, I generally take the day off. Sometimes tidy the flat. It's pretty much beyond help, to be honest. It's a bit more than a bedsit, but not quite what you'd call a pad. My desk is in a kind of ante-chamber to the kitchen, in front of a window, looking out over a few rooftops. Sometimes a cat will totter across and jump down onto the bins. I can see into a bedroom through the skylight opposite; a double bed inhabited by a young professional couple, not much older than me. They have sex with the curtains open: pedestrian, regular sex, but frequent enough that they must derive some enjoyment from it. I bet they read my column.

My desk is small, studentish, and filthy. Covered with drink-rings – wine, coffee, sugary fizzy rubbish. My Judy B beverages. I write on a middle-aged laptop; three of the keys (num lock, number seven and the plus and minus signs) are orange, sticky, and inactive, following an incident with a bottle of Taboo when I was writing Judy B's 02/07/2006 column (a fictional account of an hilarious beach holiday with girlfriends, which I, of course, never went on). The space under the desk is littered with disparate junk – my old university essays (now yellow and wilting), cupcake wrappers, Chinese takeaway menus, and the odd empty ten-pack of Marlboro lights.

Through a doorway (no door, I'm fabulously open-plan) I have a small "living area", with an obscenely large television in front of a sagging sofa, a heap of comedy DVDs (I like laughter-track studio sitcoms: *Fawlty Towers* or anything with Richard Briers and Penelope Keith), a soft chair, and a flat-pack bookshelf containing everything I should have read three years ago and still haven't. Particularly reproachful are copies of *Tristram Shandy*, *The Riverside Milton* and a small purple book called *Beginning Theory*, the spine of which is still unbroken. I have an even tinier bathroom, which announces itself to all comers as the domain of The Woman Who Has No Reason to Shave Her Legs: toothpaste, toothbrush, shower gel, moisturiser, a couple of different types of shampoo, a small and elderly make-up bag. I bulk-buy toilet roll, so have a weapons-grade stock somewhere underneath the sink. It's my big monthly outing to buy it; sometimes I even take a taxi back from Tesco to celebrate.

Out of the bathroom, across the hall, and into my bedroom, where I spend most of my time. I have a single bed with a limp, exhausted duvet in an over-washed green cover. A wardrobe full of clothes (dark, cowardly, unremarkable) including one going-out dress, a chocolate brown TopShop number that my father gave me for my birthday, two years ago now. I have three pairs of shoes: trainers, some suede lace-ups that are just one notch above trainers, and an incongruously trendy pair of heeled boots. I bought them just after I was offered the weekly column, thinking that a columnist would, inevitably, be invited to at least one party that she would want to look nice for.

And then to the rest of my bedroom, where my real life is stored. On the wall opposite my bed are three framed posters. One is what you might call a memento, a publicity poster for the Cambridge Musical Theatre Society's 2003 European Tour of *Gypsy*. It was hailed, at the time, as the most professional amateur poster ever produced for a touring student show. A1 size, my face is at the centre. I'm in costume, in character, a formidable Mama Rose with a show-stopping attitude only equalled by the power of my singing voice (I quote directly from the *Cambridge Evening News*). Next to this is a black-and-white picture of a middle-aged Stephen Sondheim at the piano. His face is rapt in concentration, eyes fierce, slightly pointed chin set, already growing a little jowly. I like to think that he's playing "Send in the Clowns" to a select audience of his peers. Below those two, forming an equilateral triangle of musical theatre glory, is a snap of Ethel Merman filling up a spotlight on the stage of Carnegie Hall, belting hard and fast, arms held high. There's no more perfect trio of images to wake up to. Below the poster display is another desk, this one larger and immaculately tidy. If you stand facing it, on the left you will see a tall pile of glossy theatre programmes, representing every musical that has been produced in greater London in the last fifteen years, chronologically ordered, the oldest at the bottom (*Phantom of the Opera*, incidentally). Obviously, most of the shows are West End staples – *Chicago, Les Miserables, Blood Brothers, Guys and Dolls, The*

Producers, *Evita*, *Whistle Down the Wind*, *We Will Rock You*, *Mary Poppins*, *The Lion King*, *Billy Elliot*, *Wicked* – but the London Fringe is not under-represented. I've got five end-of-term productions by the Italia Conti Ensemble, three seasons of lost musicals at Sadler's Well and the Pit, school plays, pub theatre, a few drama school showcases. About a hundred programmes in total. In the drawer below are my ticket stubs, seats everywhere from front stalls to the back of the upper circle, venues ranging from the Theatre Royal, Drury Lane, to the Basingstoke Anvil. I haven't been to see a show for a year or so, but the programmes remain inspirational. A lifetime of theatregoing; nights out with family, friends, alone. Fabulous, euphoric evenings that sent me reeling home, twitching with excitement, and cold, low, solitary nights of inferiority and despair at the happy, dancing poppets and their unfathomable gifts.

On the right is a signed, framed photo collage of Lorna Luft, resting on top of my CD box, wishing me "all the best for the future". Beneath the desk is my sheet music, three columns of books, about thirty anthologies and vocal scores in total: everything a female in the sixteen-to forty-five age range could ever hope to sing. I've sung it all, at some point. And perched nobly in the centre of the desk, mounted firmly on a breadboard, is the pièce de résistance, a foot-high cardboard model of a tilting larynx. It is permanently in the "tilt" position, that adopted by someone singing pleasantly in the musical theatre style. It took me five days and several attempts to make. My column that week was particularly tired and unfocused (I claimed that I'd succumbed to a five-day hangover after a rowdy hen weekend at Babington House in Somerset). The larynx looks deceptively simple, a little like a skinless rabbit. Its appearance gives no clue as to its vast, bottomless cultural significance. It could, at a glance, be mistaken for a dull or mildly revolting body part; perhaps a bit of lower colon or some hermaphroditic genitalia. But to me it represents everything that I've truly enjoyed, ever since I grew to be a sentient being. Everything that's given me a glint of pleasure, hope, or excitement, throughout my entire adult life, has stemmed from someone, on a stage, adopting appropriate laryngeal posture in order to convey narrative and emotion, ideally underneath a glitterball. Singers and singing.

Tucked quietly inside the *Musical Theatre Singer's Anthology* (mezzo-soprano/belter edition), Volume 2, is a letter. It's from the musical theatre department of a noted London music college, regarding their one year postgraduate course in musical theatre. The message is simple and direct "Dear Miss Bishop, Thank you for coming to audition for the Postgraduate Musical Theatre course. The competition has been intense, and we regret to inform you that we are unable to offer you a place on the course this year. Best wishes etc." I received this letter almost a year ago, during my final year at Cambridge. It was disappointing: a firm, resonant blow to an overstuffed ego. I recovered in the manner that one would expect of Judy B – Malibu and wisecracks – and refused to be deterred. I remain undeterred. For almost a year I have gritted my teeth and wailed into my songbooks, telling myself that this sour little bitch of a letter will not, not, not force me away from everything I love. I try to ignore the letter, its downward pull, the memento mori of life's first failure. I try to focus on the triumphs of the past; equally potent, equally valid, equally telling. I think around the letter, think of the performers in the desk, think of what they went through on the way to the spotlight. I think how like each of them I am, how I can dim the lights and become Garland, Merman, Sondheim, Streisand, Coward, LuPone, whenever I choose.

I am aware that this particular corner of my flat may be considered odd. I realise that I, perhaps, am odd. I accept that musical theatre, as a predominant passion for a twenty-three-year-old woman, is stupider than stamp collecting, more expensive than trainspotting, and often regarded with greater suspicion than, say, amateur military history or the collection of crime scene memorabilia. It's a teenage boy's obsession with science fiction, an old lady's button-box. But it is ninety-nine per cent of who I am.

The other one per cent is, of course, Judy B. Judy B, the witty urban woman with an H&M loyalty card and an acidic yet bouncy attitude towards all that her roaring twenties can throw at her. Judy B is a lie, constructed each Friday morning in a sticky, artificial rush of sugar and cheap white wine. I make my money – a comfortable amount of money for someone who leaves their unremarkable east London flat three times a week at most – by lying. Each week I dash off a first-person, autobiographical column construct-ed around a good-natured, frivolous, happy young woman, swimming brightly in the welcoming stream of popular culture. At times sharp, at times endearingly acerbic, but always, always acceptable. Mainstream. Judy B is everything I'm not, and everything that I'm determined not to be.

This perhaps makes it sound like an artful deceit, a con-scious decision to create a Sunday morning alter ego. It's not. The gap between Judy B and myself widened gradually and insidiously. Initially, the points of intersection between me and my journalistic persona were reasonable. For the first couple of months, I withheld only a tiny amount of personal information, and little that I wrote could be called an outright lie. Those aspects of myself that I was happy to turn into jokes stayed in the column; drunken slip-ups, silly portraits of my friends, the filth of my flat. I went out most nights, travelled on public transport, met the odd famous person, went to shops, watched and enjoyed telly; all this I recorded and dutifully transmitted; it was the perfect grist to my journalistic mill. I never, ever mentioned musical theatre in my column, but who cares? Even a lifestyle columnist is allowed one or two secrets. I choose to keep that which I love the most closest to me. And for a while this was fine. I was living a life, cheerful and everyday, that I was happy to share.

Then I slid quietly out of the world, and Judy B had to stay in it. I became withdrawn and eccentric, but Judy was never allowed to graduate beyond functionally quirky. She had to keep portraying a gleefully sybaritic urban life, flirting and frolicking, and I sought my pleasure in cakes, sitcom, and the great American songbook.

I realised how far the crack had opened in May, four months ago. It was a bank holiday weekend. I, little ray of sunshine, was clearly expected to write about my plans. Everything else in the supplement – motoring, gardening, food, style – was geared towards the three-day weekend: the sun, family, recreation. I had nothing. I had done nothing for a month. I had no plans. I had, admittedly, bought a Victoria sponge and a few cans of ready-mixed gin and tonic, but they were simply there to cheer me through two series of *To the Manor Born* and the original cast recording of *Oklahoma*. I had drawn the curtains on Tuesday, and planned to keep them shut for the foreseeable future.

I couldn't write that. I couldn't even put a jokey spin on it

– I, for once, couldn't see a way to capitalise on my well-sugared solitude. So I wrote a story. I wrote about a planned trip to Alton Towers with a raucous bunch of mates. We were going to eat hot dogs, and Selina the bulimic investment banker would probably be sick on the upside-down roller coaster. Outrageously gay Brian would shriek like a little girl and worry about his foundation smearing in the heat, and I was ever so excited about holding the hand of beautiful yet nervous Colin, the up-and-coming art dealer. All complete bollocks.

It was easy. Grim but easy. Like a cash-strapped glamour model giving a hand-job to a traffic warden, I jerked one out then retired into my carcass of shame. The shame subsided with each weekly pretence – the dinner parties, the insinuated shagging, the clothes, the hairstyles – it got easier and easier, and the column gradually detached itself from me.

I don't know what started all this. I can't pinpoint the moment when my job became a lie and my interest became an obsession. I can't name the day when my friends evaporated, my life started to crumble and Judy B kept on giggling across the rubble. I can't even remember when I last did laundry.

There is no excuse for my being the way I am. But this much I know: it has to change, soon. I am in the mother of all ruts; with every week that passes another exit is being boarded up. One more year and I will be trapped, alone, forever screaming out neatly formed jokes from a music-lined pit of shop-bought Battenburg cake and Sambuca. I'm nearly twenty-four; any minute now my mid-twenties will fade into late twenties, which will bloat gently along into my thirties, and before I know what's happened, I'll have crawled my way into my forties, fifties, sixties, and seventies, with nothing left but two years of eating mashed carrots in a home as a fitting preliminary to my sparsely attended DSS funeral. The clock is ticking.

There are three specific things that have to change, three starting points for the new Judy Bishop. I've had a damn good think, and these are the priorities. First, I will have sex. At the moment, I am a virgin. Not biologically – an equestrian childhood and ten years of adventurous masturbation have put paid to *that* – but I have never had sexual intercourse with another human being. I am a twenty-three-year old, overweight virgin with only three pairs of shoes. If I'd grown up in an impoverished Mormon village in rural Utah, I'm sure that I could be the subject of a heartbreaking documentary.

Second, I will triumph on stage. On stage, in lights, through song. I'm going to be in a show, a show that will send me rocketing into my real twenties, my happy twenties, with people and music and laughter. It's booked – the end of November. My singing teacher, Gareth, has sorted it out; hired me, if you will. I'm going to be in a musical revue he's putting on, at the Sydenham Bull, a fringe theatre in south east London. I don't know what my role is yet, but I have to make this work. It's my chance, my turn.

Third, with my other aims achieved and the future brightening, I will give up my column. I will steam into my editor's office and, with a throaty chuckle and a neat flick of my middle finger, hand over page 2 of the LifeStyle Review to some lissom twenty-one-year-old with three hundred pairs of shoes and a Gay Best Friend. Good for her.

It is now Sunday the 3rd of September, 2006. By the 20th of December, 2006, my twenty-fourth birthday, Judy

B will be dead. She will never, ever again listlessly vomit her post-feminist pseudo-wry bollocks over the LifeStyle Review. I will never receive another swollen cheque from News International, numerical proof that Sunday newspaper editors will chuck a few hundred quid at anything that is jaunty, accessible, female, and up for a tightly defined five-hundred-word giggle. Things must change, and autumn, as this week's column will inform you, is the time to change them.

I'm not hoping to initiate a few dozy little bursts of "self-improvement". I'm not going to cut out wheat, take up yoga, and limit myself to three caffeinated drinks a day. This isn't a fucking magazine. This is me. I'm going to bring about the Judy Bishop apocalypse. I'm going to charge into my own life and kill everything I hate. I'm going to meld together sex and songs, love and theatre, Art and Life. I'm going to get things back to the way they should have been, the way they always promised that they would be. I have fifteen weeks, fifteen more bleak Sundays to sit out until things get better. They will get better. I will get better. Steps will be taken. I write on Sundays: see you in a week.

The Days of Judy B

IT IS, OFFICIALLY, an Indian Summer. The term brings to mind a British Country House. Croquet, summer dresses. Panama hats, and the bottom of the Pimms jug. Ironed smooth lawns, faintly yellowing. The world bathed in orange and brown. Perhaps a Labrador eating a scone. All the trappings of an England that somewhere, over the rainbow at the end of the M40, may still exist. I transport you now to the sizzling sidewalks of E2. My London. We young urbanites are trying so very, very hard to enjoy the bizarre autumnal oven-blast. Legs are still bare, and jackets are still slung over shoulders. Tan lines and pedicures still matter. We should be thrilled; a country that spends ten months of the year in a slight meteorological huff is giving us a taste of the Mediterranean. Delightful.

I, personally, am not pleased. I wrote last week about back-to-school September: the sudden urge to work, to reform, to tighten up your baggy little life. This seasonal zeal presumes the cooperation of the weather. I don't need a Hebridean hailstorm battering the windows in order to clean out my wardrobe, and I accept that pelting sleet can wreak havoc with a lady's complexion. But how, how, how can people be expected to perk themselves up when the bins are festering, the cats are in the shade, and the tube still smells of curried armpit? How can you galvanise yourself into hitherto-unheard-of action when you're being environ-mentally forced to drink a long pink drink with an umbrella in it, and bare your shoulders to the sun?

It's tricky. But there is a solution to every problem that life can throw at you. Nothing is insurmountable. And the Judy B solution to the second sweltering week of September, 2006, is... wait for it... the sleeveless wrap dress. The life of the modern woman should be woven from a rich tapestry of wrap dresses. Plain, print, long, short, cheap, luxurious, vintage. No other garment can cover you up, keep you cool, take you to work, then, when paired with a Martini, subtly morph into the mother of all flirt-frocks. The right wrap can get you a non-executive directorship and a boyfriend within the same half-hour. I kid you not.

Now, in the educative spirit which you know I hold so dear, I'd like to end with a parable. Last Sunday I went to an antique sale in Buckinghamshire, with a group of fellow floozies-who-wish-to-appear-cultured. We met and befriended a charming middle-aged woman named Tamara. She told us the story of her 23-year-old son, who suffers from gender dysphoria. He had taken, in late adolescence, to wearing a basque. This displeased his magistrate father, who wished to have him removed entirely from the family. But Tamara, bless her, valued the solidity of the family unit above all else, and snuffled around plus-size clothes shops in search of a sartorial compromise. She eventually found, at the back of an unpromising Sue Ryder shop – you guessed it – a beige mock-Diane Von Furstenberg wrap dress. Her son loved it, imagining himself grinding on Andy Warhol's lap in Studio 54, and his father thought that it was an alpha-male medieval battle tunic. All were overjoyed, and they lived happily ever after, selling 18th-century chamber pots in rural Buckinghamshire.

Ponder the story, then hit the high street. If it can work for them, it can work for you. Flounce around in your purchase while the sun shines, then pair it with tights and a coat for the big chill. Happy to have helped.

Judy's Purchase of the Week: Take a wild guess – 14 wrap dresses of equal fabulousness, paid for with not a hint of guilt. I am sex!

JUDY BISHOP

2.

I'd like to describe my body. Not the way I would describe it – have described it – in my column (apple-shaped, lush, fun, Rubenesque) but the way it actually is. The sticky, contemptible mess upon which I gaze, day after day. I rarely consider my body other than in the abstract: something which holds me back, keeps me in, an unwelcome, unthinkable appendage to what remains of my life. It takes a fair bit of courage to look at it face on. To touch it, squeeze it, assess the damage that I've done.

Let's work upwards. The feet are unkempt (actually, I resent the idea that feet should ever be aesthetically maintained). No ankles to speak of. Unspeakable inches of chubby, mottled leg, knees only discernable when I bend them. The tops of the thighs bulge out, balloons swathed in uncooked pastry. This would make me pear-shaped – perhaps, pleasantly so – if it weren't for the stomach. The great, rolling hell of stomach. The sagging ball which conceals the never-considered tufts of pubic hair. My stomach, from the side, forms a great, loose, irregular arc. If I were a middle-aged man, it would be a beer gut. If I were pregnant, it would be large but fine. As it is, it is inexcusable. The legacy of twenty-three years of eating eating eating, tens of thousands of meals, countless snacks. Not a bad metabolism, nothing to do with glands. I am healthy, just uncontrolled. Not even uncontrolled; I merely decided at some unidentifiable point that I didn't need to suppress my lower urges. There's the possibility of a waist; if I were girdled and hemmed in and strapped up like a war-wound victim, I could just about conjure a waist.

And so to my breasts, my last hope of sexual redemption. Big, round, prominent, loosely youthful. Nevertheless, they are breasts for feeding children and cuddling sick farm animals up against, not breasts to shimmy in the face of an aroused man.

Up the neck, past the chins, to the face. Aggressively red cheeks. The cheeks once represented health and good cheer. Perhaps with a little touch of the rubicund, saucy drunk about them, but good cheer, nonetheless. Now, as everything else has rotted and sagged, they've glowed on mercilessly, emitting the constant stored heat of the fat person. My eyes are nice. I think they may only have a year or so more of being nice, but they do have a certain quality about them, a certain sparkle. If I wear mascara, they look, I think, fantastic. I have thick, curly, shoulder-length hair. Not cut for a year or so, and somehow unwilling to fulfil its potential as a bouncy little lion's mane. I mostly wear it tied back.

So that's me, naked. So horrendous, so unfathomable to anyone who knows my job, my background, my education, all the privilege hurled at me throughout my life. To be a physical mess is reasonable, I think, if your life is a glorious maelstrom of generous thought and activity. Start a major charity, love a large family, galvanise a generation of thinkers with a new philosophical concept and, yes, you have absolute permission to look like a sack of hammers. But when you live entirely for yourself, writing about self-image and obsessing over your own petty desires, you surrender the right to be an aesthetic and physical catastrophe. You've had the time to become beautiful. Jowls and lumps and snarls and sweat simply betray that you've followed the wrong path of self-indulgence. The sushi-guzzling Manolo-whores at least illuminate cities and fill magazines with their abs and gloss and serum. They at least provide a template, an ideal of the perfect Western woman with her perfect Western look. I, as a person, contribute nothing to the world's concept of beauty. I have nothing to do with anything. I'm just a lumpen, slothful piece of flesh, cocooned in two rooms for twelve months, bloating gently. A venom-free jellyfish.

I'm feeling, as you may have gathered, slightly low. Week 1 of the Great Overhaul has not been an unmitigated triumph. And now it's Sunday again, Judy B is shrieking up at me from my paper like a frenzied urban hyena, and my life has progressed... well, a little. A tiny bit. Not as much as it should have. I took Monday off. Not a great start, one might think, to a fifteen-week regimen of panicked, transformative dynamism, but it was necessary. And when I take a day off, it really, truly is a day off. I could teach the working world a thing or two about weekly self-annihilation for the purposes of recreation. No walks in the park, chatting or social yoga classes, not for Judy Bishop. No group nights out and fun communal hangovers. Just a day of allowing oneself to sink into the ooze of minute-by-minute self-satisfaction, devoid of guilt. A day of rest.

I began the day in tears, as I always do on Monday. Post-traumatic hangover from seeing this week's Judy B in print, and an awareness that the rest of the world hates Mondays for entirely different, far better reasons. I woke at eight, and immediately started thinking of all the mothers in the world dressing their children for school and bundling them into cars. That, naturally, got me thinking about packed lunches. I went to the kitchen, made myself a peanut butter sandwich, wrapped it in cling film, put it in a lunchbox, took it out of the lunchbox, unwrapped it, and ate it. Also a tiny little pot of Petit Filous, a carton of orange juice, a two-finger KitKat, and a bag of sherbert flying saucers (the most difficult food to eat whilst crying hysterically, I've found – the sherbert mingled with the mucus in one's nose creating a sensation not unlike snorting strong mustard mayonnaise). I went back to bed, slept until one, and woke again thinking of all the people who go to work, and are probably just beginning constructive yet amicable business lunches. So I got up and made myself a constructive yet amicable business lunch. A tomato and mozzarella wrap, chocolate mousse, and two glasses of Chenin Blanc.

Then to the afternoon's activities: an hour of staring at the cat on the bins, two hours in an internet chatroom speculating as to the possibility of Bette Midler returning to the Broadway stage (unlikely, but we anonymous members of BizChat.com are eternal optimists), and six episodes of *Fawlty Towers*. Then three hours looking for new pictures of Bernadette Peters on Google – I'm sure I've exhausted the internet's supply, a source of perverse pride at my own dedication. The rest of the Chenin Blanc to see me off to sleep, and that's Monday dealt with.

On Tuesday, I was woken at ten by the bleeping of my phone. A rare occurrence, as you'll have gathered. The synthetic doorbell noise of an incoming text alarmed me. I wondered, briefly, if there'd been some kind of disaster: my mum, my dad, my sister. But that wouldn't be a text, would it? I don't know. I'd probably send a text to convey the news that I'd been horribly maimed. My disaster would deserve little more dignity than that, I'm sure. I opened my eyes and rolled over. The text was probably from Vodafone. Or from the gym I joined three years ago and never left. Or an unwelcome round-robin limerick from someone with whom I've long since lost touch, full of smileys and emoticons. I looked at the phone.

"Judy, cud we make it 2pm today? I have to go to the doctor. Cheers, Gareth. x"

Gareth, my singing teacher. I've been seeing him once a week, every week, for just over a year. We were due to meet today at twelve-thirty, as usual at his flat in Archway. But yes, Gareth, I can move it to two o'clock, no problem. You know that. You are well aware of the flexibility of my schedule. I replied;

"Yep, fine. See you at two."

I withheld the kiss at the end. No fake affection. He'd pissed me off by forcing me to reveal to him just how empty my Tuesdays were, to make it clear that he could fling the time of my lesson back and forth as he wished, without disturbing a single other personal or professional commitment. Fucker. My phone bleeped back into life.

"Cheers Judy! Ps. I've got a new sweater. Diamond patterned. I think you'll like it….x"

Why would I like his new sweater? I've never, ever

commented on an item of his clothing, nor expressed any particular sartorial taste of my own. Then I remembered: four months ago, we had a little chat about patterned clothes. How silly they were. Golf trousers and things. I smiled at the memory, surprising myself, and replied:

"Ooh, goodee. Looking forward to it. Judy x"

Strange that I'd forgotten.

I got up to choose some music for the afternoon's lesson. I needed a lift, clearly. Something uptempo. But that's a risk when you're a bit low; if you can't pull it off then the jauntiness will just hammer away at you, taunting and poking, until a lump rises in your throat and you stand there, reddening, like a mute, pie-faced toddler as the piano bashes on beneath you. I put the Irving Berlin songbook to one side, and kept looking. *Gypsy*. Yes, *Gypsy*. That would do for today. Familiar, stewed in memories, but as yet unconquered by negative association. It's too great a show to become entrapped in, even in my web of retrospective embarrassment and disgust. The spirit of Mama Rose can bust through any mindset, stamping and belting and slamming her fists on the table, telling you that anybody who stays home is dead, and that if she dies it won't be from sitting, it'll be from fighting to Get Up and Get Out. Even on the page, even when she's just lifeless notes and suggested words, Mama Rose jumps out and screams at you to get dressed, cheer up, live your life, and stop giving a fuck whose ribs you crush in the process.

I turned to the third song in the score, "Some People". In "Some People", Rose is trying to persuade her father to give her eighty-eight bucks in order that she might take her children's vaudeville act to LA to play the prestigious Orpheum Circuit. She sings of her unwillingness to settle for the life that others sink so resignedly into, pleads with her father for the money, and when it's refused, hurls herself at him with a sound that not even the purest and most reserved of performers could stop from being cacophonous. It's meant to be cacophonous, it's meant to be the biggest, bravest noise that a woman can make, representing one of the best things that anyone can ever do: Get Up and Get Out. The song is a hymn to bullish delusion, a launch pad from which one of the mightiest characters ever created can ascend in a storm of resolution, courage and feminine grit. It's my song.

Frank Rich claimed, reviewing the 1989 New York revival of the show, that *Gypsy* was "Broadway's own brassy, unlikely answer to *King Lear*". He's wrong. *Gypsy* transcends *King Lear*, just as it transcends everything else in art and life. If that show had not been written, my life would be much, much worse. I might not even be alive any more. If it hadn't been for *Gypsy*, then I wouldn't have spent the Summer of 2003 in a state of unknowable bliss, singing, dancing, laughing my way round Europe with all the people who used to be my friends: Phillip, Adam, Julia, Maddy, Sarah, Ian, and my ex-best friend Emma. Tiny blonde Emma, who played the title role. Louise, the gauche adolescent who becomes Miss Gypsy Rose Lee. If it hadn't been for *Gypsy*, I would never have done tequila shots off a war memorial, never have persuaded the entire ensemble to board the night bus to Budapest, never have been called a legend, a belter, the life and soul of everything. *Gypsy* is a reason to go on living and, in my view, the sole reason to procreate and bring children into this otherwise flawed and unfathomable world. *Gypsy* will never die.

I'd been sitting on the carpet for some time, humming

away, before I remembered that I was still completely nude. This was not at all in keeping with the spirit of Mama Rose. I pulled on tracksuit bottoms and a hoodie, and began to gird myself for my singing lesson. It's a big deal. Still, after a year, my singing lessons are A Big Deal. They're the pivot around which my weeks spin. If a lesson has been good, then I am well. I'll tend to stay well for hours, days even, if I know that I've used everything within me to the best of my ability, impressed Gareth, surprised myself. My mind will become fractionally more open to positivity. I'll stand up straight, look shopkeepers in the eye, make my bed, brush my hair, chew my food, all the while knowing that I have a secret, wonderful skill, something which no-one would guess from looking at me. If a lesson has been bad, then the opposite will occur. Food, sludge, beer, fags, desperation. My sad little life, in savage, horrendous technicolour.

I get physically nervous about ten minutes before, when I'm on the bus. My stomach flips over and over, my chest knots. I like this – I like the adrenalin, and the sense of occasion that it generates. My Weekly Singing Lesson. I calm myself by writing out Gareth's cheque in advance, folding it neatly, and tucking it into my purse to be pressed into his sticky, grateful man-hand at the end of the lesson. I then take my music out of the folder – all loose sheets, photocopied for ease of carrying – and look over it, trying to think of some intelligent comments about the work and practice I've done that week.

I stopped learning anything from Gareth about eight months ago. We romped for a while through the rudiments of vocal quality, song interpretation, technique, and repertoire-building. Then, at some point, we both realised that we were going nowhere, and we both refused professionally to acknowledge the fact. He needed money, and I needed to keep on seeing him. Now we plod along with each other, just about comfortable. It suits us well. I'm hoping that the show, Gareth's show, will revitalise our union. It matters as much to him as it does to me; if it goes well, we'll both make strides, move towards our new selves. It's an exciting time.

I got off the bus and crossed the road to Gareth's flat. He lives alone, above a shop; a nondescript food 'n' wine emporium stocking beer, noodles, chicken tikka pasties and overpriced, inedible bricks of cheese. On a main road, teeming with buses and dry cleaners and kebab shops and old ladies in tracksuits smoking cheap cigarettes. I pressed his buzzer. No response. Tried again. Still nothing. I got out my phone, about to call, when a small, wiry, light-stepping vision sprang into view, preceded by a slightly fey tenor:

"Judy! Judy Bishop!"

The first thing that struck me about Gareth was, indeed, his sweater. Diamond patterned, as promised. Red, yellow, and green, woven from a material slightly shinier than wool, slightly thicker than polyester. A little too small, it stretched over his slender frame, the diamonds distorted. It had a shabbily widening effect, a children's entertainer fallen on hard times, or an exiled court jester on his jaunty way to the gallows. He brandished his key.

"Up we go, Miss Bishop! To the Room of Art."

He chuckled. He likes that joke.

The Room of Art is Gareth's bedsit. Tiny, really truly tiny, with the air of somewhere that has been loved too much for too long. Every space is occupied with desperate affectations of wealth, education, and gentility. Turkish rugs, Victorian tea-caddies, a record player, a 1930s hat-stand. Framed posters of operatic divas: Joan Sutherland,

Maria Callas, Dame Nellie Melba Books, lots and lots of books. Stuffed, toppling shelves of cheap romantic fiction, opera synopses, medieval poetry, comic verse, Proust, bibles, memoirs, Austen, Dickens, Jilly Cooper, Roald Dahl. Stacks of music: opera and Victorian operetta mostly, with the odd more modern songbook. Jerome Kern, Ivor Novello, Noel Coward. It's a room assembled over years to give the impression of artful whimsy, a magically eclectic cultural sensibility. It suggests, in fact, a life pilfered from a skip. A wilting student life: unfocused, scrappy, Peter Pan's weird big brother. A once-earnest twenty-eight-year-old who wishes that he knew more about opera, cheering himself up of an evening with an Edward Lear story, picking sadly at a tin of tuna and wishing it was gravadlax, wondering if he should have taken that job at the Carphone Warehouse after all.

I'm aware that it's an act of great vulgarity on my part to crash weekly into this flat, brandishing my showtunes and demanding tuition. I'm shattering a mood, intruding trashily into something tenuously contrived, a Malteser diving into a bowl of lobster bisque. Nevertheless, Gareth is always welcoming.

"And how are we today, Miss Judy Bishop?"

He speaks as if he's older than he is: old, in fact – like someone born in the twenties, a boulevardier, a cultured dandy. Perhaps he's wishing the years away, or pretending, or hankering for a place where he can never go. I like him. I pity him.

He pulled the keyboard out from under the sofa-bed, placed it on the junk-shop table, and sat down heavily on a footstool. There was a frightening moment as the stool shuddered and began to topple, its marginally shorter third leg dictating the angle of descent. I imagined Gareth crashing over sideways with a shriek and a thud, the wobbling detritus of the flat toppling down around us, choking us in mushroom clouds of dust and plaster and elderly scrambled egg. The stool stood on bravely, and the moment receded.

"I'm well, thank you, Gareth. Yourself?"

"Oh, you know," he kicked off his shoes. "Two hours in the doctor's waiting room, and you still never get what you want, do you?"

"Oh. Is everything OK?"

Why? Why did I ask that? He'll tell me. And I don't want to know. He could have worms, or lice, or scabies, or an STD. And if he does, he'll tell me, I know he will. Fuck.

"Yes, no drama. My granny's not very well."

"I'm sorry. Did you take her to the doctor's?"

"No, I just went by myself. Was wondering how long she's likely to have left. Told him her symptoms, got an opinion. All fine."

"Oh. That's… nice."

God, what a deeply peculiar little man he is.

"So, what do you have for me today, Miss Judy Bishop?"

"Um… well, I've got 'Some People'. From *Gypsy*. I already know it – I did it, actually, when I was a student, but I'm thinking of working it up again, you know, sorting it out – because – I really want that show – your show – to be good – and I don't want to fuck it up, because, I'm… flattered to be asked. It might be shit. I mean – I might be shit. Will be shit. But I thought we could look… at it. 'Some People'."

Bollocks. I'd rehearsed that. For a week, I'd been mentally crystallising my life-changing philosophy into a masterwork of rhetoric, a great galvanising speech of determination and refreshment. Gareth was to be the first blessed recipient of this monologue, and I strongly suspected that it would, in its poetic beauty, change his life as much as it would mine. Tonally, I was planning on pitching it somewhere between Winston Churchill and Henry V, with a light seasoning of Mae West. Oh well.

Gareth smiled, and replied.

"Of course. I'm delighted to have you on board. And it'd be good to have something belty under your belt, as it were. Let's have a look at this."

Gareth scanned the music, and had a quick play through the opening bars. He's not the greatest of pianists, even I can see that. He stops, oddly, in the middle of phrases, creates chords that bear little relation to the song in question, wobbles precariously on his footstool, and occasionally stops mid-flow, with a burst of uncomfortable, raucous laughter and a self-deprecating shriek. But we tend to get through it; we're not vain. He's hiring a pianist for the revue, thank goodness. He played, and I sang.

For a while, I was lifted by the music. I felt happy, easy, comfortable with the sounds I was making. The stuffy bedsit receded, and I grew in stature. My body became an instrument, for once acceptable and useful, even bordering on glorious. Noise ripped from my stomach, lashed at the curtains, bounced off the ceiling. I was winning; beating it all, doing something that I do well, and doing it fast and strong.

Then, a bleep. Once again, the synthetic doorbell of an incoming text. Gareth's phone, this time. The piano stopped, surprising me. I carried on singing for a second or two, overshooting the accompaniment. I stopped and looked at Gareth, who was groping in his trouser pocket, producing his phone, reading his text message, and emitting peals of mirth at its content. I felt myself getting redder and hotter and more pathetic by the minute. How could he answer a text? I'd been singing, belting. I'd been Mama Rose. Was I so mundane, so pathetic, so lamentable, contemptible, forgettable that I couldn't even distract my singing teacher from his phone, during the finite period when I was paying for his attention?

He put the phone back in his pocket, and played on. Everything was wrong, now. My shoulders rounded, my throat tightened, tears stung the back of my eyes. Nothing felt right, nothing sounded right. I wanted to leave; more than anything I wanted to get out of that hot little room, out from under Nellie Melba's dumb, pie-faced gaze, away from the hat-stand and the keyboard and the shrieking, unmusical Welshman still smirking at the memory of his text message. Suddenly the lesson had become a torture; singing this song, in this state, when everything was wrong. I stopped.

"I'm sorry, Gareth, I don't feel well. Ought to go, I think."

He looked concerned. Too late for that.

"Oh, love. Is it – can I – would you like some Gaviscon?"

He indicated a pink bottle of the stuff, about the size of his thigh.

"No, thank you. A migraine, I think. Best to go."

I handed him his cheque. He took it without protest, and bade me farewell.

I left his flat and got on the bus. I got off in Camden, went to the off-licence, bought a two-litre bottle of

Strongbow and ten fags, then got back on. I ogled the mid-afternoon bus crowd. Two boys in school uniform, off to rob some shops. A few nondescript, middle-sized, functional-looking women. And an old lady with a kind face. I bet she's led a long, full life. I wanedt to ask her how she did it, to know about all the relationships she's formed and the ambitions she's fulfilled. I didn't see any likely LifeStyle Review readers. They'll all be off in the City, eating Thai salads and watching the light bounce off each other's hair.

I thought, as my bus mates and I crawled idly through Kentish Town, about suicide. I've thought a lot about suicide in the last year. To be honest, I don't think it's really for me. Suicide is for the disordered, the complex, the mercurial. It requires courage – grotesquely misapplied courage, but courage, nonetheless. It is a firm, decisive act, the product of planning and diligence. And one long, deep, final breath. I'm not capable of that. I have no personal moral qualm with the idea of destroying myself – no-one would suffer that much, or for that long. My editors would be surprised and embarrassed, but so would they be if they knew about my obesity, virginity, solitude, or my Broadway fetish. I neither know nor care what my parents would think. I'm sorry about that. No, my problem with suicide is not ideological, but practical. My chubby, amorphous mind could never readjust itself to accommodate such a massive act, my grim fat body could never heave itself to the medicine cabinet, or to the top of the building, or to wherever it is that one goes to buy a gun. I don't want to die, or actively to make the transition into death. I just want to slip away, which I suppose is what, in effect, I've already done, at the grand old age of twenty-three. Congratulations, Judy Bishop.

I got off the bus, waddled back to my flat, and spent a mirthless couple of hours with the Strongbow, *Steptoe and Son*, and half a crispy duck. Then to bed, alone, curled up under the thin green duvet.

On reflection, it hasn't been a bad week. I may have stumbled into something of a trough, but I can still face the idea of climbing out of it again. I may have grown a tad more disgusted with myself, but that disgust will, surely, only goad me on into more decisive action. I think, actually, that I've been trying to attack things in the wrong order. My singing lesson, my day off, and the five borderline-bedridden days that followed were typical of my old, corpulent habits, and I can't expect to eliminate them instantly just because I think that I might want to. I need to change the thing that bothers me the most, the thing that separates me from all other secularly minded, healthy women of my age. I need to be fucked, or made love to, or shown the ways of the world, or to be transformed from a vastly overgrown schoolgirl into a working, potentially reproductive woman. I need to have sex. A long, deep, final breath. Next week, I will have sex. Wish me luck.

The Days of Judy B

LAST WEEK, 327,000 thirteen to sixteen-year-olds had underage sex – in a variety of different time-frames and locations, you understand, not all together in a sort of mad pubescent orgy. But still, 327,000 tiny little ladies and gentlemen have, in the last seven days, surrendered themselves to puerile lust.

I would bet that one or two of them are now pregnant. A few others will have diseases. Probably not many have told their mothers what they've been up to. Some of them will be smuttily proud of themselves, others will be devastated, ruined, used. One or two of them may seek to end their own lives. The midget shaggers must, surely, come from all social demographics: boarding school dormitory cubicles will be polluted as much as south London bus shelters, Boden rugby shirts will have been dropped tentatively to the floor along with kebab-stained hoodies.

I say, frankly, hooray. Hooray for all the lusty young swains and their whorish Lolitas. Good on them. Controversial, I warrant you, but I believe passionately (if not lustily) that one's first sexual experience should be dealt with when one is likely to have another seventy-odd years of life left to recover from it. One issue that modern education tends to sidestep: sex will wound you, without a shadow of a doubt, so best accept the wound while you're too off your face on snakebite and hormones to care. There are few things more excruciating than a thoughtful, respectful sexual encounter between two adults, during which both are fully aware of what is going on and of its ramifications.

I had a dinner party the other day, and as the couscous got cold, the conversation got steamy. The gin-fuelled chat lost, inevitably, whatever sheen of gentility and restraint it may once have had, and we started to talk about virginity. More specifically, losing it.

The tales would make your skin crawl. There was the investment banker who fatally stained a piece of Louis IX furniture on a school trip to Versailles, and who still has a standing order to pay for it. There was the foxy young advertising girl who set fire to a haystack with her first post-coital Marlboro, causing a barn-fire which killed three donkeys. There was the woman who believes that she may still, fourteen years on, have a male contraceptive floating around somewhere in her lower abdomen.

And then, of course, there's me, Judy B. And I'm not telling. Even a boozy lady has the right to a couple of secrets.

And that's the moral to this sexual tale – don't tell. It's probably too horrendous for others to cope with. My friends all humiliated themselves roundly by revealing the price they paid for giving free rein to their loins, and I wisely kept schtum. Let me just say this; either get it over with when you're fourteen and shit-faced, or don't bother. Ever.

Judy B's Purchase of the Week: A peep-hole bra and some French knickers with no arse. Hilarious.

JUDY BISHOP

3.

If you can't get laid in Ipswich, give up. The same is true, apparently, of the passing-out ball at the Sandhurst Royal Military Academy. There are certain places where, if you make yourself completely available, you will get fucked. And if you can't, then you are for some reason unfuckable, and you must live with that fact.

Let me talk you through my decision to spend Wednesday night in a Novotel in Ipswich. This week, as you know, I had planned to have sex. I wondered, idly as ever, where precisely people go to do such a thing. A lifetime of late-night TV and dull misinterpretation of other people's conversations led me to believe that easy, no-strings sex happened either in the marital bedroom (not an option), or in Soho. So, on Monday morning, I went to Soho on a recce. Not promising. I trudged up Greek Street, ducked in and out of Shaftesbury Avenue, walked passed clean, shut, unfriendly clubs in alleys. I saw herds and herds of lean, clean, honed young people; people of lattes and taxis and chats and the media, their spectacular clothes irrelevant when pressed against their mainstream sex-bodies. I would not have sexual intercourse with any of these people. Quite apart from the fact that none of them would want to have sex with me, I have no desire to enter their lives, to add any more sensual or anecdotal texture to their already gleaming, thrilling, artistically corrugated evenings. We are a different species, they and I; entertaining as it would be to throw a bison into a goldfish pond and watch it flounder, I'm staying well away. They can fuck themselves, and each other.

I walked home, glum and fetid, and pondered my possible sexual milieu. I have, in the past few days, forced myself to believe that everyone has a sex-place, and they must simply be willing to trawl the depths of the recreational world in order to find it. I considered my own position on the sexual ladder. I concluded that I could, with time, commitment, and enthusiasm, haul myself up to the bottom end of "mediocre". I do have one thing strongly in my favour: I am very, very available. A gift, if you like. A slightly embarrassing Christmas gift from a tasteless aunt, but a gift, nonetheless. I'll even buy my own drinks. I don't want to chat, I don't want to know you, I just want a brief and perfunctory seeing-to. It doesn't have to be good. I wouldn't know whether it was or not. I am the opposite of picky. That must count for something, in Sex World. No-one need know that I'm twenty-three, or that I live more alone than most lucky, functional people can even imagine. No-one need know that I'm shagging to a deadline. I'm perfectly content just to be meat – quite bad meat, a burger from a van or a £2.99 kofte kebab. I am very, very easy.

As I neared Bethnal Green – wondering where in the world ease of access to a slightly dodgy erotic funhouse might be most appreciated – I saw a wheelie-bin, the contents as bad as those of any wheelie-bin I have ever seen. Leaking bin-bags, noxious fast-food containers and – the icing on the shit-cake – a roll of old, orange-and-brown patterned carpet upon which someone had vomited lavishly. I stopped and stared, and thought of Ipswich.

Ipswich, the town of my unsuccessful adolescence, of my first badly aimed alco-vomit. I remembered my first Big Night Out, aged fourteen, with three bootfaced, hair-gelled schoolgirls who scared the life out of me and whom I wanted to impress more than anything. I remembered the sixteen-year-old GCSE dropout who had bent me over the post office railings and rammed his furry, wet, flaccid tongue down my tragically welcoming throat. He had wanted to have sex with me. It wouldn't have taken a moment; we were both wearing tracksuits. I wouldn't even have had to take anything off – merely yanked down my elastic waistband, moved my clean white pants a few inches down or to the side, waited draughtily while he fumbled with a condom, then stood there and taken it. But I didn't; I said no. Like a child stamping its foot on a school morning, I Said No. I thought that I could do better, that within a few years I would be ready for someone who was ready for me. Idiot.

So now, almost ten years later, I must admit my error, and go back to Ipswich. I decided, on Monday afternoon, that I would find the tongue-boy, or someone like him, and I would, if necessary, beg him to do what so nearly got done to me, so long ago. Everything would be sorted out in Ipswich.

I packed a bag on Wednesday morning. Functional underwear, plain black. Nothing fancy; no point sugaring the pill. A going-out outfit, carefully selected from the trash-racks of Matalan: short skirt, gold strappy top, enormous pleather belt, heels. Clothes designed for a pixie, copied and blown up by a rip-off shop to pander to the delusions of fat women. Polyester, nylon; trash. I will be trash. I am trash. I am throbbing, dancing, grinding, shagging, shameless trash. I topped off the bag with three bottles of Cherry Lambrini and a couple of vodka miniatures, just in case. As an afterthought, I added an old pair of devil-horn deeley-boppers that I was given for a party in my last year at Cambridge. The plastic has begun to perish and they no longer flash, but the design is, I think, evocative and timeless.

Armed and ready, I boarded the five-thirty from Liverpool Street. I squeezed myself between two middle-aged, suited city workers, doubtless on their way back to cherubic children and a glossy Suffolk wife. Sad acts. Conformists. Fuck them. I downed a vodka miniature, closed my eyes, and concentrated on making my loins throb. Trash. Shrieking, throbbing, grinding trash. A sexual behemoth, a big juicy lust-monster. Judy Bishop: animal. The other vodka, some more thoughts, and I was there. Ipswich. Home.

The panorama that faces you when you step out of Ipswich station is one of benign provincial bleakness unsurpassed, I think, by any other British town. Peterborough makes the runner-up position, and Stevenage does its best. But Ipswich seems to be the end of a certain road, a vortex of boredom and mediocrity. The effect of the great knot of roundabouts, the immediately visible proliferation of carpet shops, and the joyless hostelries is one of insidious stultification. This becomes, within hours, strangely appealing. Stroll around the station car park, peer over the edge of the multi-storey, maybe vandalise one of the pay and display machines, and you can quickly see the appeal of becoming an Ipswich Person. You get up, hop in the Mazda, drive around the roundabout for a bit, purchase miles and miles of carpet, then sit, catatonic, in the Station Hotel, inhaling local bitter until the next dreary little day rolls along and whacks you in the back of the head.

Perhaps, I thought, as I wandered out of the station, I'm meant to be an Ipswich Person. Perhaps I've been setting the bar too high for the last eight years. Not just sexually; perhaps I, in all aspects of my life, am more suited to the grimly humdrum. Here in Ipswich, my life wouldn't be so incongruously pathetic. Many, many people here live in quiet little boxes, eating, sleeping, and watching things they like. No-one here has to deal with passing flashes of urban colour. Fat people here aren't tormented by physical perfection and by the preoccupations of London: progress, creativity, fun. In Ipswich you just get on with it. Maybe always a couple of notches below happy, but existing contentedly. If I moved back to Ipswich, I might become integrated; I could live on the Kesgrave roundabout and watch traffic accidents, I could make a few glum little friends, perhaps take a pottery course at Suffolk College. I could meld seamlessly into the globular indolence of fast food, half-empty cinemas, Woolworths. I could join coach parties and see *Mamma Mia* once every six months. I could grow old and fade away, comfortable in the knowledge that no-one would ever think about me again. Moving to Ipswich would, in fact, be the perfect Judy Bishop form of suicide.

But I'm too stubborn even for that. This week, at least, I was feeling grimly pig-headed. I will not do what's best for me and best for London. I will take whatever Ipswich on a

Wednesday night has to offer in the form of 0.2 fluid ounces of semen, then leave, returning to London a better, more functional person.

I went to the station toilet, downed half a bottle of Cherry Lambrini, and checked into the Novotel. The receptionist was a full-on Ipswich Person: nylon shirt, chain-store shoes, make-up applied with a bacteria-caked flannel.

"A double room, please, one night only."

"And how many people will be using the room?"

"Two."

She tapped my sexual destiny into her computer.

"OK, and when will your partner be arriving?"

"Not until late."

The transaction completed, she pasted on her best I've-got-a-GNVQ-in-hospitality smile and commenced professional chat.

"Are you here on business or pleasure, Miss Bishop?"

I stared at her – jaw locked, heart thumping.

"Business."

A bottle of Cherry Lambrini exploded in my bag.

• • •

I spent two hours in my room – my boudoir, if you will. I watched the local news: a farm machinery fair, a new flyover, and four non-fatal knife attacks. I then trashed myself up. Swigging all the while at the sticky pink fizz, I smeared my face in base and shadow and gloss. I rammed my lard into the sparkly baby elephant outfit – taking a certain surprised pleasure in the oddly firm contour of my breasts – and let the shoe-straps pinch through the skin of my unaccustomed feet. My hair was basted down with cheap, harsh, spray; facial heat made my foundation a glaze. I didn't give a shit. I was in Ipswich, I was drunk, and I was a fat bird on the lash. Perhaps this is my niche. God bless East Anglia.

I went to Liquid. Liquid arrived in Ipswich when I was in the sixth form, and Suffolk's youth rejoiced. The arrival of Liquid was more of a compliment to us than Suffolk College being awarded university status, more of a shove up the national ladder than the restoration of the Norman church. The Liquid chain's selection of our humble town for a new nighterie was a true recognition of our communal worth; it placed us on a par with Harlow, Wrexham, Lancaster, and Nuneaton. It proved that we could shag and grind and stab with the likes of Newbury, Mansfield, Hanley, and Wigan. It was a glorious day; you're not a true provincial shithole until you've got a Liquid. Admittedly, I didn't see myself back there at twenty-three, still hunting for the same shag I was hunting for at fourteen, but there you go. Life is full of surprises.

I paid my three pounds and tottered into the main arena. To my surprise, it was Foam Night. Every Wednesday, apparently, is Foam Night. A side room was given over to heaving waves of wet synthetic fluff, spasmodically illuminated with strobe. I wondered briefly about the omnipresent electrical equipment, then had three shots of Sambuca and stopped caring.

The music was as loud as one would hope. Pop, cheese, soft hip-hop. I could only make out a few tracks: Girls Aloud's "Jump" – a throbbing exhortation to hurl yourself about if you want to taste their kisses in the night – Christina Aguilera, old Atomic Kitten, some "classic" club tracks from the mid-nineties. A great mash of a playlist, all desperately geared towards a wicked night out.

The clientele were not threatening. Little girls, fuzzy teenage boys, a hen night, all of whom were fatter than me. Gangs of beery lads, too sad and floppy to be carrying knives or guns. Not scary. Not cool. Not interesting. Perfect. I decided to keep drinking and see what happened. Over an hour or so I worked up a routine. I would get a drink from the bar and circumnavigate the room once with it, scanning the room, smiling a little, meeting as many eyes as possible. This had a dual effect; I looked as if I were searching for my temporarily mislaid group of friends, and I could try to build initial bridges with the Man Who Was To Shag Me, wherever he may be. As I worked the routine I violently suppressed great waves of sadness that kept threatening to send me out into the night; thoughts of all the evenings, worlds away, when I actually was out with a group of friends. Friends whom I loved and trusted and was comfortable with. Nights where a snog was something silly and a kebab was a joke rather than a biological necessity. I had to forget them. I had work to do. Two beers and an Aftershock.

The Man arrived quickly. He caught me off guard, in the foam room. The first thing I saw was a spot, a red, half-healed adolescent spot looming at me through the pink-and-white sea, then a rolling bumfluff chin, a shaved head, some piggy, baggy, half-closed eyes, and finally a pair of pursed, chapped, swollen lips. They met mine. They moved around. Then in with the furry, flaccid, cold, beery Ipswich tongue – just like it had been on the Post Office railings, nearly a decade ago. We pressed our bodies together; I felt a gut, a fat back, the top of a loose, baggy arse. All through a soft and shiny Ipswich Town supporter's T-shirt. We stayed like this for a while. My lips were dry and sore, and I had trouble breathing through my nose. He put his hand up my skirt, drove my black pants aside and put some fingers inside me. Fine. We're on our way. Let's get gynaecological. A little more of this, and he's shouting in my ear.

"D'you wanna...?"

He flicked his head, suggesting that we exit. I nod.

"Yep."

And we're outside the club. I grab his arse-cheek through his outsize jeans, forestalling any possible conversation. I can taste beer and Sambuca and fags and *him*. This is what I need to do. At least I'm doing something. Oh, shit, he's talking to me. Slurring at me, retching his vile Suffolk accent in my face.

"If we're going to mine, we have to go on the bus. Have you got two pounds?"

I can't look at him. He disgusts me. If I look at his face, I'll have to imagine his life, his parents, all the fat birds he's fucked before me. I grab his crotch instead.

"It's fine, I've got somewhere."

We reach the Novotel. I've lost a shoe. He follows me up, looks round the hotel room, looks at me.

"I'm not paying."

He thinks I'm a whore. Does he? He can't, surely. Not that it makes any difference.

"You don't have to pay."

"Wicked. Sorted."

I close my eyes briefly and sit on the end of the bed. Everything spins: lights, foam, Ipswich station, gold sparkly tops, Lambrini, and That Spot, moving in on my face. He places his body on top of mine, smothering, a bouncy castle slowly deflating. Oh, marvellous, he's got an erection. Well done him. The tongue is back, flapping and weaving, still oddly cold.

I lie sprawled on the bed, a gymnast crashed on a mat, akimbo. He moves his head down between my legs, pulls the pants off, manhandling my drunk limbs with a certain deluded authority, if not exactly finesse. He rams his clumsy, bulbous, shaven head between my thighs. Oh, don't bother, sweetheart. Just get on with it. You have a moderately willing receptacle: use it, then leave. This isn't going to get any better. Clothes have been removed. Fat on fat.

He stops.

"I don't have a condom."

I scream back at him, fury rising.

"Do you think I give a shit? For fuck's sake. Just DO. IT."

"Alright."

And he does. I barely notice. I notice the smoke alarm on the ceiling, I notice the orange car park light peering round the edges of the curtain. I notice the tastes in my mouth. And then, suddenly, I can't keep the thoughts down any longer, and they're rising and rising and washing over me, and I cry. Great heaving sobs, working their way through my upper body, stopping when they reach the fat stranger who is fucking me like a rubber doll.

I think of Cambridge. I think of friends, hope, potential. And then, inevitably, I think of Emma. Now, while the fat man is penetrating me, is as good a time as any to tell you more about Emma. Emma was my friend. As I said, she played Louise in the Cambridge tour of *Gypsy*. She hailed from Cheshire, a binge-drinking Venus who'd sing Ave Maria at a funeral then bottle a choirboy at the wake. She was perfect. She had spent her life in theatres, in the children's choir of *Evita*, the chorus of *Joseph*. It was her life, and we both, I think, believed that it was going to be mine, too.

From the end of my second year, we were friends, of a sort. We'd meet for coffee, send each other stupid little presents. It was fun. Sometimes we went clubbing; we were at the centre of the most central group of people in the city; drinking, dancing, flirting, chatting, storming on into our throbbing, twinkling, welcoming lives.

She kissed me. Outside a school hall in Nuremburg, after the last performance of *Gypsy*. The show finished with the two of us on stage, holding each other, quiet in each other's arms. She was tiny. I used to look forward to holding her. I told her as much: she didn't mind. She snuggled into me, her hair pressed against my mouth, my hand in the small of her back. I loved that – the small of her back. I drew her into me night after night, feeling her little, soft body and smelling her neck and her costume. I loved it; I loved her.

Then she kissed me. I don't know what happened, what either of us thought. But she kissed me, and we kissed, warm and soft and safe, all night. We lay in our hostel, kissing on the bunk bed, one duvet wrapped around us. Then we flew back to England, next to each other, speaking only in necessities. Our separate parents picked us up from the airport, and we went away, separately.

She's dead now. She died in a car crash about a year ago. Driving along a B-road, something happened; the car rolled and flipped and landed wrong. Killed instantly, apparently. Nothing's that instant. There must have been a moment of knowledge, of shock or fear or acceptance, before her hair and teeth and brains and skin were burnt, or crushed, or mashed. Anyway, she's dead.

And I, Judy Bishop, am alive. Drunk, but alive. And an obese clubber, whose name I don't know, has just ejaculated all over my glitter-swathed breasts.

• • •

On Thursday morning I threw a coat over my sex-costume and checked out of the Novotel, stealing ten little tubs of jam from the breakfast bar on my way out. I pottered back to the station, make-up ground into my puffed face, strappy top glittering on defiantly, a small area of my chest crisp with congealed semen. I purchased the obligatory cheese and tomato baguette from the Upper Crust kiosk, shoved it into my bag, and flopped, again sweating – always sweating, like a shaved bear covered in oil – into a seat on the train.

I wasn't as unhappy as you'd imagine. I didn't exactly ride back to the capital in triumph, but I was somehow unable to enter the great black sucking hole of misery that my sick, sticky, hungover, violated, lonely, embarrassed state technically warranted. I felt, in fact, a sense of achievement. Joy, even. I had had sex. Sex! Me, Judy Bishop: shaggable, shagging, shagged. Huzzah. I'm a woman, really, truly. Glowering thoughts of dead friends and plastic mattress covers and the liquid rumble of my paramour vomiting into his pillow aside, I had had sex. I had become a member of the biggest club on earth, a club established only shortly after the first genitals were attached to the first people at the dawn of time. The Shagged Women Club. A club that includes Brigitte Bardot, Margaret Thatcher, Bernadette Peters, all my old university friends. Absolutely everyone, save for the Virgin Mary and a few of her most devout followers.

The train trickled unenthusiasically through Chelmsford, Kelvedon and Shenfield, and I thought about children. I had become, in the last twenty-four hours, a potential child-bearer. A good thing, surely. I'm the perfect age to pop one out. I now know that I have a relaxed, undemandingly accommodating vagina, and you could fit a well-built polar bear in the space between my hips. I'd handle the pregnancy with great aplomb, taking lots of rest, giving in generously to food cravings and confining myself to only the most child-friendly of alcopops. Vodka Mudshakes, perhaps. I wouldn't know what to do with the sprog when it arrived, of course, but who ever does? Children are weird, and people turn out wrong. Maybe it's because of the way we raise them. The ever-ready nipples and milk and tiny little velour jumpsuits and bits of primary-coloured plastic paraphernalia that are supposed to be entertaining may be the principal mistake of the Western world: feeding tiny humans unrealistic expectations of ongoing love; cuddles, food you can eat lying on your back, hilarious toy post offices that you can be in charge of.

No, my child would be different. It would have a start more truly reflective of life as it would continue. It could live in the bath and eat crisps. I could take it for walks through Bethnal Green and let it look inside wheelie-bins. We could listen to musicals together, and I could name it after my favourite musical theatre stars: Elaine Paige Gypsy Rose Lee Merman Garland-Bishop. I would have another little weirdo to play with, for ever. It would have to sort out its own education and transport, of course, but that would teach it independence from a young age, improving its future employment prospects. Yes, I could have a child.

And as for the sex itself: well, it was dreadful, but dreadful can be worked up into an anecdote. That's what the old Judy Bishop would have done, the Judy of almost five years ago. She would have seen the ridiculous in the horrible – the way he was, the way I was, the moment when he choked on a pubic hair, washed it away with a swig of Lambrini, then worried that I thought he was gay for drinking it, or the mutual, unspoken realisation that his bosom was a fraction bigger than mine. Once upon a time I would have drunk a bottle of house white, gathered ranks of friends, got red-faced and larky and laughed the wounds better in All Bar One, much like the Judy B of my column. I would have pretended that I hadn't planned sex, that it wasn't important, that I had just had a few too many and it had happened, and how absolutely hilarious that it had.

Now, finally, I have the raw material for a good story, a bawdy story, and the inclination to share it with people. Not with my readers – they can all fuck off back to Islington and have a soy latte. No, I want to share this with real, laughing, three-dimensional people, round a table, I want to have drinks and dinner and allow people to enjoy the giggling spin that I choose to put on my exploits. That's the way to be in control: not by leading a functional, admirable life of which you can be proud, but by sculpting your great mire of stagnant life experience into a smiley face and letting people laugh at it. I can do that, I know. I just need to find the people. New people, or old people; anyone who wants to come. I'll find them, soon. They're out there, and I will be, too.

I ate my Lambrini-smeared baguette (a cheeky flavour, cherries and cheese – slightly continental), got off the train at Liverpool Street, and walked along Bishopsgate, through Shoreditch, towards Bethnal Green. For the first time, I wasn't concerned with the people around me, and with what they were thinking or doing. I had had a day as interesting as any of them would ever have; the milling, mid-morning bankers in the City or, as I trudged further east, the spunk-haired ooh-look-at-me-I'm-so-fucking-cool-I'm-wearing-a-scarf-as-a-belt-and-I'm-probably-about-to-do-a-line-of-Fairtrade-coke advertising and media pseuds. I just wasn't bothered. I had my own Thursday morning story, undoubtedly fresher and more energising than any of theirs.

I turned into my street, and stopped abruptly on the doorstep of my building. There was a black bin-bag, a label attached reading "FAO Judy Bishop". I looked at it, gave it a quick kick. Soft. Not soft like pillows, but not hard like a bomb. I bent down and ripped open the bag. Another layer of black plastic underneath, then another, then another, then a white Waitrose carrier bag containing a surprisingly large amount of fresh horse manure. Shit. A bag of shit, on my doorstep.

I picked it up, took it into the flat, and set it down on my desk. This needed some examination. I picked up a fork, sat in front of the shit and began to pick through it, much as one would go through a Chinese take away looking for prawns. Nothing there, except shit. No note, nothing nasty, no diamond engagement ring sparkling at the bottom. Just shit. I rinsed the fork and put it back in the drawer, then hopped in the shower to wash the semen off my breasts. Plenty to think about, this week.

The Days of Judy B

I LOVE PRESENTS. What classy young London Lady doesn't? Disregarding birthdays and Christmas – I don't want 16 bath-bombs, a book of George Dubya's faux pas and a sixties compilation album, I'm sorry but I just don't, Dad – presents give me a buzz like no other. I've spent years engineering pointless arguments with dear friends, simply because the tearful girly making-up process is so joyously sodden with designer-stamp coasters and Gucci ice-cube moulds.

There's a reason for my current gift fixation, aside from my approaching birthday (for which I'm demanding a Vivienne Westwood corset and a Big Night Out at Bouji's). A school friend is getting married. Hitched, shackled, coupled. Good for her. She – let's call her Jacinta, her real name is too dull to bother with – hasn't been much of a presence in my life over the last few years. To be honest, the last time I saw her was walking out of our history A-level, weeping convulsively and trying to pierce her own jugular with her kings and Qqueens of England ruler.

She wasn't ever really in my gang. Not cool enough, I'm afraid. I remember her as a rather sullen figure. I have no idea what she looks like now, or where she lives, or what she does, or who she's marrying. All I know is that she's getting married, I'm invited to the wedding – which I feel minded to go to as it just might be interesting, from a columnar point of view – and I'm expected to bring a present.

I'm stumped. There's no wedding list, no guide as to her current financial or social status, no clue as to her tastes and interests, nothing. Just a big, nagging hole where a present should be. What to do? I could be generic and get a trinket, a charm, or a little silver jug that's too small to put anything in. I could be wacky and adopt her a panda. Or I could be cowardly and ignore the invitation altogether. So many options, all a bit dreary.

As ever, I trotted down to the Slug and Lettuce to consult my 15 best friends. They, between gulps of Kir Royale and thoughtful fags, came up with the following: Jacinta, having failed to put out a list of must-haves carefully drawn up with her new beau, clearly doesn't mind what she gets. So I must respond to this by getting her a present that's all about me, The Fabulous Judy Bishop. Something that will give *me* more satisfaction, albeit perhaps malicious, than it will her.

So I went out and purchased a trio of ferrets. Three wriggling, squeaking, biting little animals which will interbreed and blight her honeymoon with their demonic rodent presence. I'm looking at them right now. They're horrid. I'm going to put them in a huge Tiffany box and persuade her to open it at the buffet table.

Oh, alright, I'm not really. I didn't get her ferrets. I got her, if you must know, a scented candle and a photo frame. There are social standards to be maintained, people. But didn't you enjoy that little fantasy? It's nice to imagine the thrill of behaving badly, the deviant buzz of doing something impolite or unattractive, on purpose. We know we'll never actually do it. We know that we'll always brush our hair and smile and send thank-you notes after dinner parties. But please take five minutes each day to imagine the thrill of momentarily Unleashing the Beast, of giving free rein to your nastiest thoughts and desires. Then put on your perfume, get to work on time and give up your seat on the tube to a sweet old lady. There's a good girl.

Judy B's Purchase of the Week: Alas, not ferrets. I walked past H&M the other day and couldn't resist a pair of truly fabulous pink pleatherette mules. Trashy, I know, but I must look nice for Jacinta.

JUDY BISHOP

4.

24th September, 2006

Another bag of shit came yesterday. It arrived in the morning, when I'd popped to the shop. It was similar enough to
the last package – a note saying "FAO Judy Bishop", several layers of black plastic, a Waitrose carrier bag, and a quan-
tity of reasonably fresh horse manure. It's not frightening. It
should be – a stranger tracking my movements and leaving
excrement on my doorstep – but it's not. It's horse manure,
for goodness' sake. It's made of healthily digested grass and
hay and oats, and it smells like an August afternoon in
Suffolk. Old people put horse manure on their roses, and
farmers sell it at the roadside for 50p a bag. It's really rather
lovely.

In fact, I've started a window-box. The window just
above my Judy B writing desk has a midget balcony, which
I'd artfully filled with fag butts and discarded prawn crack-
ers. Now, thanks to the phantom shit-sender, I have a little
rose bush, growing more attractive daily. I add a new layer
of manure each morning. I'm no horticulturalist, but I feel

that the bush must surely blossom after a youth spent wallowing in such decadent amounts of fertiliser; it's getting, in my little window-box, the plant equivalent of Eton, Oxford and home-grown peaches.

I've had no clue as to who could be sending the shit, despite some intricate detective work. On Tuesday morning I got out my fork, rooted through the Waitrose bag, and found a receipt for some shopping. Three Thai ready meals (chicken and beef based – he or she is clearly not a vegetarian), some milk, red wine, salad, a medium-sized Brie, meringues, and a guava. The shopping list suggests a lonely, civilised, moderately affluent person. An impulse buyer who fancies themselves as exotic (guava), someone susceptible to food cravings but with a certain regard for their health and dignity, someone who attempts to follow an ethnic menu (Thai green curry), whilst fatally misunderstanding the central tenets of flavour balancing (following the curry with wine, cheese, and meringues). Someone trying, perhaps, to have a good night in, or to alleviate a bad one by a well-judged stop at the supermarket.

That's been my only clue as to the shit-courier's identity – the receipt. Further to this I know, for sure, that they're delivering the bags in person. No Parcel Force-type service has been engaged, and I've never been asked to sign for it. Someone is waiting, watching, depositing, and leaving. With considerable care, it seems. Good for them.

What does one do, in this situation? Very little, is the obvious answer. You discard the shit, as far away from your flat as possible, and think nothing of the receipt. Maybe you panic, you assume that you're being sent offensive parcels by a lunatic. You detach yourself from them, make yourself safe by calling friends, family, colleagues, police. You let the world, and yourself, know that poor functional, mainstream little you has been the victim of a mad stalker, someone on the periphery of society, perhaps someone who's going to run at you in the middle of the night with a knife. You cocoon yourself instantly in the safe, sober, sensible world, asking a dear friend to come and curl up in bed with you, holding you tight around the middle and stroking your shoulders when you get anxious, kissing you on the top of the head, and telling you that everything's going to be OK, we won't let the mad person get you.

Or, if you're Judy Bishop, you sit for a little while, have a think, and greet the shit with interest. You light a fag, look at the lovely new flowers in your window-box, and decide to be happy, curious, flattered by the attention. Why the fuck not? After all, the alternative reaction, the panic reaction, is one based upon a series of imaginative leaps. A parcel, a lunatic, a door opening in the middle of the night, a glinting knife, your own grisly and reluctant death. To assume that events will progress thus is irrational and paranoid. It makes just as much sense to let your imagination romp off, puppyish, in the other direction; a parcel, an admirer, a romantic picnic on a lake, a sparkling ring, a long and blissful life in the arms of a horticulturally minded and generous equestrian. That could happen. It might happen. Wait and see.

In the meantime, I had an appointment. A social engagement, if you will. Anna Cook.

Anna I know from university. Rooms near each other, a shared cupboard in the kitchen. Little in common, other than basic geographical proximity. We led wildly different lives. As I rocked in of a morning – drunk, smoking, the latest verbal warning from the Thames Valley Police ringing in my ears – Anna would be heading out in a neatly pressed outfit: to the library, for a jog, to the early morning meeting of the Student Union, or the Social Committee, or the Homeless Foundation or, for all I knew, NATO.

Anna loved a project. Always something on the go, something inarguably fibrous and worthy and obscurely beneficial to some previously forgotten subsection of the community. We exchanged pleasantries from time to time, and she once persuaded me to walk down the High Street in a gorilla suit to raise awareness of the illegal bushmeat trade (I got carried away and pretended to attack a gang of shoppers – Anna blanked me for a month and I spent two hours in the cells). But apart from that, our contact was minimal.

We graduated and I imagined, with faint delight, that she'd left my life for ever. Then Emma died, and back she came. Out of the blue, ready with her nods and her smiles and her religiously sensitive expressions of sympathy. I remember it well; two weeks after the funeral, I was sitting in my flat in Muswell Hill, the flat that I'd shared with Emma. Just sitting. Staring. All quiet. I heard the key in the lock, and a cheery greeting.

"Hello-oo? Judy?"

She couldn't have sounded less like Emma. Emma didn't do greetings. She'd just storm in, seemingly in mid-sentence – "Can I just say" – ranting cheerfully about something bad that Transport for London had done to her that day. She'd rant her way across the living room, pausing only to give me a kiss. She'd stop when she got to the kitchen, and put the kettle on. That completed, she'd settle herself cross-legged on the worktop, often with a foot in the washing-up bowl, come to the end of her story, exhale, and smile. Then, without fail:

"So, JB, how goes it with you?"

Every day she'd do this. And I'd be sitting on the sofa, looking up at her, taking in her clothes, the bounce of her hair, trying to guess from her complexion how cold it was outside. I'd generally be smiling. Always smiling, in that situation.

So you can imagine the offence I took when Anna made *her* entrance. Clutching a box of tissues, a roll of binbags, milk, rubber gloves, and a Tupperware container of potato salad, in she came. No excuses, no explanations. A brief word to the effect that she'd spoken to Emma's parents, got the keys, offered to come and sort things out. "It was the least I could do, considering all they're going through. And I thought that it would be lovely to see my favourite Judy Bishop again, after all this time!"

She set the tissues and the potato salad down in front of me, put the milk in the fridge, donned the rubber gloves, and set to work with the bin bags. Clearing Emma away. Smashing through her room, closing her magazines, wiping her surfaces, stripping her bed, folding her clothes, plumping her pillows, tactfully disposing of her underwear. The grim reaper's chambermaid. Anna had offered to perform this task having, I imagine, read a pamphlet on how to help the bereaved. It all boils down to potato salad, bin bags and the awkward embrace. She asked me – quietly, for volume offends the bereaved – whether or not I had any "plans for Emma's things". Well, actually, Anna, yes. I had plans, rather good plans. I'd planned to sit very, very still for ever and ever, breathing as little as possible, letting her dust settle slowly on my body until one day I was found, there in Muswell Hill, mummified in what remained of Emma. But those plans are flexible, by all means. Proceed with your rubber gloves, Anna. Do the right thing.

She had no place there, but still she came. Because of her apparent birthright; a seat by the side of the suffering, the right to enter any room she chose with a mop and bucket, the right to don her halo and pity those less good than her. She cleaned, sterilised, junked, and left, leaving me nothing but her "best wishes". We hadn't spoken since.

Then she called me. This week, as I was spreading manure on my roses, she called me. Wondering if I wanted coffee. I was in no position to turn her down, truth be told. No human contact this week, apart from the man in the corner shop, and my usual hour with Gareth. Curious, I clutched at the social straw, and agreed to meet her.

I got the tube to Leicester Square. Anna had selected a patisserie on Charing Cross Road, Chez Marie: a sterile, non-smoking tourist hell. She said that the maroon velvet banquettes make it "cosy". I thought it looked like the saloon bar of a cross-Channel ferry.

I arrived at Chez Marie a touch late, pumped up and edgy, everything still throbbing with the ghost of my Ipswich trip. I wasn't on peak conversational form, to say the least. In fact, I was a human sewer, my vocal folds still clotted with Lambrini, the inside of my mouth clammy and furred, like a deep, hot armpit swathed in orange wool. Every few seconds a great wave of flashback would yank me out of myself, the bustle of the coffee shop punctuated by the image of a shaven, bobbing head, a stiff nylon pillow, and a bottle of Aftershock rolling serenely onto the brown patterned carpet. I didn't mind. It was only Anna – the residual whiff of drink and the healthless pallor would confirm her existing view of me: funky little Judy, always up to something louche.

She was already there, sitting primly on the banquette. Dressed as she always used to be: Converse sneakers, semi-designer jeans, fitted, zip-up hoodie, necklace from Accessorize. Scrubbed face, conspicuously clean hair. Beanie hat sitting on the table in front of her. Clean, apple-cheeked, preppy. Fit to tour an old people's home then march into a CEO's office and demand increased funds to develop it. She got up to give me a hug. It was an entirely one-way affair; I stood immobile as her earnest little arms encircled me.

"Judy!"

"Hi!"

"Long time no see! You look so well!"

"Right back at you!"

She laughed. She thinks I'm so hilarious.

"What are you having? I'm feeling a bit naughty. Shall we share a slice of tarte aux fraises?"

No. I want a whole fucking tarte aux fraises, not just a slice.

"That would be lovely."

We ordered. Hot chocolate for her, black coffee for me.

"So so so" – she drummed the table with her fingers, her whole frame zipping with well-channelled energy – "what have you been up to since we last met?"

Well, Anna, let's see. I moved into a small hole in Bethnal Green, began a long, slow process of solitary stagnation, resolved to change myself for the better, went to Ipswich, checked into a Novotel, got completely paralytic, went to a Foam Night, and then allowed an obese teenager to penetrate me while I wept. Ever since, I've been sitting in said hole eating cheese and taking regular delivery of anonymous sacks of excrement. But I did finally get around to paying the electricity bill, so that's something.

"Um... well, I suppose I've been quite busy with the column. Research and stuff."

"Oh, yes. I loved your last one. So wry."

"Thanks. I do my best."

She laughed again. For God's sake, neither of us are being amusing. End this.

Her expression twisted into something like curiosity, or suspicion.

"Do you ever struggle to find material?"

She knows. Shit, she must know.

"Oh, not really. It's just life, what I write about. All there in front of your nose."

Now it was my turn to laugh, albeit nervously.

"Because, if you ever do, I know of some really interesting causes that need to be brought to wider public attention. A lot of it isn't, you know, glamorous, but it's all worthwhile. There's a foundation I'm working with at the moment, delivering medical supplies to –"

"Really, I'd love to, but I think my readers are more after a bit of fluff. You know – shoes, hair, clothes, dating."

"Well, you could always try. You might convert them."

"Honestly, Anna, I wish I could, but I'd never get it past my editor. I really am sorry."

"Oh, go on. Please? You're a big brave girl."

"Really, no."

She wasn't offended. Anna is impossible to offend. A smack addict once bit her on the nose; she just chuckled and gave him some more soup.

"Well, actually, seeing as you're keen to help, there is something that you could do for me. For us. That's sort of why I wanted to see you –"

Oh, Oh, Oh, God. It's all over. I'm going to have to spend every Saturday for the rest of my life sponging mildew off the walls of a recreational centre.

"Oh?"

"Well, in December, I'm doing some work for a new charity."

"Mmm-hmm?"

"It's to do with the reduction of heating bills for the elderly. But we're not just lobbying; we're aiming to install a number of solar-powered storage heaters in homes across the country. That way, bills are reduced and, should the project really take off – which of course it will with help from the likes of yourself – then it could start a trend for more eco-friendly heating worldwide. It's an environmentally aware and humanitarian scheme, which has the potential to genuinely benefit humanity both right now and for centuries to come."

Can't really argue with that.

"And how would you like me to help?"

"Well, we're holding an Auction of Promises. You know – a grand or so to the charity, and a company director takes you for a spin in his light aircraft, or someone gives you a free marquee, or a facial. We've got some celebrities involved," – she leant in and lowered her voice – "if you bid high enough on a certain lot, then a certain TV personality will *come round to your house*." She smiled, her trump card produced.

"And what will said TV personality do when he gets there?"

She sat back, loud again.

"Well, you know, it doesn't matter, does it? He's just there, and that should be enough. Anyway, I was hoping you'd be one of our celebrities."

"But, Anna… I'm not famous."

"Well, no, but you are. You may not think it, but in real terms you are. You're in the papers. People love you, Judy, love you."

Oh, fuck.

She went on.

"And what might be really, really nice would be if you were to, say – and stop me if this is an imposition – allow someone to bid for the privilege of shadowing you for a week, then allow them to be present while you were writing your column. So that way they could see a columnist gathering material, then eventually watch them form that material into the neat Sunday paper package that we all know and love!

"What do you think? It'll be such fun. No weirdos, I promise."

Except me. I'm a weirdo. And she knows it. How, how, how could she ask this of me? She *knows*. She knows the putrid excuse for a woman that I am, she surely knows that I must lie and cheat and debase myself in order to produce what I produce, week after week. I can't do this.

"Really, no. I'm sorry. I just can't, it's too difficult."

Her face sank, then hardened, her eyes taking on the demonic glint of the wronged Samaritan. She reached into her handbag, pulled out a photo of an old woman, and slid it accusingly across the table.

"This is Ada. She lives in Langtoft. She recently lost her council house to subsidence. Without new heating, she will die. She will die, Judy. She will be dead."

She folded her arms. QED, apparently. I felt nervous.

"Do you, um, know Ada?"

"We all know Ada, Judy. Or someone like her. Come on. Be kind. It'll be easy."

"Really? Will it?"

"Yes."

"When is it?"

She told me. Near the end of November. A flush of relief – it was the week of Gareth's show. The night after, in fact.

"Ah – I'm afraid it just won't work dates-wise. You see, I'm performing – singing – the night before. A new musical at the Sydenham Bull. The rehearsal schedule should be pretty fierce, and –"

"Oh, well, that's OK. There'll be no commitment to the auction before the day itself. And we can all come and watch you in your show! How exciting!"

I stood firm.

"No. I'm sorry. I still can't do it."

"Well, that's a shame, because some people you know are involved, Charlie Rogers is –"

"Wait – Charlie Rogers?"

Another smile, and a nod. She knows she's got me.

"Charlie Rogers."

Charlie. Charlie is an actor. Two years above me at university. We performed together in a production of *Guys and Dolls*; he played Skye Masterson, I was one of the Save-a-Soul Mission ladies. We had, I believe, a brief flirtation. It could have come to something, back then. He always smiled at me, and I always responded.

He's beautiful. Six foot one, broad-shouldered, flat stomach. Not quite muscled, but lean. Lovely, lovely hips that sway easily with his walk, complete comfort in his own body. Always trashily low-slung jeans. No belt, the waistband of his boxers two inches visible. A T-shirt or sweater which suggests a casual, freelance, sporty life; perhaps a thin fitted hoodie, zipped up, or a clinging, subtly Hawaiian shirt. Once, three years ago, he wore a child's Rainforest Café T-shirt. It was hot; the palm trees and the giraffe clung sweatily to his chest, his nipples discernible through the cartoon foliage. I envy him, I always did – I imagine his morning routine, so simple. Hop in the shower, stroke your abs for a bit, get out when you smell beautifully of man-product. Fling on your boxers, jeans, any T-shirt. Then go about your day: stalking through London, turning a few heads, maybe having a sandwich or a coffee, knowing on some subliminal level that you look just fine. There's no risk whatsoever of a stranger taking it upon themselves to tell you that you're fat, or sad, or badly dressed, because you're not. You never have been. You've never even considered the possibility that you might be.

I think about Charlie a lot, more than he'd be comfortable to know. I look at pictures of him on the internet. I listen to the *Guys and Dolls* cast recording, imagining his abdomen tensing beneath his green Rainforest Café T-shirt, producing that round, pure, clean tenor voice. I see the pattern of his sweat – a trickle at the neck, moving down, spreading out in the small of his back, softening and dampening and moulding his green shirt to his body until he becomes lush, ripe, verdant. I fantasise about my life being different, with him more than ever a part of it. Sometimes I fold the bedroom curtain in two, press it up against the wall, and stroke it, imagining that I'm stroking his chest. It passes the evenings.

I want to see Charlie again, more than I can say. I want to exchange pleasantries, smile back at him, receive my peck on the cheek with coy merriment. Then perhaps, through this auction, we'll become friends. Soon enough, as I am changed for the better by our friendship, we'll kiss. Make love. Move in together. Children. Parallel careers. Walks in parks, dogs, tiny disputes over wallpaper that we'll recover from quickly. We'll grow old, one of us will die. The other, grief-stricken, will die shortly afterwards. It'll be perfect. And all because of Anna's Auction of Promises.

I wiped a bead of sweat from my forehead, feigned breeziness.

"How is old Charlie? It's been a while."

"He's doing really well. *Measure for Measure* at the Barbican, bless him. Haven't seen it. His promise is rather fun; he'll take you for a walk on Primrose Hill and recite some sonnets. We're imagining that it'll be a nice present for a youngster, a GCSE student perhaps."

Or a fat, horny twenty-three-year-old who'll grab his crotch in the middle of 'Death Be Not Proud'.

"Anna… perhaps I could do it. The auction thing. A bit of fun. But no weirdos, you promise?"

"Cross my heart promise."

"Alright then."

She smiled, victorious.

Nice work, Miss Cook. All Hail Anna.

• • •

I went to the bus stop by way of the off-licence, where I bought ten Mayfair Menthols and a litre of Kronenbourg Blanc (light, fruity, tastes like peaches, can elevate any mood beyond recognition). Back on the bus, surreptitiously slurping beer from my handbag, and home.

Another bag of shit, waiting on the doorstep. I decanted the usual amount into the window-box – which, by the way, is turning into quite a little Eden – then threw half a sack out of my living room window and into the street, like a medieval housewife. It was a wonderful thing to do. The rounds of manure separated as they flew, forming a rich brown hailstorm. Each little bolus hit the ground separately with a dull thud, the combined impacts producing a sound like a volley of arrows hitting a battlefield. One of them narrowly missed a young couple, walking hand in hand. The man swerved, squealed, and ducked, shielding his face. I shook out my shit-streaked Waitrose bag, raised my bottle of Kronenbourg, and gave them a little wave. I felt better, an odd kind of momentary, elated wellness flying in the face of the facts.

I was glad of that lift in mood. I was going to need it to deal with what I found when I went downstairs to put the plastic sack in the wheelie-bin: post. Mail. A letter. Not junk mail, or a cheque, or a bill, but an envelope with my name on it in curly pink handwriting. Stiff. I took it upstairs and ripped it open. It was a card, a thick pink card with gold writing on it, and a pair of silver-sprayed raffia fairy wings sticking out rudely from each side.

Clare Bishop invites you to celebrate her 21st Birthday.
Date: Wednesday 27th September, 2006.
Venue: The Old School House, Glemham, Suffolk.
Time: 7:30pm till late
Theme: Flowers, Fairies and Castles.
Dress: As if you were made of magic.
RSVP

I put the card down, and sat. Clare. My sister, Clare. I made myself shudder; it seemed the appropriate response. How dare she? How dare she send me an invitation, formally inviting me to return to my childhood home, no doubt dressed up as a battlement or a portcullis or some such wank, just so that I can drink cava and tell all her friends from Durham University that, yes, she has always been this beautiful. And, to heap insult on top of insult, the party is only a week away; my invitation was clearly some kind of afterthought. Perhaps our parents made her send it. I picked up the invitation again, and saw a scribbled note on the back: "Jude, Am sure you're really busy but would be lovely if you could make it. Going to be a great party and there will be miniburgers. Lots of love, Claz xxxxx" Oh, marvellous. "Claz" is laying on miniburgers to lure her fat sister down to Suffolk for a midweek Mardi Gras in aid of her own fabulousness.

Well, I'm going to go. She won't be expecting that. I'm going to turn up and lift the fucking roof off that marquee. I'm going to drink and dance and play the only trump card I have: I am two years older than Clare. I'm going to be the embodiment of maturity, and no-one will dare to doubt me. Never mind that Clare lost her virginity at eighteen, in a rather lovely way to a rather lovely man who told her she was gorgeous and bought her flowers the next day. Never mind that she spent her gap year in Kenya digging a well so that hippos could drink. Never mind that she's a size ten, with a smooth chestnut mane and a face that could melt glaciers. I'm older than her. I win.

I'll tell you where it all started to go wrong between Clare and me. I was seventeen. Our father had, for our respective birthdays, bought us each a rather special present.

"Something which we could treasure for years to come," he said.

Clare was given two beautiful beagle puppies, Sugar and Spice, which she kept in a basket in the conservatory. I was given driving lessons. While little Clare romped adorably with her two furry, pool-eyed beauties, I sweated down the Wickham Market bypass in a Ford Mondeo, the fetid breath of an obese racist forming bubbles in the side of my face as he rasped "Mirror, signal, manoeuvre".

What happened was not my fault. To this day, I passionately maintain that it was not my fault. It was the end of a long day's driving, and my father shouldn't have let me go up and down the drive in the old Land Rover. He just shouldn't. I was tired, he should have seen that. Perhaps I was even a bit dehydrated, I don't know. I don't remember much. All I am certain of is that one of my feet slipped, the pedals got mixed up, perhaps they even moved, and I couldn't find the handbrake. The steering wheel meant nothing any more.

I was a passenger in that Land Rover, as much a victim as the puppies. I just sat, helpless, as the vehicle barrelled on, quite slowly as I recall, through the conservatory and over the dog basket. The Land Rover nosed, majestic, through the glass, over the wicker chairs, past a sofa, then unmistakably over the yielding, yipping bodies of Sugar and Spice. I came to a stop about a hundred yards on, fully aware of what had just happened.

I didn't cry. Clare cried, for a whole fucking week. We had to have a little funeral for the dogs, at which I was allowed to hold the spade and lead the singing. She called me "Judy the Dog Killer".

It stuck. We fought. She cried. I still didn't, even

though I had more reason to cry than her. I was the one who had to live with what I'd done, had to be blamed for the general unhappiness and horror; she just had to weep under a black lace mantilla and accept sugared almonds from Granny.

Clare says that she's over it now, that it's all terribly sad, but how funny it is when you actually think about it. She says that it's fine, that of course she's not upset, she hasn't been for years. I'm just her lovely big sister Judy. I don't believe her, not for a second. But I'm going to her party, nevertheless. She can't stop me. It's family time.

The Days of Judy B

PRIDE IS, WITHOUT A DOUBT, the worst of the Seven Deadly Sins. Without wishing to thump a tub in your poor bleary Sunday morning faces, I think that Pride may well be the scourge of our society. Gluttony, Sloth, Avarice, coveting a neighbour's ox, and all the others that you'll have to look up yourself because I can't be bothered, are, for the most part, quite pleasant little quirks. The odd muffin, a weekday morning lie-in, not really wanting to share your Jo Malone bath gel: that's all OK. Endearing, in fact – our flaws make us human. I'm sure that Moses, or Jesus, or whoever it was, knew that.

But Pride: now, that is the one that will secure your ticket on the down train to Hades. Pride will alienate the humble, belittle the meek, and make even the most well balanced of your friends quite seriously cheesed off with you.

I came to this conclusion, as ever, after attending a series of parties. As if Jacinta's present-thieving wedding bash weren't enough for Poor Little Me to contend with, certain members of the shambolic circus that constitutes my social life have decided, flying in the face of the facts, that they are Bright Young Things. They believe, suddenly, that their existences are worthy of celebration. So they're throwing parties – birthdays, engagements, book launches, house-warmings.

When someone calls upon us to come together in a Central London Venue and pool our joy at their own success, we trot along obediently. It'd be rude not to, and anyway, there might be sushi and a slightly-too-small glass of Perrier Jouet to be got out of it. But are we actually happy for them? Of course not. Every time a promotion is accepted, every time a couple buy a house, every time a new baby pops into the world, a little part of me dies. I think that most people feel this way. Not because we begrudge our friends their joy, but because the raw, unsheathed sight of someone standing tall and proud, clutching a glass and revelling in themselves, drives a red-hot poker of latent malice into our usually generous hearts.

Whatever love we once had for them suddenly turns into a cowering bitterness; we see their good fortune as an act of aggression. We don't want to sit them on a lily-pad and fan them with congratulations. No matter how lovely we are, we still want to smash their blini in their face, send their mother an offensive text message, and make off with their car tyres.

Of course we do. Because we're human, and *they're* human, and humans, particularly urban 20-something female humans, should not be inclined to gloat. The odd moment of joy – a birth, a marriage, a job – should never be a source of pride. Gratitude, perhaps. Chances are you were just lucky. And even though one good thing has happened, the rest of your life is probably still a bit fucked, a fact which you'll realise as soon as you take off your party make-up and stare at your face in your merciless bathroom mirror. Pride is a delusion, and never again will I buy a new pair of shoes and eat satay sticks in order to pander to it. Party-throwers, take note. Judy B is off the list.

Judy B's Purchase of the Week: Alka-seltzer and a fried egg ciabatta.

JUDY BISHOP

5.

Have you ever heard of Donald Crowhurst? If not, I'm shocked. Everyone should know the story of Donald Crowhurst the Doomed Yachtsman. I was told about him by my babysitter Lucy, when I was eight. She spun the yarn with a certain Halloween relish, darkening the bedroom and shining a torch up her face, much as other, less nautically minded babysitters would speak of decapitated horses or ghostly highwaymen, or axe-murderers on car roofs. Lucy wasn't the finest of storytellers – her near-impenetrable lisp detracted somewhat from her gravitas – but she loved to talk about Crowhurst. Sometimes she'd even don a sou'wester hat and yellow wellies to create an ambience.

Donald Crowhurst was an amateur yachtsman, a week-end sailor. In 1968 he entered the *Sunday Times* Golden Globe race, a single-handed, round-the-world yacht race. He hoped to win a cash prize to aid his failing business, convinced of his imminent triumph. His faith was largely down to the fact that he had invented, he believed, a revolutionary control computer for his boat with self-built marine navigation system (Lucy went into considerable detail here, sometimes employing diagrams and a scale model. The story tended to flag at this point).

Yet when Crowhurst set off on his voyage, he was far from ready. His boat, the *Teignmouth Electron*, was barely seaworthy, his revolutionary navigation system merely a jumble of disconnected wires. In fact, none of his proposed safety devices were complete. He departed in a tense confusion on the 31st of October, realising, as he recorded in his log, that as things stood, he had only a fifty-per-cent chance of surviving the trip. Yet off he went, to face the ocean.

Almost immediately, Crowhurst's fears began to be realised; he discovered leaks in his boat, his bilge pump wasn't working, he was going to be unable to work the necessary safety devices. He considered the journey before him – the treacherous southern Ocean, Cape Horn. It wasn't going to work.

So he started to lie. He radioed back false reports of his location; he claimed to be making heroic, groundbreaking progress. By early December, he was being hailed worldwide as the likely winner of the race, a record-setter, even. In fact, he was drifting erratically in the southern Atlantic, confused, floundering. He spent hours, days, weeks composing his fake log: complex mathematical equations and feats of bogus celestial navigation.

Crowhurst began to fall apart. As those at home cheered his triumph, he disintegrated. Perhaps he was crushed by the weight of his own deception, perhaps he became unable to function in a state of such acute, desperate solitude. We'll never know. All we know is that sometime in early July, Crowhurst jumped ship. The *Teignmouth*

Electron was discovered, adrift, on the 10th of July. The interior of the cabin was squalid; on the chart table lay his logs, real and fake, arranged for all to see. Two halves of a man, exposed. One of the entries in Crowhurst's tortured log contained a phrase, a scrawled phrase which, from time to time, pops unbidden into my head: "it is the mercy". It is the Mercy. Opaque, terrible, indecipherable.

I've always been entranced by that story, since I first heard it. I loved the artfulness of the deceit, and recoiled from the horror of the reality. I imagined the increasing filth of the cabin, the disorder of Crowhurst's mind, the carefully constructed perfection of his messages to the world. Night after night, as my parents dined with friends, or went to the cinema, or worked late, I begged Lucy to don the oilskins and tell me, just one more time, the tale of Donald Crowhurst.

Years later, I relayed the story to Clare. She didn't get it. She just said something like, "Oh, how sad", and went back to watching *Friends*. I put on a sou'wester and tried again. Still, no response. She heard the tale with a remote detachment, perhaps seeing the poor man as one of a different species, worlds apart from nice, normal Clare. To her, he was a mad person from a film, a quite nasty film which makes you want to hide behind your princess-scented pillow and hold your adolescent boyfriend's soft, little hand for comfort.

I, on the other hand, was right there with Donald, on the boat. I felt his determination at the start, his delusions of brilliance, his realisation of defeat, the impulse to lie, the breakdown. I held his hand as he leant over the stern rail and went forward, forward, forward into the dreadful curls of foam. There, I stop. What happened next – some kind of death, probably not fast – is outside the scope of my pissy little Sunday-supplement imagination. And thank goodness. For up to that moment, I *am* Donald Crowhurst. Right down to the bilge pump.

Lucy and I took to using a phrase, "Crowhursting", meaning to relay false positives about one's life in order to comfort loved ones far away. We came up with it the day I left for a two-week horse-riding camp, aged twelve. "Now, Judy, no Crowhursting. If you're unhappy, you must tell us."

Fat chance. I have never, ever confessed unhappiness to my family. Friends, perhaps, back in the day. And occasionally Lucy, before she joined the Merchant Navy. But family – never.

What would be gained? They'd worry, and I'd feel like shit in the knowledge that they were on to me, that they knew about my abject failure in yet another supposedly pleasurable field. I just apply a merry gloss to events, varnishing over the cracks until my life gleams enticingly. On the train – Liverpool Street to Ipswich, once again – I thought about Crowhurst, and about all the untruths I've told my family over the years. Tiny little fibs, which congeal, in time, to form one big, insurmountable lie. I must be frank; my family do not know much more about me than my readers. They know where I live, they know that I still hope to perform professionally, and they know that I am a tiny bit bigger than I sometimes let on. The rest they deduce from my column.

I did tell Clare about Emma, though. I had to. Clare had spent three days in Cambridge after my finals. Together we'd passed a fair bit of time in Emma's company: walks, meals, chats, wine. Emma had described Clare as "almost offensively fit", an observation which ties in well with my own view of my little sister. Clare had adored Emma. Most people did.

I remember telling her the news. She was watching *Top of the Pops*, and a taxi had just brought me home from the hospital.

"Clare?"

She didn't look at me.

"Yep."

"You know that girl?"

Still watching telly.

"The blonde one. Quite small. We went to Quod together and you had steak?"

She perked up.

"Oh, yeah, Emma. She was lovely. How is she?"

A little pause.

"Dead."

I felt a mixed pang of pity and guilt, not so much for the news I'd just conveyed as for the way in which I'd conveyed it. I softened the blow a little.

"I'm sorry."

Clare froze and stared at me, looking exactly as people should look when they hear of a death.

"What? Oh, Judy, I'm – what happened?"

"Car crash."

Clare's eyes began to widen and shine, always the preliminary to a flurry of rather fetching little sobs.

"Oh... oh... I – what?"

"The car went wrong, it skidded, over and upside down and things. It was all pretty quick. Nothing much would have registered."

"Oh, Judy, I – it can't – oh –"

She was properly crying now. This was, as ever, a

situation that called for a hug, but why the hell should I? I was annoyed. This was my friend, my sadness, my life. I wished that I'd never invited her to stay in Cambridge, then I wouldn't have had to tell her about Emma and we wouldn't be performing this impromptu grief-masque in our parents' living room, backed by the plastic bounce of *Top of the Pops*.

She leapt up and ran across to me with her arms open, face distorted with sorrow. She crashed firmly into my abdomen. I wrapped my arms around her – for physical support as much as anything – and together we toppled smoothly backwards into Dad's tank of tropical fish. The back of my head hit the edge of the tank; water and weeds and broken glass and fish cascaded forward, rinsing the newly seething gash on my skull.

Clare – dry as a bone – ran screaming to the kitchen, sobs backed up in her throat, voice shifting in pitch until it became a perverse, animal wail:

"Mum! Dad! Judy's friend died in a car crash... and then she fell over, and she cut her head, and the tank broke, and the fish are everywhere, and we need to put them in a bowl of water now or they'll die! Mum! MUM!"

I sat on the floor, stunned, and dropped a hysterical angel fish into a mug of cold peppermint tea. Emma was dead, my beautiful Emma whom I loved better than anyone in the world, and Clare was screaming about buckets and fish and water weed. I heaved myself off the floor, shook the ornamental pebbles out of my hair, and went to comfort my weeping little sister.

• • •

I dragged my luggage off the train at Ipswich. I had opted for a one-night-only visit: Wednesday to Thursday. I would be there for the party preparations, the night itself, and the hangover breakfast.

I'd brought about twenty disparate items of clothing, which between them could probably be spun out into two or three passable outfits. Among them was the gold strappy top from my previous Ipswich visit, two weeks ago. Teamed with some black trousers, a big shawl, and my one pair of decent boots, it would, I felt, add a touch of mature yet frivolous glitter to my evening-wear. I'd sponged off the residue of Ipswich, and cancelled the nightclub smell with a six-year-old bottle of Ck One I found under the sink. I was ready to mingle.

Clare met me at the station in the old family Volvo. Black, battered, still bearing the dent where I once threw a wheelie-suitcase at the boot in protest at being driven back to school. It smelt violently of car, conjuring fifteen years of putrid memories: travel sweets, bickering, school runs, nausea, fist-eatingly dull caravan holidays in the Dordogne. I wanted to run, screaming, back to the Novotel and get revved up for this week's Foam Night. Anything but the car. I was certain that if I got back in that car, I would suddenly become thirteen again, gravid with wine gums in the back seat, already sniffing the indolent despair of the life that lay ahead of me.

I determined to be polite, mature, effusive. I pushed my bag into the back, leant over to the driver's seat, and greeted Clare like the lovely big sister I am, flinging my arm around her shoulder and kissing her noisily on the cheek.

"Clara!"

"Judith, my lovely!"

"Hello!"

"Hello!"

We let out girlish squeals of delight, like pigs at a bucket. Clare looked great. Glossy, healthy, bouncy, quite the little butcher's dog. Her clothes were perfect: magazine-friendly faux-casual rustic with a polished urban sensibility. Skinny jeans, dark green wellies, and an apparently baggy brown jumper that clung pervily to every honed contour of her petite-model torso. Around her neck was an artfully dishevelled string of obviously plastic pearls. A little touch of mascara and thick, tumbling sheets of poker-straight mahogany hair completed the picture – the girl who every man wants to shag up against the stable door then take back to his parents for a white wine spritzer. We drove off, past the Novotel, past Liquid, and out onto the A12.

"Nice pearls, Clare."

She let out an airy little laugh.

"Oh! Ha ha. They're ironic."

How hilarious.

"You look well, Judy, have you lost weight?"

No.

"Yes! Thanks for noticing. A couple of pounds, per-haps. I've been busy."

"Gosh, lucky you, being in London. Durham's starting to feel ever so tiny. But there are lots and lots of hills, and that keeps me fit. There's this one big hill that I have to walk up every single day to get from my college to my library, it's ever so steep. I suppose London must be quite flat. I can't wait!"

Why is she talking about hills? I don't care about hills. Oh well, as long as she's yammering on I don't have to say anything. I smiled pleasantly.

"Yes, it is quite flat. And there's the tube, which is handy."

"Gosh, yes, I bet."

"Or buses. Sometimes I go on the bus."

"Gosh, yes, absolutely."

We continued in this vein for twenty minutes. We covered the relative gradients of all the towns in which we'd lived, compared favoured methods of transport, and addressed the issue of practicality vs. aesthetics in different types of footwear. We even touched on travelcards. Just as we were going into the details of how best to stroke one's Oyster card against the top-up machine, I was brought up short. We turned into the drive of the Old School House, Glemham, and I caught sight of an enormous pink marquee. Not just pink, but Hot Pink – the pink of the 1980s, of Cyndi Lauper, of the Eurovision Song Contest, of Gaviscon. I interrupted Clare's stream-of-consciousness monologue about the Newcastle metro.

"What the fuck is that?"

"It's the marquee for my party. Do you like it?"

I was dumbstruck.

"Yes, yes… it's quite… fuck."

"We've got a chocolate fountain and a pink champagne bar and a huge bathtub full of Turkish delight cubes. It's going to be brilliant. Are you excited?"

I thought back to my own twenty-first birthday party. Me, Mum, Dad and Clare went to the Old Orleans Mexican restaurant in Ipswich. We had to leave at 8pm because Clare burnt her arm on a sizzling platter.

"Yes, it's amaz – hold on. A bathtub full of Turkish delight?"

"Yeah."

"Why?"

"Well – duh – it's Flowers, Fairies and Castles, isn't it? The Turkish delight is for the fairies."

But of course.

"And the chocolate fountain's got battlements. We found a company in Lavenham that does them. We got it half price because Mum did the flowers for their daughter's funeral."

"Brilliant."

"I'm so excited, Jude, honestly. It's going to be the Best. Party. Ever."

"I don't doubt it for a second."

Also, possibly, the most financially unfeasible party ever. Even my tiny little town centre guacamole-fest had come close to breaking the parental bank. The Bishop finances have always been a source of great pain and hilarity. Mum and Dad – she's a florist to the moderately affluent, he's the deputy headmaster of a shrinking private day-school – have a certain flair for making deeply unwise monetary decisions. They've spent their entire marriage flinging themselves, lemming-like, into investment opportunities advertised on pieces of junk mail, setting up compassionate yet misjudged standing orders to "charities" whose very existence is questionable, and selling property to the lowest bidder because "he looked a bit like Grandad." Our Great Depression was brought about by the arrival of the "farm". We, as a family, own five elderly sheep, a Red Poll cow, and an albino donkey called Esther. The plan was to increase the number of sheep through breeding, shear them for wool, then use their offspring for meat. The Red Poll cow – one of a registered rare breed – was bound to be a lucrative tourist attraction, and Esther could offer rides to local children for a small sum. Problems arose immediately; no-one knew how to shear a sheep and we loved them too much to eat them, no-one gave a toss about the Red Poll cow, and Esther turned out to have the temperament of a pre-menstrual SS Officer. So for the last seven years the animals have stood quietly in the paddock, staring implacably out at the world and eating money.

The Volvo crunched up the gravel, and we had arrived. Home. You have to keep calling it "home" until you have children of your own. It's the rules. If Mummy and Daddy still live in the place where you grew up, then it's your home, and don't try to pretend otherwise. You can say "Mum and Dad's", or "My Parents' Place", or "Where I Grew Up", all you like, but one day someone will catch you out and ask you where you're going for the weekend, and you'll say "home". As long as Mum and Dad are there, boiling the kettle at the Old School House, Glemham, then you will always have a default address, whether you like it or not.

Home, when I arrived, was the same as ever. So little had changed that every difference had to be remarked upon. Dad took me on a tour of the refurbished woodshed, introduced me to the new log basket, and told the tale of the patio heater. Mum let me try out the salad server and rattle the newly acquired bottle of feline thyroid pills.

Then we had tea. We always have tea, whenever anyone arrives or leaves, whenever anyone feels happy or sad. We take our seats at the scrubbed little kitchen table and have tea, just the four of us, back in our old chairs. Mum had made a fruit cake as a concession to my presence. Dad ate most of it. Since he got the "farm", he's taken to eating like a grizzled son of the soil, using mealtimes to aggressively slough off his mundane rural schoolteacher status. He grasped his slice of cake in his open palm, obscuring it entirely, and then rammed the whole thing into his mouth, chewing as if he'd just returned from nineteen hours of intensive tilling. He's a big bear of a man, six foot three and broad: a physique that could give you a brilliant hug then heave you smoothly into a ditch. Mum twittered and chewed, hopping around like a fragrant little robin, smelling, as ever, faintly of plant food. We drank our tea, and chatted as if we'd never been apart: awkward, stilted, nagging, affectionate.

Then they took me up to my room. My Room. At the top of the house, with low-slung beams and Roald Dahl books and rosettes pinned to the board. They'd made up the bed with a flowery duvet cover, which was nice. Dad surveyed the room, put an arm round my shoulder and said "Good to have you back, Judy. Thought we might never see you again, off in London." A little Dad-chuckle.

Suddenly I wanted to fling my arms around my Dad and tell him that I'd like to stay for ever, curled up under the flowers in my little single bed, eating apple crumble and stroking the cat. Here, Glemham, was where I was meant to be, where I could be happy. I felt my nose and eyes fill up, and a lump rise in my throat. I stepped into the room, away from him, and dumped my bag on the bed.

"Don't be so silly, Dad. Anyway, I can't stay long. Just till tomorrow. Thanks for sorting the room. You can go now."

"Come down and see the animals! Esther's in a good mood today. She just ate a cabbage."

"In a bit. I've got some stuff to sort out up here. Bye."
"OK."

He left, offended. "I've got some stuff to sort out."

Honestly. What could I possibly ha e to "sort out", in my childhood bedroom, with nothing except fifteen Roald Dahl books and a slightly disgusting bag of clothes? Christ.

I lingered a while in the bedroom, for form's sake and to stop myself from crying. I went to the living room and found Mum, Clare, and a selection of aunts and neighbours stuffing pink carnations into gold-sprayed ramekins. On the wall, in a polythene bag, hung Clare's party dress, a silver, backless concoction which screamed "princess" but whispered "whore".

Clare presided over the festive sweatshop:

"OK, so we've got the champagne bar by the entrance – has anyone distressed the silk for Birthday Avenue? Good, thank you. Then we go in, chocolate fountain to the left, dinner tables in a horseshoe, and the Turkish Delight bath will be on the plinth in the centre. Dinner to be cleared no later than eleven – it must be eleven – and the space freed up for dancing. White chocolate fairies on every placemat – did you hear that, Sheila? *Everyone must have a fairy* – and the Durham Barbershop Boys must sit near the sound equipment so they can get up and sing straight after dinner…"

• • •

I sat down and sprayed a couple of ramekins. The air was noxious with gold paint, everyone and everything glistening gently under a light sheen of ornamental toxicity. This was going to be hell. Does Clare think she's a Rothschild? Has she spent so much time at Durham wearing a pashmina and eating venison and talking about beagles that she's started to believe her own snobbery? My way of life, squalid as it is, is at least honest. Our social status is more suited to Lambrini than it is to Krug. Good-natured moderation with the odd glint of lunacy, funded by a workable bank balance that you can see the bottom of: that's us. Yet here's Clare, spending Dad's donkey-food money on Amanda Wakeley and aggravating Aunt Sheila's asthma with spray-paint, simply so she can be more like her hooting, squealing, braying acquaintances. For a moment, I felt superior. I was glad to be grubby and shambolic and aimless and greedy. I grabbed another hunk of fruit cake from the kitchen, and went to don my multi-stained Matalan evening-wear.

The guests began to arrive at seven. Lissom posh girls in ethereal dresses, boys done up like their fathers in dinner jackets and cummerbunds. Lots of silver eye shadow and self-conscious ornamentation: Flowers, Fairies and Castles, a sexualised Disneyland. I grasped my flute of pink champagne, and felt my age. Not in a bad way – I still couldn't place myself alongside the proper adults who were standing to one side, drinking Pinot Grigio and talking about dinghys – but I did feel a certain seniority, a detachment. I was relieved to belong to neither party; happy to float, unnoticed, through the fun.

Clare had prepared a militaristic table plan. To my left was Lucinda, the only large girl, I think, in Clare's circle of friends. She wasn't so much fat as solid, five foot nine, meaty, possibly a student of veterinary science. She'd made an effort with her appearance, which only added to the tragedy of the thing.

Some people are not meant to wear dresses. With her hair in a severe up-do and her body encased in a stretchy steel-grey dress, she looked slightly like a grain silo wrapped in clingfilm. She was quiet, sweet, obviously accustomed to being put next to the fat sister at parties.

I wondered whether or not to break the ice with a compliment. "You look lovely", perhaps. She didn't, but I could still say it. She'd clearly made an effort. Maybe a kind word from me would improve her evening, give her the touch of confidence that would actually make her look lovely. Or perhaps it would just give her false hope, perhaps she would try misguidedly to form a romantic or sexual relationship this evening, bolstered by my compliment. She'd then be shatteringly rejected, confidence in shreds for the foreseeable future. Nevertheless, she did look better than I did, so a compliment from me was plausible:

"You look lovely."

She smiled shyly.

"Thanks."

To my right sat a small, tubby, sweaty, bearded man of about thirty. Adrian Simmons. Mr Simmons. Dear God. Clare had, unknowingly, played a bit of a blinder with the old placement. Mr Simmons and I go back quite some way; he was a junior history teacher at mine and Clare's secondary school. He spent years being mercilessly bullied by twelve-year-old girls, and was rarely seen without a wounded expression, having had yet another packet of crisps smashed in his face by a pre-pubescent rude-girl.

Our relationship was remarkable because of one incident; the great Belgium shit-fire of 1998. Mr. Simmons was escorting my sixth-form history group on a tour of the First World War battlefields of Belgium and Northern France. During a particularly dull weaponry lecture just outside Ypres, he – ever the professional – nudged me in the ribs and suggested that the two of us sneak off for a cheeky fag.

We went through a copse, to the edge of a farmyard,

where we sat atop a soft earthen mound and fired up our Marlboro lights. We couldn't have known at the time what that mound consisted of: two tons of agricultural manure, left tinder-dry by months of arid weather. Thus we couldn't have known the potentially devastating effect of any hot cigarette ash. We'd been there about a minute when I first smelt burning, at least two before I realised that it wasn't just the fags. By then it was too late; heat was spreading through the muck-heap, flames starting to lick its lower edges. We jumped and ran, making up in sheer, burbling panic what we lacked in athleticism.

The damage totalled one small field, two outbuildings, and a memorial dedicated to those who had lost their lives at the Battle of Passchendaele. Also, Adrian's job. He was sacked shortly afterwards, as much for sharing his cigarettes with a sixth-former as for the ensuing carnage. I saw him at the bus stop as he left town. He shook my hand.

"No hard feelings, Judy."

"Thanks. Bye, Mr Simmons."

That was eight years ago. I hadn't seen him since then. I'd heard vague reports, some accurate, some apocryphal; he'd married an heiress, he'd moved to France, he'd lost weight, he'd become obese, he'd taken up scuba-diving, he'd gone mad and killed a horse. The only certain, solid thing I knew was that two years ago he'd briefly tutored Clare in preparation for her history A-Level. Hence his presence here, I supposed.

He sat down. We stared at each other for a second, then chuckled.

"Judy. Judy Bishop. Bloody hell. So good to see you. Kiss me?"

A peck on the cheek. He was sweating lightly, as was I.

"Eight years. God."

"Eight years, Mr. Simmons."

"Adrian, please."

"Oh, I couldn't possibly."

I was being coy. No idea where that came from.

"So what are you – well – the column, obviously, but, what else do you – God."

The words trailed off, and he beamed at me. I beamed back, for a while. There was a little pause. He unfolded his napkin, refolded it, and began to dab his face. It was, honestly, lovely to see him. Far from easy, though. Seeing him again set off a train of niggling little feelings: guilt, embarrassment, surprise, affection, nostalgia. I wanted to know what had happened to him, how he'd been, which of the vicious rumours were true. I wanted to chat, but I couldn't; he remained my schoolteacher, and a man who'd lost his job because of me. Never the finest of conversationalists, I was now completely stumped. We sat for a few moments, toying with our cutlery. He broke the ice.

"I'm divorced."

"Really?"

"Barbara. You met her, I think. The bursar's cousin."

"God! Wasn't she –"

"Nearly fifty, yes."

He smiled, bless him, and went on.

"She had a twenty-four-inch waist."

"How small is that?"

He made a shape with his hands.

"That's pretty small."

The starter arrived. Melon, and a little scoop to eat it with.

"Where do you live now, Mr Simmons?"

"London. Do you know – um – Elephant and Castle?"

"I know – I know of it. Why did you choose to live there?"

Why did he choose to live there? No-one would choose to live there. It's a motorway intersection and two hundred kebab shops.

"Well, largely necessity. I own a business, the rent's affordable –"

"Oh, what business?"

"Mashed potato. Catering. It's a café."

I brightened.

"Sausage and mash?"

"No, just mash. Or variants thereon. Barbara hated mash. Wouldn't eat carbohydrates. 'Carbs'. I love mashed potato."

"Good for you."

Another pause, longer than ever. Dinner continued, interminable. I chatted to Lucinda, Mr Simmons chatted to his other neighbour. Mid-pudding, he picked up with me again;

"You know, Judy, Elephant and Castle is actually a very historic area."

"Oh?"

"No, really. Its original name was Newington – unrelated to Stoke Newington, ha. The name 'Elephant and Castle' is, apocryphally, a corruption of the Spanish Infanta de Castile, meaning the eldest daughter of a monarch who landed by royal barge in Newington some time in 1501. There's so much to learn about the area, people don't see that."

I imagined Mr Simmons, alone, eating mashed potato and reading books on the history of the SE17 postcode. It was rather lovely.

"Do you enjoy local history, then?"

"Oh, yes. I live near the Michael Faraday Memorial."

"What's that?"

"Essentially, a stainless steel box. It also contains an electrical transformer for the Northern Line, which –"

His flow was mercifully stemmed by the arrival of Clare, on the brink of tears.

"Judy, oh, my God, it's all gone – sorry, Mr Simmons, hope you're having fun – it's all gone wrong – there's no-one to sing, and someone has to sing because if they don't then there'll be a gap between dinner and speeches and I was counting on the Barbershop Boys for a smooth segue, and now we're fucked, and it has to be a capella because there's no piano, and you have to help."

"Alright, calm down. What happened to the Barbershop Boys?"

She gulped, desperately. I thought for a second that they might have drowned in the chocolate fountain, or been communally kicked to death by a red-eyed Esther.

"They're drunk."

Mr Simmons suppressed a chuckle, and spoke.

"All of them?"

Clare's voice sharpened, and she all but hissed at poor Adrian.

"Yes, Mr Simmons, drunk. They had a competition. I hate them."

She began to cry.

"Judy, would you sing something? Just one song, to fill the gap while the coffee's put out?"

It seemed to matter to her. I was light-headed with cava. I felt warm and friendly. Yes, I could sing.

"Yeah. Alright. Just one song."

Adrian perked up again.

"You sing, Judy?"

Once again, I was coy.

"Yes. Sort of."

Clare grabbed me by the hair.

"OK, now."

"Now?"

"Yep."

"But what shall I sing?"

"I don't know. Something… something… something after dinnerish. Not too bouncy."

I weaved up to the rostrum. "Something after-dinnerish." So something soothing, something sad, something momentarily arresting, yet without too much flash about it. I delved into my vault – the happy place of songs and feelings, appropriate moments. I found it: "If Love Were All". By Noel Coward, originally, then subsequently covered by every wounded diva under the glitterball. Halfway between a shrug and a suicide note, "If Love Were All" is an entertainer's moment of indulgence, of introspection, of softening self-awareness and vulnerability. It requires a certain qualification to sing it which, perhaps, I lack. It needs a life leading up to that first note: true pain, true trial, true stardom. Nevertheless, I thought, it would do. It was soft and calm and pretty.

Clare tapped a fork against the edge of her glass, and a series of "shhh" noises ran round the room. I held the microphone, kept my eyes resolutely open, and sang. Light, breathy, tremulous. In tune, in time, connected, the notes climbing gently to meet the feeling, my free hand rising slowly with the sensation generated by the cadences.

I believe in doing what I can,
Crying when I must,
Laughing when I choose,
Hey ho, if love were all
I should be lonely.

As I sang, I believed it. Or wanted to believe. Wanted to believe that these lyrics could be a summation of all that I was really about, that my humanity mirrored that of the greats – Coward, Garland, Merman – as much as it did the boy in Ipswich, or the shrieking post-adolescents in front of me, or my journalistic persona. I could be great. I am great already. That veneer of magnificence may conceal a void, a glamorous, smoky, boozy, gnawing void, but still it's there. I am singing, as I should.

But I believe that since my life began
The most I've had is just …… a talent to amuse.

I let my breath catch, left a pause, before I sang "a talent to amuse". That'll show 'em. Not a dry eye in the house. This brave woman, they'll think, this beautiful, beautiful thing that she's doing, showing us all that she's more than just a Sunday Paper Scribbler. I maintained the tension, letting my voice quieten so that my people had to strain to hear it.

Hey ho…… if love were all.

I finished, eyes shining, and looked around the room. I clocked numerous variations on attentiveness, embarrassment, surprise, and polite vacancy. A predictable reaction to an anonymous chubby woman getting up to sing, apropos of nothing, the peaceable lament of a wounded star. Mr Simmons just sat there, interested, smiling slightly, completely still, watching and listening.

I could see Clare clearly. At the back of the room, talking to the caterers, arranging coffee, clinking cups. As I sang, she weaved through the tables, got up onto the rostrum, and stood at my shoulder. Coffee was evidently ready. I finished, and she cut short any applause I might have received by steering me off the rostrum and tapping the microphone flirtatiously. It was time for her speech.

She took out her cue-cards – pink, gilt-edged, most likely scented – and began to speak. She was thanking people. She was thanking Mum and Dad, thanking the guests, thanking God, thanking the fucking caterers. Thanking everyone except me. Me, her sister, who paid fifty pounds for an open return ticket to Ipswich, who sat uncomplainingly between the two dud guests at dinner, who got up and sang like a choirgirl in front of two hundred pissed twenty-year-olds just so there wouldn't be an awkward pause between pudding and coffee. Clare finished speaking – to a barrage of applause – wiped away a beautiful tear, and sat down, clutching her pretty little heart like an Oscar winner.

The towering blackness descended. I wanted to scream, to run at Clare and rugby-tackle her to the ground. I wanted to pound my fists against her and pull her hair and cry, like I did when we were little. I wanted to shriek and wail, just so that someone would ask me what was wrong. I wouldn't know what to say when they did, but I'd stand a chance if someone would just fucking ask me.

I didn't scream. Instead, I drank. I drank and drank

and drank. I moved alone between the tables, swallowing the last inch from everyone's glass. I went into the kitchen and begged for spirits. I slept briefly in a bush, had a glass of water, then carried on drinking, like a Roman, like a film star, like a tramp.

Mid-binge, I remember a conversation. Mr Simmons. He approached me, as I slouched against the canvas at the side of the tent, accepted my offer of a swig of blue curacao, congratulated me on my singing, then blushingly asked me a question.

"Judy, have you – ahem – have you been receiving any strange… any strange parcels lately?"

Oh. Yes. I had. I told him so, only capable, by this stage, of monosyllables. He chuckled.

"Have you been enjoying them?"

"Yes. I'm growing flowers."

"Well, all I can say is, you're welcome."

I was too drunk for this.

"What?"

"You're welcome."

A creepy little smile. Aha. So he was the sender. Of course. The fire. Belgium. I get it. It's funny. And when something's funny, you laugh. I felt laughter bubbling up, a little shrieky hysteria, foam rising above the murk. I lurched forwards and hugged him, laughing into his shoulder, tears streaming, knees weak. I thanked him, over and over again, for creating such a brilliant, life-enhancing joke.

He blushed deeper, puce.

"Well, as I say, you're welcome. I – I – got the invitation to the party, and thought that I might like to get back in touch, so I got your address from Clare. Then I remembered our funny thing from Belgium, and thought that I might be a bit, well, creative about it. Hope I didn't scare you. I'm surprised you didn't guess that it was me."

I laughed harder, held him harder. What a wonderful man. More drinks now. Cheers.

The rest of evening is, to say the least, fuzzy. I remember dancing, dancing round and round like a furious dervish, until I was dancing around Mr Simmons. I remember kissing him and kissing him and kissing him, pulling his beard and biting his lips and holding him tight around his lovely yielding middle.

I remember us ascending, together, onto the plinth, in triumph. I remember us nestling together in the tub of Turkish delight. I remember climbing on top of him, pushing him down, unzipping his flies. I remember stuffing handful after handful of Turkish Delight into his pants. I remember lowering my head to his crotch and biting and licking and sucking and giggling, my mirth turning to wails of thwarted fury as I noted his flaccid genitals and mounting discomfort. I remember the bath tub sliding slowly and majestically off the plinth, trapping a half-naked man underneath. I remember Clare crying, I remember the paramedics laughing.

Then I remember waking up the next morning, in a bush in my parents' drive, my Dad blackly revving the family Volvo, ready to take me back, once again, to Ipswich station.

• • •

On the train, my phone rang. A voicemail, left early in the morning. It was Adrian Simmons, mumbling something about how lovely it was to see me again. He then asked if I fancied meeting up back in town. You know what? I think I might say yes.

The Days of Judy B

THE THRILL of the First Date is a well-documented phenomenon. Books, magazines, chat shows, sitcoms: since the dawn of courtship lads and ladies have been recounting the thrill of those initial hours, and the gleeful horror of preparing for them.

This week, I am proud to have been one of the preening many. I spent two days choosing my outfit, chucking great waves of my hard-earned cash at the salespeople in TopShop and Ravel, sucking in my stomach until I became vaguely concave, and wondering whether lilac eyeshadow will make the difference between an awkward evening and a lifetime of happiness. I've been shifting between practice postures like a ballerina at the barre, trying to find the perfect physical angle to flag up my sexual availability, without crossing the dirty border into Slutsville. I've been contemplating and dismissing conversational topics with the focus of a political speechwriter.

All in preparation for The Big Evening Out, with The Man (of my dreams?). Those three make-or-break hours which allow the tortured single lady a glimpse into the shimmering Elysium of coupledom.

And, I'm happy to report, it all went marvellously. He joked, I laughed. We enjoyed our sushi whilst gently mocking it, we drank enough sake to keep us bouncing along nicely. We shared a finger-bowl, then he offered to walk me home. It was perfect. I was already imagining the tender kiss followed, in all likelihood, by the cheeky and misguided shag.

But it was not to be. In my desperation to play the vamp, I'd purchased a pair of flirty-pointy red kitten heels in the only size available – a size too small. A mile from my flat, the pain became unbearable. Half a mile later, all the skin had gone from my heels. Then, as we reached my door and blood bubbled over the sides of my initially alluring purchases, I lost it. I dropped my date's hand and burst into tears.

He – ever the gentleman – enquired as to why I was hopping and weeping. Certain that I couldn't tell him the grim and bloody truth, I sobbed, "I already have a boyfriend. I'm so sorry. We can't see each other again." This is untrue. I have never been more single.

But because of my ever-reliable womanly vanity, I had to lie. And, to be frank, I'm not ashamed of that. Better to be thought of as a two-timing wench than as someone with ugly feet. We must make sacrifices for our looks, ladies, and remain uncomplaining. Just take a quick stroll in your new heels before the Big Date, that's all I ask. Listen to Aunty Judy, she's rarely wrong when it comes to dating.

Judy B's Purchase of the Week: A good shoe-tree. I'm not giving up on those pointy red bad boys.

JUDY BISHOP:

6.

8th October, 2006

Is it possible to fall in love with a man who leaves bags of shit on your doorstep? I think so. We all have our quirks, and faeces-based stalking must surely be one of the least alarming. It's encouraging, even. It shows creativity, an undeniable level of originality combined with a poetic acknowledgement of the filth in which we all exist. And it's the perfect starting point for a human relationship: the only way to go is up. A courtship that begins with flowers, candles, picnics, and loving chatter must eventually descend into the sordid minutiae of ongoing companionship; here we're starting with the worst of life, and as time passes, we'll be allowed to glimpse better things, and be glad of them. But we will start with the shit, and live in hope. It's all we can do.

It should have been obvious that it was Mr Simmons who was romancing me in this strange, earthy way. I should have guessed, if not immediately on receipt of the first bag, then as soon as we remet at Clare's party. He shouldn't have had to tell me. We have a shared history of manure, and he's a strange enough man to think that anonymously offering it is the key to my affections. But I must admit that his name didn't immediately occur to me; there are many, many people who could wish to send me shit: all those whom I've hurt through my actions, or annoyed through my column. I'm a sitting target, and I'm lucky that my parcels were, this time, the result of philanthropy rather than hate. Anyway, the mystery is solved, and on we go with our lives. Case closed.

Hence my surprise when, on Monday morning, another bag turned up on my doorstep. I imagined that Mr Simmons had already made any point that he was seeking to make, and that my morning post-fetching visit would now be free from excrement. But no, my parcel arrived in the usual manner: two layers of black plastic, Waitrose bag, decent shovelful of reasonably fresh manure. But this time, atop the pile, adhering valiantly to the smooth brown rounds, sat a yellow post-it note: "Surprise! Good to see you last weekend. Just thought I'd send over one final load, to help your roses! Call this number, go at 11 on Wednesday, and I'll meet you outside for lunch. 0207 892 4371. Adrian S." That was all: the note, then "0207 892 4371." I put the note down, lit a fag, and had another think. So far, the shit had been my friend. It had added flavour to my days, taken up some thinking room, and nourished a charming window-box. Now, it had brought Mr Simmons officially back into my adult life. I felt odd, initially. When the shit had been anonymous, it had been a curiosity, something onto which I could project my oddest and most lively imaginings. Now that it was attached to a person, a funny little person from the past, it had become somewhat frightening.

There were people involved, emotions, futures.

I looked at the number. Central London: it must be civilised. Should I call? Should I go to this thing – whatever it is – and meet Mr Simmons outside it for lunch? What warped and hellish seduction tool has he got lined up for me now? A humorously annotated selection of my old school reports? A tub of gunge? A historically themed torture garden? All possible, knowing his ways.

I picked up my phone and scanned my last few calls. One each from my editor, my mum, and Vodafone. Four calls to Jamal's Indian takeaway (they're doing a two-for-one on chutney when you order more than three dishes). I looked through my texts – the three-week-old rearrangement text from Gareth, one from Anna, and one from my sister calling me a "cock-sucking whore" and asking that I never call her again. I thought of Mr Simmons. He must like me, really like me, maybe even love me. He'd found out my address, clearly had a good long think about how best to reintroduce himself to me – aha! he'd been prompted by receiving Clare's party invitation, and thought he'd add an interesting little preamble before meeting me again on the night; yes, that was it! He had then acquired some horse manure and spent two weeks delivering it to a flat on the other side of town, simply so that he could romance me – is it romance? What a man. I glanced back at the number. Yes. I should call. 0207 892 4371.

Two rings. A soft, Scottish woman's voice.
"Hello, Quietus?"
"Hello?"
"Hello, how can I help you today?"
"I… um… who is this?"
"This is Janine, I work on reception here."

"Oh."

"Are you a patient?"

"A patient?"

"Are you currently seeing one of our practitioners?"

Patient. Practitioners. Quietus. Aromatherapy? Massage? Palmistry?

"Um, no, I'm just… calling."

"Would you like to make an appointment?"

"What kind of appointment?"

"An appointment with one of our practitioners."

A pause. She spoke again.

"Hello?"

"Hello."

"Have you been to see us before?"

"No. Who are you?"

"As I say, I'm Janine. May I ask why you're calling?"

"I found a number, on a parcel I got, and I wanted to… call it."

"Of course. If you're actively seeking therapy, we can offer an initial consultation with a psychotherapist, a cognitive behavioural specialist, or a consultant psychiatrist. Might any of those interest you?"

Oh, I see. It's a head-shrinking firm. Psychiatry. What? Why was Adrian Simmons sending me to therapy? The party? The blow-job? The song? Well, who cares. It might be worth a punt. Obey the shit.

"Perhaps the consultant psychiatrist."

If I'm going to do this, I'm going to do it right.

"Doctor Goldberg has actually had a cancellation this week, so he could see you on Wednesday at eleven, if that suits?"

"That suits very well, thank you."

"Great, and your name is?"

"Judy Bishop."

"Judy, lovely, thank you. You know where we are?"

"Uh, no."

She gave an address just off Harley Street, and we parted amicably. Janine the receptionist, and Judy Bishop: soon-to-be mental patient. And why the hell not? Why shouldn't I pop in for an hour of one-on-one with a mental health professional? Talking is, apparently, good, and this will be a low-stakes conversation. Whatever I give him, he will quietly and uncomplainingly receive and dispose of. It'll be like emptying a septic tank.

I've always refused counselling in the past. I find the concept alien – non-judgemental sympathy isn't a useful reflection of the way the world works. It's dangerous to speak unguardedly, to make verbal aspects of oneself which should remain inaudible and invisible. It's enough merely to smell the maggots: I don't need to open the bucket and watch them writhe.

But just this once, I thought, I'm going to give it a go. I'm trying actively to change myself, so it might be nice to have my progress monitored. And someone cares, someone cares enough to send me. If he cares, then others will too. It's all promising stuff.

On Tuesday, I went to my singing lesson. Gareth was on rare form having, he believed, unearthed a distant familial connection between his ailing grandmother and Dame Joan Sutherland. He produced a pair of photos – one of the six foot bel canto diva in full flow on the stage of La Scala, the other of a tiny pickled Welsh woman eating a biscuit. He explained the similarity: "It's in the jaw, dear. They both have the soulful Welsh jaw. And it's not entirely implausible, you know. Sutherland had the Spirit of the Valleys, in abundance. Her mother could have had a sister there, or a half-sister, and it makes sense that if she did, then I would be descended from her. You see?"

I didn't see, and I didn't care. I had no time for Gareth's deluded yammering. I needed to know about the show, the revue. I needed to focus on that prospect. I was concerned that Gareth hadn't mentioned it recently. Perhaps he'd dumped me in favour of someone else, another pupil. That didn't bear thinking about. The show was a light at the end of this grim autumn; a brilliant blank canvas onto which I could project my best fantasies, the shining, radiant Judy Bishop.

But Gareth wasn't mentioning it. It was going away, slipping, as everything so easily can. I breathed, relaxed, and – ever the professional – got ready to sing.

I'd chosen my repertoire for the lesson with more care than usual, settling on languid jazz standards which I felt I could make my own – "The Way You Look Tonight", "Embraceable You", "My Funny Valentine". Songs which couldn't be less relevant to my experience or attitude, but songs which could, if performed well, move me another rung up the sexual ladder. I bet Ella Fitzgerald never had to get her jollies in a provincial Novotel. Singing, I've decided, is my key to a functional sex life. Everyone has their selling point: mind, body, wealth, attitude. Mine is my voice; it must be, it couldn't feasibly be anything else.

I've been thinking a lot about sex lately. Real sex, sex between two people who know each other's names, on sheets that one or other of them owns, in a familiar room. Now that I've cleared the first sticky, drunken hurdle, there's no reason why I shouldn't progress to the next level, the level where there's eye contact and chat, and no-one throws up afterwards. I've made a decent start; in the space of a week I managed to rack up one fully penetrative act and an abortive attempt at fellatio. There are provincial hookers who couldn't have managed that.

And I can still see that the good kind of sexual relationship, however brief, may well be as much my entitlement as it is anyone else's. I just need to get a tiny bit better, in any way I can, to give the prospect of good sex something to latch onto. Singing is the answer, singing in public, in shows, in Gareth's show. To be able to do one thing admirably well elevates you in the eyes of others, throwing your flaws into soft focus and making the whole of you more appealing, if only for a few minutes.

I remember the first time I saw Ethel Merman performing on film. I was fifteen, on my parents' sofa. It was a school night, two days after the dead-end Ipswich boy had snogged my face raw outside the post office. I was babysitting my little sister Clare, then thirteen. It was about half past ten – the mischievous dead of night for a rule-abiding fifteen-year-old – and Clare was asleep upstairs. I'd poured myself an illicit glass of pudding wine and was looking for a video to watch before bed, perhaps an episode of *Steptoe and Son*, or a nostalgic, comforting children's show: *Muffin the Mule*, or *Bertha the Big Machine*. All the videos in the cupboard were over-familiar and dull, nothing I wanted to commit to for half an hour or more. Then I saw a quiet, dusty box, the cover a ratty olive-green, with an antiquated picture of two women: one small, honed and boxy, the other taller, swan-necked, and princess-like. The princess was holding the shoulders of the ballsy dwarf, both had their eyes forward and their mouths open, utterly engaged.

The sounds that they must have been making were being picked up by a 1950s microphone hovering low over their coiffed little heads. I looked at the title: Ethel Merman and Mary Martin at The Ford Motors 50th Anniversary Show. Recorded in 1953. I slid it into the machine and sat back.

One's first intense sexual feeling is always going to be the cause of some confusion. Even if it's a run-of-the-mill twinge on seeing a boyband, or a slight yearning for your best friend's older brother, there will still, undoubtedly, be a certain tense puzzlement connected to the experience. Mixed feelings. Hope, fear, embarrassment, frustration or, as the years roll by, relief. Whatever the time, location, or stimulus, no matter how ordinary you know on some level that you are, your first move in that direction is going to be a worry. Imagine, then, the upset that someone might suffer if suddenly they find themselves, at age fifteen, pinned to their parents' sofa, incapacitated with lust at the sight of a dead American gnome singing "Boogie-Woogie Bugle Boy". I didn't know that it was lust. I didn't know what it was. All I knew was that this woman was amazing, a physical presence above and beyond anything I'd ever seen. Taut, brassy, and loud loud loud.

I was far from ready for my first sexual bowling-over. I was wearing tracksuit bottoms, a rugby shirt, old slipper-socks, and an Alice-band. I'd just eaten uncomfortable amounts of shepherd's pie and an expanse of chocolate sponge. My maths homework was unfinished on the table in front of me. My aspect and situation couldn't have been less suited to the sudden heat and pressure, the dampness and throbbing, the big, hefty, inappropriate hello from my sexual organs. I wanted to pause the video, run upstairs, and change into something fabulous, something ornate and sculpted, something that conjured whisky and smoke and orchestras and dancing boys. I knew then that I would do anything, anything to place myself alongside this amazing woman. I wanted to drag her off the screen and touch her. I tried to touch myself, to masturbate – I'd read about it in *Sugar* magazine – but I didn't know what to do and it just felt a bit weird and grubby. I was hot and cross and impotent. I took the video out, got a bag of chocolate buttons from the treat cupboard, and settled down to watch *Muffin the Mule*. You know where you are with *Muffin the Mule*.

Once, at university, I tried to recreate that moment. With Emma, actually. We were drunk together, at an open mic night in a beer cellar. Persuaded by friends, giggling and stumbling, we got up to sing "Little Lamb", from *Gypsy*. It's a simple nursery song, slow and pure and contemplative. Yet when Emma and I took the mic, we might as well have been singing "I Touch Myself". Both facing outwards, an arm around each other's waists, we sang. Her clear soprano mixed comfortably with my rich brassiness, her cool, soft, heart-shaped little face nestled against my hot cheek. I was Ethel Merman, she was Mary Martin.

We turned to face each other, leant in. Emma – ever the show-off – improvised a harmony, which momentarily threw me. But still we sang, and moved closer, our eyes locking and just an inch of air between our lips. The song ended. Emma truncated the last note, smiled, moved closer still. Her lips touched mine. Everything in me knotted and flipped; I felt that same throbbing. I thought of Ethel Merman and of the song and of the audience, and then I couldn't think of anything but Emma, and me. I exhaled, and kissed her, my hand, once again, in the small of her back.

A vast, raucous cheer erupted. A hundred rugby-playing recruitment consultants-in-training bellowed with laddish glee, unable to believe their luck. Girl-on-girl action, always a winner amongst the viciously heterosexual. Someone threw a plastic cup of beer, someone else hurled a crisp packet corsage. Emma released me, raised her arms in triumph, and took a bow.

"Told you I'd do it."

She grinned at the audience, gave me a slap on the arse and a cheeky wink, and scampered off the stage to greet her fans. I stood there: mute, sweating, throbbing, shocked. Nearly had it, that time.

On Tuesday, with Gareth, I sang from the groin. As I slid through the lounge room lyrics, I conjured lovers and broke their hearts, flew from Broadway to Vegas to Carnegie Hall. For that hour, Gareth was my slave, my prattling piano-boy, the second-rate underling to be left in the dressing room after the show. I was the centrepiece, the work of art, the diva of the Archway Road. Sound flowed and resonated, every lyric doubled in meaning. It was a good lesson. Only loins of stone could have remained unmoved.

And all, perhaps, because I was due to meet my old history teacher for a sandwich the next day. It's peculiar what can lift you. I wasn't yet attracted to Mr Simmons, but I could see that I could be. He is old, fat, and strange. I am young, fat, and desperate. We could melt disconsolately together like two scoops of vanilla ice cream. I would be in a relationship and thus sorted, he would talk with affection and pride about his "younger woman". And he was my teacher. There's nothing sexier than a teacher, and nothing more enviable than going out with one. And I'm doing it. I have plenty of reasons to be positive about this.

Similarly, Gareth. As I sang, I felt that he could love me, and that I could love him. This was new; in the past he'd merely been a means to an end, a useful tool on my way to the spotlight. But as I sang before him – statuesque, in control – I saw his potential. A small man, an odd man, but a young, bright, engaging man. Perhaps that's what happens when you're happy, when you're using yourself to the full. You become, effectively, porous, soaking up all the joyful possibilities of life, and being lifted by them. So it was with Emma. That night after *Gypsy*, then singing together in the beer cellar; I was happy, I was open, every box contained a treasure. Bisexual? No. Expansive, questing, avant-garde. When I sing, I regain that joy. Keep it coming, bring it on. I can do this.

But first, therapy. The timing was good; I'd spend a cathartic hour with a mental health professional and then emerge – phoenix-like, healed – to face my romantic future in the form of Mr Simmons.

The offices of the Quietus practice were tucked away amongst the gaudy red mansion blocks of Marylebone. The area around Harley Street felt elderly, hushed, respectful. I looked at the gleaming black doors and the blinded windows, and wondered what was going on behind each one, here in this enclave of high-end medicine. Stomach cancer, electro-shock, breast augmentation, facelifts. People chucking vast sums of money at their own minds and bodies, giving themselves the best of everything in an attempt to keep on living. Good for them, I say.

I was there in a spirit of exploration, driven only by a buccaneering desire to play a cheery part in Mr Simmons' warped courtship. No pressure; I was strictly undercover. I reached number 84 and pressed the third floor buzzer, "Quietus". Someone buzzed me in – the noise continued for at least quadruple the amount of time it took me to open the door and pass through it. I imagine that the chronically mad do take more time than most to enter a building; they probably have to do their quirky little mad-things – touch the floor six times, put on a big rabbit hat, burst into tears.

I was greeted by Janine (a delightful woman, petite and fresh-skinned, just the sort of nurse I'd want swabbing my brow as Dr Goldberg strapped me to a table and passed high-voltage electricity through my juddering form) and directed to the waiting room. I took a seat and suspiciously eyed the mad people. Two of them. A beautiful young Indian woman in a cream-coloured business suit, reading e-mails on a Blackberry, and a short, shy-looking man flicking through a copy of *Good Housekeeping* magazine. They both looked fine. Still, you never know. She could be halfway through a sex change, he may have four hundred hamsters and speak only in vowels. They're a stealthy bunch, the mad.

Before long, I was ushered into a consulting room. Grey, gloomy, larger than you'd expect. The blinds were drawn to create the effect of dreadful privacy; I imagined all the pain that's trapped within those four walls, all the terrible secrets and destructive tragedies and unspeakable desires that have been forced out of people in a spirit of medical confidentiality. Against one wall was a long black sofa, and a tartan rug, neatly folded. On the table was a box of tissues. Everything was geared towards tears and pain, towards yanking out the darkness that the psychiatric profession believes lies within us all. I sat down on the sofa, and suppressed a near-overwhelming urge to get my money's worth by wrapping myself in the rug, keeling over sideways, and sobbing hysterically into the tissues.

I didn't. I sat tall and faced my new nemesis, the good Dr Goldberg. If asked to describe him, I would say that he had a beak. A long, hooked beak beneath a domed, ovoid head. His features had already settled into a sort of death mask – folds and furrows and shades of grey – and his mouth formed a ruler-straight line, perhaps consciously fashioned in order to convey neither disapproval nor encouragement. He sat in a maroon leather armchair, moulded over years to meet perfectly the contours of his body. I couldn't imagine him ever leaving that chair; motion would surely inhibit his air of sedentary omniscience. He looked as though he ought to be shrouded in clouds, gazing down over a mountain vista.

I sat for a few moments, trying my hardest to appear sane. I instinctively raised my finger to my mouth, then realised that nail-biting could be seen as a symptom of anything from general anxiety to a yearning for the nipple. I withdrew my hand and sat on it – a move I reconsidered when I saw the potential for auto-erotic association. Hands folded in my lap, I sat. He sat. Face-off. Years passed, then finally:

"Hello, Judy." A little smile.

"Hello, Dr Goldberg."

More silence. God. What do I do? Is the ball in my court? How can it be? I'm paying him, for heaven's sake. Guide me, Dr Goldberg.

"Why have you come to see me, Judy?"

I must be honest. This is a Space for Honesty; a sign in the waiting room said so.

"I – um – well… a bag of shit told me to."

He raised an eyebrow, heaved an eyebrow north until his floppy stone face reached "quizzical".

"Yes?"

"Yes. I've been receiving parcels of horse manure, anonymously, at my flat. Except they're not anonymous any more, because I know who the man sending them is, and I tried to suck him off in the bathtub. But I was getting the parcels every day. And then one of them had a note, with a phone number on – your number – well, Janine's number, and I thought that I should call it. And then I made an appointment, because I thought it might help me find out who was sending the shit."

Psychiatrists are not literal people. I should have known that Dr Goldberg would interpret my practical quest for information as a more generalised cry for help. He quizzed me, probed me as to how long I had been receiving the parcels, who I thought could be sending them, why I believed that coming to him would be beneficial. I answered briefly and factually, and he dug deeper. Had I ever been stalked in this manner before, what was my relationship history, did I have many friends, what were my interests, was my job fulfilling? No? Why? How did I get on with my family, do I still see them, do I like the way I look, do they like the way I look, how does that make me feel? Every ten seconds, "how does that make you feel?" And then the crunch question – "Would you say that you were depressed, Judy?"

Well, that came out of nowhere. I was completely pole axed – I hadn't mentioned the D-word, nor had I suggested that any kind of black dog might be straddling me. I'd merely furnished Dr Goldberg with my personal history and ongoing world-view, and he'd taken an inappropriate leap in the direction of a clinical conclusion. And he was wrong. I've never been depressed, surely not. Depression is a downward dip, a grey Tupperware lid placed on an otherwise good nature, impairing judgement and motivation. That didn't apply to me, it just didn't. Sure, there's plenty wrong with me, but that's only to be expected. I have a richly corrugated personality, and some of the grooves are bound to get rusty from time to time. But I'm taking steps to remedy that problem, I'm shaking things up, bounding energetically forward. That's not something a depressive would do. She'd just examine her pallid face in the cracked mirror, then sit back and have another flick through *The Bell Jar*. No, that's not me.

"No, Dr Goldberg, I don't think I am."

He made a sort of harrumphing noise and crossed his arms. Stalemate. Once again, we both sat. I scanned the room with mounting panic, searching for an escape, a possible digression, some form of stimulus. Suddenly I caught a glimpse of a framed photo on one of the bookshelves. I gasped.

"Is that a Welsh cob?"

It was a Welsh cob! Without a doubt, the same sort of pony I used to ride, once a week, at the stables back in Suffolk. And Dr Goldberg had a photo of one. Well, he couldn't be all bad if he had a photograph of a Welsh cob.

"No, it's a fell pony."

"What?"

He was wrong, he was just wrong. There was no way it was a fell pony. It was too tall, for a start. It's almost unheard of for a fell pony to be higher than fourteen hands. And its coat wasn't thick enough. That photo looked as though it had been taken during a frost; a fell pony would look like a little round Furby in that sort of temperatures.

"It's not a Welsh cob, Judy, it's a fell pony."

"It's a Welsh cob! I know!"

To my dismay, I felt my voice twisting, moving into my nose. My face became hot. Tears sprang to my eyes. Fuck. I was crying. Why? Dr Goldberg leant forward, his face melting gently into a mask of compassion. He offered me a tissue. I took it, ripped it up, and tried to speak again.

"You're wrong! It's a Welsh cob!"

The sentence twisted and stalled, juddering to a wet finish a good ten seconds after it had begun. How dare he? I know ponies. I may not know psychiatry, or Jung, or the ins and outs of the human mind, but ponies, I know. They're my childhood area of expertise, one of the very few oases in my mind that I can go to when things are at their worst. And now I was being made to doubt my own knowledge. What next? Was he going to produce a picture of Patti LuPone and try and tell me that it was Michael Ball? No, fuck this, I'm off. I know that therapy is meant to make you question yourself, but this is ridiculous.

I stood, scooped up my bag and coat, and charged out of the room, through reception, and down into the surprisingly, gloriously, clean new air of the street. Knocked backwards with relief, I sat down on the steps of the building. My sobs subsided, and I breathed. I lit a cigarette; the smooth, invasive smoke only increased my enjoyment of the cold air around me. I shifted to the side and lay down along the step, like a draft excluder. Still forty minutes to go until my lunch with Mr Simmons. That was fine. My plan to rise serenely from Dr Goldberg's lap and embrace the world of male possibility had, I think, been officially scuppered. I needed to regroup. Keep breathing. Repeat after me, "You were only crying about the Welsh cob. It's what anyone would have done, in that situation. There is nothing wrong with you. Nothing at all." Breathe. I felt the panic depart, replaced by the healthy, physical satisfaction that one feels after tears. Tiredness, serenity edged with euphoria, a dull glow. Shame, embarrassment, and fear will edge their way in later, I'm sure. But, for now, I'm lying here on the steps, comfy on the cold grey stone.

Then, a voice from my left.

"Quite full-on, isn't he?"

I sat up, twisted round. Peeping over the low brick wall which separated these steps from the next was the round, half-furry face of Mr Simmons.

"Mr Simmons."

"Adrian."

"Whatever."

I slumped forward again, resting my head in my hands. I couldn't handle him, not yet. He rested his chin on the low wall between us, and kept on looking at me.

"Aren't I punctual?"

Head still firmly in hands.

"Yes. Yes, you are."

Still that smile, that beard-splitting rictus of misplaced affability. He beamed on.

Silence. I spoke, still to the floor.

"Mr Simmons?"

"Yes."

"Why did you send me shit? Why didn't you just phone me?"

"Well... our joke. It was funny. You laughed, remember, at the party?"

"Oh. Yes. So I did."

I did remember Belgium, of course. It all made sense. How hilarious.

"And why Dr. Goldberg?"

"Oh, well. I wasn't going to do that. I was just going to put something funny on it – a photo of myself, or of the war memorial, or something. But then we met at the party and you sang – you sang that song so… so sadly and then you – then we – ahem, did that – in the bathtub, and I thought that perhaps you might like the Quietus number instead."

"Why?"

He shrugged.

"They really helped me out after the divorce. Got me seeing clearly again, you know. If it hadn't been for Dr Goldberg I'd never have had the courage to ask you out for lunch. He's great."

I kicked my left foot with my right, petulant.

"I hate him."

"I know, he is tough. But it's all to the good, you know. Are you seeing him again?"

"No."

I felt the tears re-emerge. Mr Simmons shuffled a bit, uncomfortable. He reached over the wall and patted my shoulder, like a seal hitting a block of ice with its flipper. We resumed the awkward pause. He perked up a little, and spoke.

"Hey, you know what?"

"What?"

"I saw your name in print the other day."

"Um, yeah. I'm in print every week. In the paper."

I'd regressed to adolescence, gum-chewing, hormonal sarcasm. Lovely. What a brilliant first date.

"No, no, something *about* you, not *by* you. Theatre

listings. I subscribe to this thing, a sort of a round robin cultural freesheet about the arts in South London. You were mentioned – a musical revue, in Sydenham? You were listed as 'ensemble and soloist'."

Oh, my God. *Oh, my God.* This was wonderful. Word was spreading, Gareth was plugging the show, it was listed, official, approved. And I was in it! A professional show, in a London newspaper! And just as I'd despaired, just as I'd thought my hope was being ripped away, in swings Mr. Simmons with this wonderful news. What a man, what a day! I sat up, smiled. The tears running down my face now seemed entirely incongruous; I couldn't think how they'd got there.

"Well, that's great news. Thank you, Mr Simmons."

"I'm definitely going to come and see it."

"Good stuff. I'd book your ticket now. It's only running for one night, and there's already quite a lot of heat under it publicity-wise. I'd hate for you to miss it."

I really would. I'd hate for him to miss my big night. He's part of my life now, he must see my triumphs.

"Of course. Hey – you can thank Dr Goldberg in your programme notes. For giving you pain and anguish on your way to the top."

I giggled. It wasn't that funny, but, giddy with tears and pleasure and affection and relief, I giggled; girlish, comforted.

At that moment the door swung dramatically open, and Dr Goldberg strode out, a sweeping, vampiric presence in a thick black greatcoat. Adrian shushed me and we sat up straight, like naughty children in the back row. Dr Goldberg nodded to each of us in turn.

"Adrian. Judy."

We nodded back and spoke in unison.

"Dr Goldberg."

As the good doctor powered off along the street, Mr Simmons and I looked at each other. A moment of silence, then we simultaneously burst into laughter, raucous, abandoned, yelps and hoots and wails of pleasure. I laughed until my abdomen tightened and I could take no more, until further tears coursed down my cheeks.

Eventually, we quietened. Adrian stood.

"Hoo. Fuck. Time for lunch, I think?"

"Oh, I don't know. I've had quite a morning. I should go home, really."

"OK."

He extended a hand to pull me up from the pavement. I used it gratefully, allowing him to take my whole weight as I swung up into a standing position. He took my hand and held it as we walked. I didn't mind. It was nice, actually.

"Let's get you a pasty, Miss Bishop."

"Alright."

I giggled again. I felt coy, submissive. We selected our pasties – for which he paid – and agreed to meet again some time soon.

I smiled, turned, tapped my travelcard against the barrier, and strode wordlessly off into the murk of the station. I think he likes me.

The Days of Judy B

SO, THERE HAVE been developments. I'm imagining that you, loyal followers, remember last week's Tragically Aborted First Date. In fact, you've probably been thinking of little else. Well, I am pleased to report that things have taken a Turn For The Better.

Reader, he called me. Well, let's be clear: he texted me first, as one would hope. A phone call out of the blue may be a stunningly romantic concept, but in practice it could be a disaster. The call might arrive when I'm in the bath, or when I've just run up some stairs, or when I'm in some other kind of aurally unappealing position. So he texted, I gave him the OK to call, I put on some Nina Simone and made a few restaurant noises, and we talked. We talked and talked and talked. We talked love, we talked life, we talked films, we talked family, we talked dirty. Yes, dirty. Little curls of filth peppered our otherwise civilised conversation, leading me to believe that there could really be Something Between Us.

Because that's where it needs to begin. With the Hint of Sex. I'm sorry to have to say it, I really am. Friendship, companionship, compatibility are all very well, but if that groinal spark is lacking, then you're going nowhere, I'm afraid.

I'm something of an authority on these matters. My first boyfriend – aged fifteen – was a deeply lovely person. We shared interests: the Spice Girls, movies, cheap cider cocktails. We were even in the same GCSE group for food technology. We kissed, of course we did. We kissed in public; we were so delighted to have each other as a mark of adolescent status that we grabbed and poked and made an exhibition of ourselves for the benefit of anyone who cared to look. In public, it was lovely. We were envied and revered. Everyone wondered whether or not we'd "done it".

And we tried to, my God we tried. But, whenever we reached the critical moment, one or other of us would have an infinitely more appealing idea – let's bake a cake, watch some telly, play on the computer. In the end, we broke up, touchingly and to the sound of Westlife singing "Flying Without Wings". I'm sure that we were both sexual beings – after we broke up he started going to life drawing classes and I got more seriously into horse-riding. But we just weren't into each other that way. And that way is not something you can control. It's either there or it's not.

And I'm pleased to announce that with The New Man, it most definitely is. I've started shopping for our next date, and this time I'm digging deeper. Underwear, new perfume, candles for the bedroom. It's the boy scout school of sexual optimism. I'm not going to push anything, but at least if it happens I shall Be Prepared.

My columns have been slightly down on the whole sex thing lately, I know. But that may simply have been the glumness of enforced chastity. Now that I'm climbing the rose trellis into Loverland, hypocrisy reigns. Long live it.

Judy B's Purchase of the Week: A red satin bedspread. Sorry, I just couldn't help myself.

JUDY BISHOP

7.

I thought, this week, that Gareth was trying to murder his grandmother. A big step, I know, a big splash into man's darker waters. But, perhaps, it's been a big week; a week of shocks and alarms and reconfiguring what I previously thought to be true. It's easy to assume that people are essentially benign; that they mean well and act only upon the most positive aspects of their nature. When you're walking along and a stranger touches your back, or shouts at you, or grabs you around the shoulders, your instant, momentary assumption is that it's a friend messing about. Someone who means you no harm. Not until the dagger is at your throat do you accept that you're in the presence of an aggressor. We assume that he must be alright, because everyone's alright really.

It's time to dispense with this Winnie the Pooh mentality, and to make ourselves alert to the constant presence of evil. Not merely lurking, but actively pursuing its wicked aims, minute by minute, second by second. Only by being aware that everyone has the potential to kill can we stop them from doing so. Unlikely as it may seem, right now Evil could be sitting above a shop on the Archway Road, eating a takeaway burrito and ploughing through *The Cole Porter Songbook*. And so I decided, this week, that I will carry a knife around with me, everywhere I go. I will never use it – cowardice – but I'll be glad to know it's there.

On Monday, I had a shock. An e-mail shock, from an old university friend. One of the many who'd petered out, drifted off, left me behind. Adam, who'd played a small part in our production of *Gypsy*. He sent round a general news e-mail, to all of us, the old gang. Just telling us what he was up to – training to be a music lawyer – and letting us know his new contact details. He'd included some photos he'd dug up from the *Gypsy* tour. A few of me in action, on stage and off. One in particular stuck out: a picture of me standing on a table, drunk, with my top pulled down. I am flanked by two couples, two happy pairs, holding hands and smiling up at me with affection, admiration, amusement – everything except envy. I have a stein of beer balanced on my head, and a large bratwurst protruding from between my manually accentuated bosoms. Red-faced, corpulent, beaming, merry – Sir Toby Belch on a Club 18-30 holiday. Adam's caption reads "BAPS! Judy Bishop – UTTER FUCKING LEGEND".

I remembered the night that photo was taken. Somewhere in Germany, a couple of stops before Nuremburg. We'd done a matinee, and afterwards I'd wandered off to get a sandwich. I stood in the street, eating it, and a group of German teenagers passed. They stopped, nudged each other, giggled, pointed, then laughed together. I stood in silence, watching, eating, a victim. I caught a few words, one in particular. "Fett". Fett. Fat.

I threw the sandwich down, and ran back to the hostel. Fat. The fuckers, the little fuckers. I'd just sung Mama Rose in front of 450 people – un-miked – and I was hungry, of course I was, and I'd earned a fucking sandwich. And they'd ruined it. I couldn't eat now. I couldn't eat ever again. I went into the toilet and stuck my fingers down my throat, got rid of it. Then went, did the evening show, retired to a bar, got raucously drunk, climbed on a table, and shoved a bratwurst down my top, just so everyone would know that I was still a legend. Then a long, lonely, drunken wander round the town, lost, sick, crying, before curling up in the bunk bed, underneath the prettily slumbering Emma. And now that night, that horrible, typical night – which meant nothing to anyone else – was preserved for posterity as being one of my finer moments, a treasured communal memory.

I was angry; angry with Adam, angry with all of them for not knowing how unhappy I'd been, for not acknow-ledging that I was changing, growing up. Hence the knife. I deleted Adam's e-mail, closed my laptop, and picked up a medium-sized kitchen knife from the worktop. I slipped it into a side pocket of my handbag, and sat back, calmer. The knife was a tangible sign of my difference, my experi-ence. It made me special. None of them carried knives, none of the lager-swilling *Gypsy* gang, or the bullying German teenagers.

The next day, knife still tucked firmly in bag, I headed out to my singing lesson. I was on high alert – the previous day's e-mail had made me aware of life's capacity to discon-cert, of the nasty surprises to be found in each new minute. The first half-hour of the lesson passed smoothly; unusual-ly, disorientatingly smoothly. It was exciting, even. We were choosing potential repertoire for the revue. I'd learnt a bit more about it; it was to be a smorgasbord of show-stoppers, chosen by Gareth. He would narrate the piece, mingling music theatre history with a sort of emotional memoir – his own personal responses to these songs, and the way in which they'd informed his world-view. I was to sing one solo number – as yet undecided – and join in with the end chorus.

Both Gareth and I were working with an alarming degree of what must have been professionalism: assessing the relative merits of various uptempo numbers. I sang thoughtfully, he listened and commented with an intelligence and focus that I hadn't before seen in him. Usually he'll break off in the middle of phrases to tell me about his new recipe for bread-and-butter pudding, or to recount some winning but irrelevant anecdote from his music college days. Sometimes he'll just rock back on the piano stool and laugh and laugh and laugh, made giddy by the dusty, glittering contents of his own head. Not this time. There was a certain grimness about him: beneficial to my vocal progress, but unnerving, nonetheless.

Midway through "Blow, Gabriel, Blow", my nose began to bleed. These things happen; small physical peculiarities suggestive of a more general cosmic rot. Sometimes my hair comes out in clumps, occasionally I get bouts of shooting pain, bullets ricocheting around my abdomen and exiting through the top of my skull. The nosebleeds are by far the least convenient. I adopted the inelegant posture of the human blood fountain. Head tipped back, wadded tissue clamped against my face, still making breezy, muffled attempts at conversation to prove that this wasn't a big deal.

Gareth seized the brief recess and began to chat. He started, predictably, with a nosebleed anecdote; he once suffered a similar torrent whilst performing a scene from *Rigoletto* at an old people's home (uninvited, I imagine). He continued bravely with his song, "Like Kathleen Ferrier, you know. She sang Eurydice with an exploded femur. We can all learn something from that, Miss Bishop." I nodded as best I could whilst keeping the tissue rammed against my face.

Gareth sighed, and walked the three steps across the room to the bookshelf. He picked up a framed photo of his grandmother sitting by a fire.

"Look at her."

I peered down over the tissue and made an appreciative noise.

"Ummph."

It was an image of unmitigated human frailty; a tiny, fading form engulfed in a rug, her face a decrepit walnut of confusion and decay. She sat by a fire so large and thriving that it looked almost predatory, ready to engulf her with its energy and youth. Gareth spoke, his eyes fixed on the photograph.

"She's going, you know, she's on the way out. Sooner than she thinks, even."

"What?"

I pulled the tissue away from my face, then rammed it back within seconds as I felt the blood start to trickle, metallic, over my lips.

"Dying."

He laughed again, his usual, unhinged laugh, never less appropriate than now. I often think about his laugh: hard, shrill, scattergun. It's a camp affectation which slightly misses the mark, staggering sideways into manic desperation or cartoon villainy.

"We all die. Dust to dust and all that. It's her time."

I spoke through the tissue.

"How long do you think she's –"

"Not long."

A pause.

"I'm thinking of going to Wales."

Again, through the tissue:

"Really?"

"Yes. There are things to do, you know, with a death. She's wealthy. There's a house to be thought of, acres and acres. Complicated."

He sighed again, moved back to the bookshelf, replaced the photo, and started fingering one of his objets. A poker.

God. God. My head lightened, my stomach knotted. My peripheral vision blurred until all I could see was Gareth, and the poker. Spotlit in a splash of red. Glinting. Demonic. I shuffled and coughed, not wanting Gareth to hear the portentous thudding of my heartbeat. I had to say something, change the tone, lighten the mood, before he realised that I was on to him and he brought the poker crashing down against the top of my head. He could dispose of my body quite easily, here in Archway. Bury me under the kebab boxes in a skip, or put a hat on me and sit me down dead on the bus to Kennington, unnoticed until I failed to disembark at the terminus.

"Whereabouts in Wales are you from, Gareth?"

"Just outside Cardiff."

"You can get there and back for a pound if you go on the National Express."

He's going to take that advice, isn't he? Great. Now I'm an accomplice.

His manner changed again; he brightened and breathed.

"Have you staunched the flow, dear? Shall we sing?"

Never has the score of *Anything Goes* been sung with such an acute awareness of the proximity of death. I belted out the crisp 1930s numbers as if I had a gun to the back of my head. The musical comedy became tempered by a need to deceive the villain who sat before me at the keyboard; I was singing for survival, taut body, rictus grin firmly in place.

My dread solidified, the terror became more elaborate, more justified. Gareth. I should have known. He may have been planning this for years, gathering objects, books, furniture, stacking them in his bedsit, just waiting for the moment when he can decant them into his grandmother's vast mansion in the Valleys. Finally he will have her massive wealth as a foundation for his own floundering gentility; he'll become the person he imagines he now is. He can buy a grand piano, a vintage Steinway perhaps, and first editions of all his Edward Lear books. He'll be able to entertain, have people for dinner, then kick back with a bottle of brandy and discuss Proust by the fire. Perhaps his granny is so rich that he'll be able to get himself a little opera house somewhere, or convert a barn, and stage productions of the great operas, starring himself. What a wonderful life. And all he has to do to get it is hop on the National Express with a bunch of grapes and some soothing magazines, pop round to a relative's house, and hit an old woman on the head with a poker. The crime will be easy to conceal – he can say that she tried to stand up and fell, that in her state it's no wonder, really, is it? He can feign enormous sorrow at her passing, sing at the funeral, leave it a few months before he moves into the house, then sit back and smile with the silent thrill of a job well done. It's horribly understandable, this crime.

Then – it stopped. As if at the end of a storytape; silence. I was wrong. I had to be wrong. I glanced at Gareth as I sang, his good, kind face, concerned for his grandmother, his soft musician's hands, his silly jumper. He was no killer. I replayed the lesson in my head, divested of horror. He'd merely expressed concern for a loved one. I was the one who'd turned him into a killer, albeit briefly, and what did that say about me? The terror remained, but now the focus switched. The threat was not Gareth, but myself. For the first time, I feared my own mental capabilities, thought of the knife in my bag, the morbidity, the crashing waves. I thought of Donald Crowhurst, and wondered just how far out to sea I was.

I sang the final note, slipped him his cheque, and left, barely waiting for the piano accompaniment to finish. Slowly at first, quietly, gently down the stairs, then I crunched up to fifth gear and sprang into the street. I ran to the bus stop, ran as I haven't run since primary school; liberated by panic, animalistic, desperate. I got to the stop – no bus. I kept running. South, west, whatever, just away from myself, my own thoughts. The contents of my bag bounced onto the pavement as I ran: sheet music, cigarette lighters, Munchies, hairclips, a bangle. I didn't care. I didn't need the hairclips, and I certainly didn't need any extra weight impeding my flight. I kept on going, wing-footed, down Holloway Road. The kebab shops and dry cleaners and Poundstretchers and crime scenes flashed by, a kaleidoscope of urban squalor. Soon, as one postcode merged into the next and the image of Gareth's flat subsided, I slowed. I sat down hard on the pavement, knocked out with exhaustion. The mid-morning human traffic surged around me like water round a rock. A few glances were cast my way, some derisive, some amused, most merely acknowledging the presence of a fallen human in the middle of a pedestrian thoroughfare. I shuffled to the left and adopted a tramp-like posture in the doorway of an office building.

I took stock of myself. Handbag still intact, approximately nine personal items missing. Left knee of jeans ripped, small amount of blood from the fall. Mobile phone still in left pocket, still operative. No messages received. Most music still present in my folder, give or take the last few pages of "I've Never Been in Love Before".

And sweat. Gallons and gallons of sweat, all over me. As if my body had been so surprised by the sudden physical activity that it had started to melt. A trickle ran down my back, forming patches here and there, pooling into a swamp-like wetness at the waistband of my jeans. I glanced at my face in the shop mirror: a mottled hell of vivid red and mauve, illuminated by a beaded glaze of glutinous moisture. I scrabbled through my bag in search of anything to stem the flow, a handkerchief, tissues, an old McDonalds napkin. All I found was a Hello Kitty ruler, 15cm long. Fuck knows what it was doing there.

A peculiar hangover from childhood, or something which I'd borrowed from someone three years ago and neglected to return. I remembered my adolescent Latin lessons, the satisfying repetition of clauses interspersed with gobbits of ancient history. Slaves in Roman baths used a small, curved, metal tool – a strigil – to scrape the dirt and sweat from their clients' bodies; I proceeded to do the same to myself with my Hello Kitty ruler. The moisture swished away from my skin as the ruler made its tracks, hitting the concrete around me with a defiant splatter.

Now dry, I began to feel marvellous. I relaxed, leant against the door of the office. I had, albeit fantastically, escaped a killer. Or, at any rate, I was experiencing the relief of one who had. I created him, believed in him, feared him, and then destroyed him. My terror had been real, even if its foundations hadn't been. I'd earned a little euphoria. I'd run to safety, just as a good human should. I scrambled up and treated myself to a copy of *Yes Please!* magazine for the tube. *Yes Please!* is one of the finest periodicals on the market today. I look forward to its weekly publication – Tuesday is generally one of my better days. I tend to wake up with a slight Christmas-morning feeling, knowing that it's about to hit the shelves. *Yes Please!* is a slim glossy, around fifty pages long, which specialises in True Life Stories. It's a receptacle for human filth, horror, and quirky triumph. I had a quick flick through before I left the newsagent, just to whet my appetite for the immeasurable treat in store.

This week's edition was no disappointment. There, on page 3, was a woman whose toddler had mashed up her head with a claw hammer, only days after her vicious ex-lover burnt all her clothes in a stolen skip. There's a picture montage: the left side of her head – perfectly attractive – and then, shock horror, the right side, caved in and bloody. Between the two pictures is a snap of the offending toddler eating a cheese-and-pickle sandwich, little devil-horns superimposed onto his glossy blonde locks by the *Yes Please!* picture editor. Then page 7: "Autistic Sister Shaved By Lesbian Vicar". Only her head, but it's still quite a tale.

Then stories, stories, stories: women with two vaginas, mammoth weight loss, devastating weight gain, tummy-tucks, exploding boobs, wasp stings, more domestic hammer attacks, and a woman who triumphed over lupus to become a pole-dancer.

All of the *Yes Please!* contributors hail from the grimmer parts of provincial Britain, weepy little towns which make Ipswich look like a Renaissance heaven. Row upon row of terraces and bungalows and council houses, heartlessly photographed under grey skies and whacked between chunks of text with the caption "HORROR", or "BATTERED", or "RAW SEX". Impoverished readers are invited to submit lurid accounts of their racily filth-ridden lives to a large, prosperous office in Chelsea. Perhaps the contributors are hoping for some kind of catharsis, or closure, or untold financial rewards. Instead they get a cheque for £250 and the chance to see their most unguarded words cut, pasted, and whacked up in neon. I wonder what they feel when they see their stories in print. Disappointment, a sense of violation, giddy pleasure at being on the periphery of the media world? Regret? Perhaps, once the money has gone. But by then they're forgotten, their story a press cutting which only they will keep.

Yes Please! is a act of thoughtless, pseudo-journalistic cruelty by the calculating middle classes, pandering to idiots like me who can't get on the tube without at least two slashings and a sex change op in their handbag. And I adore it. I lose myself in the stories as I chug along the Central Line; I'm reminded of the mercies of my own life, and reassured that what I do doesn't quite represent the true bog-end of popular journalism.

Just as I was wondering how I'd word the story of

Gareth when submitting to *Yes Please!*, my phone buzzed. A text. Anna. She'd wanted to meet me again – further details of the auction, apparently. Shit. When activity suddenly enters an empty life, it's easy to get lost in the maelstrom. I had precisely two appointments scheduled for this week, and I'd managed to forget one of them. I looked at the text. "SO sorry hun, I'm running late. Can we meet at Chez Marie in half an hour? Can't wait 2 C U! A xxxx."

Ah, OK, I can do that. I hopped on the tube, sinking gratefully into the empty midday seat, and dived into my magazine. Five zippily recounted personal tragedies later, I arrived at Piccadilly Circus. The sun was out, it was unseasonably warm. I like Piccadilly. No-one actually lives there; we're all just passing through, allowed to enjoy the fun, free of obligation or expectation. Most are tourists, so no-one really knows their way around, nor could they be expected to. I smiled at some Japanese families, took a photo for someone. I looked at my watch: twenty minutes in which to walk the 600 yards to the café. What should I do? This is the perpetual question of my life: what shall I do? Not what shall I do in the grand scheme of things, but what shall I do Right Now. I was, admittedly, quite dirty from all the running and falling. I needed a bath. Yes, a bath, or at the very least a damn good wash.

I wandered over to a fountain, across the square from the imposing statue of Eros. Four metal horses charged out of the wall, frozen in positions of bounding combat; huge, noble, cresting the waves of the fountain beneath them. Tourists gathered round, taking photographs, appreciating the aquatic might of the equine fixtures. I inched my way to the front of the crowd, knelt down, and began to splash my face a little. The water was a touch below blood heat. I wanted more. I sat on the wall by the water's edge, and began to smooth the liquid onto my hot little arms, splashed it up to the nape of my neck, smoothed it through my hair like a man applying gel. Wonderful.

I felt my body cooling and relaxing, steaming and melting softly back into a place of comfort and assurance. I inched my way over the low grey wall until I felt the water rise to meet me. I continued, lowered myself, and sat fully down in the pool. This was lovely, absolutely lovely, the best I've felt in months. I splashed a little, giggled, like a child in the bath. The jets of the fountain shot out over me, a veritable water carnival and all, it seemed, in my honour. I wished I had a rubber duck. I reclined until I was fully horizontal and stared up at the metal horses as water lapped at my peripheral vision. I imagined them coming to life, trampling over me as they charged up Shaftesbury Avenue. That wouldn't be a bad way to die: swept up a in a miracle of metal and water and clattering hooves.

I was happy, in the water underneath the horses. I felt, for the first time, in harmony with my city. I was enjoying something that it had to offer, honestly and openly.

"Excuse me? Miss?"

A voice from the blue. How could they be talking to me? I'm far too peaceful to be talked to. I sat up.

It was one of those policemen, one of those annoying policemen that aren't quite policemen, but whom you still have to obey because they've got uniforms and the power to make a citizen's arrest.

"You have to leave the fountain, Miss."

I stared up at him like a wet cat, mute and furious. I started to get worried. He might take my name. Then what? I'm in the papers. People know me. I'm a very minor public figure. I absolutely cannot be found upside down in a fountain, contravening a by-law. I needed to disguise myself.

"Sprechen Sie Deutsch?"

Ha! Fooled him.

"What?"

"Sprechen Sie Deutsch?"

"Miss, please get up and leave the fountain."

He held out my bag and coat, which I'd thoughtfully left on the ledge. I stood up, minding the treacherous slime underfoot, and doggishly shook the water from my body. I took my bag and coat from the fake policeman, threw him a look of dignified condescension, and flounced away, rather wishing that I had a fur stole and a little pillbox hat.

Five minutes later, I steamed wetly into Chez Marie. Anna was sitting primly in front some green tTea, flicking through the *New Statesman*. On my arrival, she looked up, gasped, spilt a little tea on herself, and hurried towards me. She took in my vast wetness.

"Judy! What happened?"

"I got mugged. On Piccadilly Circus. Someone pushed me into the fountain, under the big horses."

Then, as an afterthought:

"I'm really upset."

"Oh, Judy, you poor, poor thing. Did you call the police? Shall I call them now?"

"Oh, no. It's too late. It was just a gang of kids. They're probably miles away by now."

"Some people."

She shook her head.

"I know. They were probably urchins."

"Urchins?" Where did that come from? This was beginning to sound like a mugging in a musical. Anna spoke.

"Do you want to leave? Or stay here and get warm? You could sit on this."

She held out her magazine. I took it, arranged it on the banquette, and sat. She handed me a menu, which I perused with care. I wanted a drink, a post-bath tipple. That's a civilised thing to do, isn't it? Having a quiet drink after a relaxing soak? The waitress came over.

"I'd like an Irish coffee, please. And do you have tequila? Yes, a shot. Thank you. And some toast."

I handed back the menu. Anna raised an eyebrow.

"I'm sorry. I'm just shaken up from the mugging."

She was accommodating, caring, courteous.

"Of course you are, love. Goodness, what a nasty shock. How much did you lose?"

"What?"

"How much stuff did they take? Wallet? Keys? Phone? This is all on me, by the way."

"Thank you. No, they didn't actually take anything. It was more of a random assault. A playground sort of thing, you know."

"Oh, Judy. How terrible. Did anyone help you?"

I needed to get off this topic. I was reluctant to embroider my fib any more than was strictly necessary. I'm not terribly cunning. I knew that I'd catch myself out before too long, perhaps get my geography wrong, or invent implausible identities for my assailants.

"Yes, plenty of people helped, thanks. It's all fine. Really, I'll be fine. Just a bit embarrassed."

"Of course."

She leant forward and grinned, briefly drumming her hands against the table to signify a conversational gear-shift.

"Shall we talk about something lovely?"

"By all means."

"The Auction of Promises. It's all coming together."

"Oh?"

"The date is set. Saturday, November the 18th. We're having it at the Union of Words, near Piccadilly. Do you know it? You did debating at school, didn't you?"

Yes, I most certainly did. I remember it well. The Union of Words was where you were taken for the finals of inter-school debating championships, when you'd powered through the first eight rounds and had cultivated stronger opinions about rail privatisation and green-belt development than any seventeen-year-old should. It's a musty, pompous building just off Piccadilly, an enclave of unnecessary administration and adolescent boys in ill-fitting suits. It was the perfect spot for Anna's evening of worthy jollity.

"Yes, I know it. What a great choice of venue."

"Yes, it is, isn't it? It's no-smoking, I'm afraid, but you can always pop out onto the terrace."

"Thanks."

"Now, Miss Bishop, I need a little something from you. All of the 'lots' – of which you are one, ha! – are producing a little biog for the programme. Just something about you, about what you're offering, why people should bid for it, that sort of thing. I've got some examples here; this is one."

She held out a brochure for some kind of designer leg-wax, and some biographical notes about Fabio, who would be administering this expensive torture. He'd grown up near Naples, then moved to England to start up a waxing salon in Mayfair. He now regularly de-furs the drinking buddies of minor royalty. I handed back the brochure.

"Lovely."

"And this is Charlie, who you know, of course."

"Ah, right."

My stomach descended fast as I took the paper. I was nervous – there was clearly a photo attached. What if he'd become better-looking since we'd last met? Then I'd have no chance. Or what if he'd shaved his head, or pierced his ears, or done anything to destroy the image that had sustained me through the last two and a half years? What if he was married? If he was, I'd cry. I knew it. I couldn't countenance him having done anything, having developed at all. He was mine. I downed my tequila shot and looked at the material.

The photo sent a buzz of heat through my body; the warm, familiar glow from a log fire which narrowed and hardened until it became the shooting pain of lust, homing in on my groin. The ideal reaction one should have to one's husband, I think: comfort, security, warmth, and the physical unsettlement of yearning. His face was the same as ever: slim yet cherubic, mouth relaxed into a half-smile of benign amusement, an adorable discomfort in front of the camera. His hair a darker blond, it seemed, and shorter, but still curled like the inside ear of a golden retriever. Smooth, soft, careless. I would do anything, anything, to be touched by him, held by him, loved by him. I would stop all work, not that he'd ask me to. I would change my body, my mind, myself. I would perform the most obscene and frightening of sexual acts, and love him all the more for asking me to do so. Whatever it takes.

I turned to his biog. "Charlie was educated at Cambridge University and L'Ecole Phillipe Gaulier in Paris. Since then he has worked as an actor in theatre and film, at the Barbican, the Sheffield Crucible and in the recent BBC adaptation of Fanny Burney's *Evelina*. His interests include walking, reading, five-a-side football and the operas of

Richard Wagner. He is delighted to be supporting Eco-Heating for the Elderly, and to be offering a guided sonnet-walk in a London park of the buyer's choice."

I looked up at Anna.

"Can I keep this? Just so I know what kind of thing you're looking for."

"Oh, yes, of course."

I tucked the beautiful document into my handbag, and ascertained that she'd like my biog e-mailed to her within the next couple of days. The conversation was about to move on, when she jerked in the direction of her diary.

"Oh, by the way, are you free a week on Wednesday?"

"Yes, why?"

"Around six o'clock. There's going to be a very brief drinks thing for everyone involved in the auction. Just so you guys can meet the reps from the charity, get to know a bit more about it. It's by no means mandatory, but I'd love it if you could attend."

"Will, um, will everyone be there?"

She smiled. I imagine she thought herself "knowing".

"Yes, Charlie will be there."

She does make me furious. She thinks that I have an adolescent crush on Charlie. How dare she diminish my feelings for him in this way, reducing a real love, a passion, a *knowledge*, into her idle-minded magazine-think?

For all her ostentatious "charity" and manifest Good Works, Anna is self-centred and idle. She doesn't engage with those around her, she doesn't attempt to empathise with her peers. She simply "ropes us in", abuses our good nature, blackmails us, makes us the mindless victims of her "projects". And all for the greater good of that ever-present figure "humanity", who Anna has certainly never met and probably wouldn't like very much if she did. I hate being shackled to her as I am. But I can see the hint of savagery behind those shiny honest eyes, I know that it would take very little for her to turn against me, to use all the vicious little facts that she's accumulated over the years. She's hateful, in her way. But so am I, and we must stick together.

"Ah, OK, sure. Of course I'll come. It'd be lovely to see him again, and to meet all the charity people."

"Good stuff."

"Coach and Horses, Soho, six o'clock."

We chatted for another ten minutes or so. She asked me if I was still singing, whether I was auditioning for "that little place" again. She said how much she was enjoying my column and that she couldn't wait to meet "the mysterious man" I've been mentioning.

I left, and headed back towards my flat. The wetness had dried to a clammy residue; I felt cold and dirty. As I walked along Charing Cross Road, it occurred to me that perhaps I should prepare a little bit for seeing Charlie again. Show him that I was on his wavelength, that I was a suitable life partner. I really am a suitable life partner for him, if only he could see it. Him so mainstream, so clean, so polite, so acceptable. And me so grubby and belty and loud. We're duck and orange, fruit and cheese, one of those magic combinations that rein each other in and bring each other out. Him, perhaps not quite enough fun, and me, slightly too much fun. Together, we are perfect.

I looked at his biog again. I had little to work with. He likes "walking". Well, I walk. I waddle almost everywhere. I can always fabricate a passion for the Pennine Way, if necessary. "Reading". I have an English degree, that ought to clinch it. "Five-a-side-football" isn't really an area I should trespass upon; that's male territory, something that he can go off and do with the boys on Saturdays when we're married. And "the operas of Richard Wagner". Now that is something I can tackle. I dived into one of the second-hand bookshops and headed down into the basement. "Opera". Hmm. Books on musicology, history of opera, criticism, biographies of composers. No, all too dense. Not enough time. For now, all I need are a few points of cultural reference. Conversation starters, perhaps.

Then I saw a slim, faded, blue hardback. *The Stories of Wagner's Operas*, by one J. Walker McSpadden. This looked promising. I skimmed through. Large print, lots of illustrations, a fairytale-by-the-fire sort of a narrative thrust. J. Walker McSpadden's other work, apparently, includes the *Boys' Book of Famous Soldiers*. Perfect, this would sort me out nicely.

I handed over three pounds, tucked the book into my handbag, and tottered on home. It was nearly 5pm. A wave of exhaustion hit me like water as I entered my flat. I undressed between the front door and the bedroom, on a downward trajectory to sleep. I took the photo of Charlie out of my bag and propped it up against the cardboard larynx on my desk – tucking it between the vocal folds to ensure that it didn't fall – then collapsed into bed. I pulled the little green coverlet over myself, and relaxed gratefully into the warm, dry cocoon. As I began to drift off, my phone bleeped. Mr Simmons: "Hey Judy, sorry not to have seen you since Weds. Lunch soon? Adrian x."

Fuck off, Mr Simmons. You've been usurped. Just like my column says, there's a better man in the picture now. And I'm exhausted. Adrenalin, terror, euphoria, heat, baths, Eros, horses, muggings, murders, tea, and romantic hope. I need to sleep. As I drifted off, I heard some children laughing on their way home from school, imagined that the couple opposite weren't even home from work yet, remembered that it was still light outside and that some people will be out of bed for another eight hours. I need to join the world, to swim along with everybody else. I'm getting there. I will get there. Wagner, that will help. Yes, Wagner. Goodnight.

The Days of Judy B

OH, DEAR LORD, it's all Getting Complicated. Last week we established that my love life has been growing somewhat hot in the Bedroom Department. You may, in fact, have assumed that there would be no column at all this week, as I would be firmly ensconced in the Chamber of Shag, talking sweet nothings and making sweet love with the man who has staggered so willingly into my den of sin.

Well, I am slightly worried to inform you that things have got even hotter. And more complicated.

My love life is a veritable pan of fresh spaghetti, writhing and bubbling, giving out the tantalising prospect of eventual nourishment. But first I must rein it in, gather it, and untangle it to the best of my ability.

For, ladies (and, perhaps, surreptitious gentlemen), there is Another Man on the scene. I met him, shockingly enough, when I was shopping for my sex-date with the initial beau. I dropped a pack of chewing gum onto the pavement, slightly knocking someone to one side as I bent to pick it up. I looked at the man I'd bumped, expecting a middle-aged face of hostility.

Instead, I got The Full Works. Calm blue eyes, raven hair, muscles rippling beneath a Calvin Klein suit. He smiled, and spoke, a rich American accent, dripping with money and culture and Sex Sex Sex.

"Hey, baby, whaddaya need gum for? I've got a piece you can share." He stuck out a perfect pink tongue, on which rested some half-chewed gum. And it wasn't even gross. It was sexy beyond anything I've ever seen. He drawled, I drooled. He took my number. I'd walked 300 yards up the street when my phone rang. Him. Asking me for a drink, Right Now. And I went. We kissed. Nothing more yet, but we're having dinner next week.

How, you might ask, did I muster up the confidence to go through with this? How did it happen in the first place? Well, you see, I was looking good. I was looking good because of the affirmation I'd received from the man I'd planned to go out with (and still am going to go out with – I told you it was complicated). I felt sexy enough to attract, and reciprocate, the attentions of the Bloomberg Cowboy. Is it true that all you need to snag a man is, well, another man? One man for validation, one for the actual relationship? Can the two switch roles as they like, no questions asked?

Gosh. What a conundrum. I'll keep you posted. Right now, I'm going to get my hair done by my Gay Best Friend. That shouldn't be too romantically complicated. That said, at the rate I'm going, I'll be carrying his child by the end of the day. Watch this space – it's about to get saucier.

Judy B's Purchase of the Week: A larger flat in which to store all my newly acquired exotic underwear. I'm going to be needing it.

JUDY BISHOP

8.

22nd October, 2006

I'm suddenly feeling the pressure of my fifteen-week deadline. The number fifteen has become something of a mental
focus, and it needs to be made visible. This morning, I took
a lipstick from the bathroom cabinet, an old lipstick,
unused for months. I went to the mirror, and wrote the
number fifteen in foot-high letters. Not wrote, drew. I
adorned the two figures, illuminated them like a medieval
monk illuminating a bible. I then went round the flat with
the lipstick, drawing a "1" here, an "5" there. Fifteen, my
number – it's inspirational. And inspiration, at this stage, is
necessary.

It dawned on me, as I tried to acquaint myself with the
works of Richard Wagner for the sake of romantic further-
ance, just what a difficult task I've set myself. The initial
three goals are, well, doable. I've done one of them already.
The sex thing. But it didn't feel quite enough, somehow.
Having had the sex, all I want is more. I realise that to lose
one's virginity is not a triumph in itself; the triumph is in

building up the track record, learning the craft, getting some moves down. I need to learn my style. I need someone to practise on until I'm ready to take off the stabilisers and head out into the heaving, adult world of lust. I'm considering Mr Simmons for this position. I think he's game. I think he's more than game. I think he's a forty-five-year-old, middle-aged divorcee with a hankering for flesh. Bring it on.

And then the singing. Improving enough to make a real splash at the revue, learning new songs, progressing. I can do that. I've been thinking a lot about the show, about how lucky I am, and how huge it's going to be. I can't wait to find out what my song's going to be. Whatever it is, I'll make it shine, and it will do the same to me.

Finally, the column. That must be the last thing to go. For now, I need the money. It's not too bad. I have the writing-time down to a tight fifteen minutes, during which I tend to consume a bottle of wine and three/four donuts. It's OK. I file my copy, sleep it off, and I'm then able to use the paper's money to fund my personal overhaul. But I do panic, of course I do. I'm acutely aware that I'm halfway through my allotted time, and that sort of deadline breeds anxiety. I don't know what will happen if I'm not where I want to be by my birthday. The date looms so large, so significant. I circle it in my diary, every day, draw another little "15" on the worktop. I have so much to do, and I am being given opportunities left, right, and centre.

The *problème du jour*, though, is mouth cancer. At least, I think it's mouth cancer. I woke up on Monday with a burning tongue. I hadn't been drinking. I hadn't, for once, had a curry. It was just red, and burning. Patches, smooth red patches that got brighter and brighter and more and more painful as I stood in front of the bathroom mirror.

Then my voice, my beautiful voice. It's periodically hoarse and grainy; the finer notes of "Everything's Coming Up Roses" are, for the first time, starting to elude me. It gets worse; I'm having difficulty swallowing. I used to be able to swallow a whole plum without taking a bite. It was my party trick. I'd start with a grape, work up to a cherry, gulp my way through a series of small tomatoes and then, by way of a finale, down a plum. It made my sister laugh. But on Monday morning my breakfast pizza had to be forced through a protesting oesophagus, pounding its cheesy way into my poor ailing body.

I did some research into my condition, found my way onto the website of a small American hospital specialising in Oral Cancer. There were pictures, page after page of close-ups of tongues and gums and teeth and tumours. There's a sort of game you can play. You look at the picture, try to guess whether or not the patient's lesion is cancerous, then "Click for Diagnosis" to confirm your worst suspicions. Nine times out of ten: Squamous Cell Carcinoma. And my tongue is no better than that of those poor people. Mouth cancer is the worst thing that could possibly happen to me. No more singing, no more music. Massive facial disfigurement. It's ugly, it's deadly, and it's happening.

Yet what can I do but put my tongue back in my mouth, dry my tears, and stagger stoically on? I have so much to do, no time for the doctor. I have my deadline, and the possibility of my imminent death only reinforces that. I started with the Wagner on Tuesday. I felt, given my condition, that it would be wise to work from bed. It was pleasant, exciting. I felt, as I read the stories, a sense of togetherness with Charlie, a merry companionship. Perhaps one day we'll read the stories to our children as an early introduction to our favourite composer, in the hope that they'll grow up to love him as much as we do.

McSpadden's book is fantastic. Knights and witches and castles and powerful yet deadly magicians named Klingsor. People shooting swans and questing and dying of a broken heart. Strong stuff. It made me wonder what the music's like; pretty bloody loud, I imagine. Booming, possibly a trumpet and drums.

My favourite story is Parsifal the Pure, about a hero "superior to every enemy and every temptation to the end". He, as I gather (even McSpadden's bumptious prose can't simplify the convoluted plotting), was essentially questing after the Holy Grail, as all the best knights should. His purity and energy knew no bounds, he laughed in the face of obstacles. When faced with the smothering voice of reason he'd say something like, "Nay, but tell me now! Why should I pause when I am not faint? No good deed was ever done by stopping on the way," and then smite someone. Damn straight.

I put the book down, picked up a jar of mayonnaise from my bedside table, and downed a contemplative spoonful. A dollop fell off the edge of the spoon and landed with a splat on my cleavage; I lowered my head, hoisted the sullied breast up to chin level and licked off the mayo, mouth-to-nipple, natural, earthy. I swallowed, licked my lips, let the thoughts run. I think I'm quite like Parsifal. Questing, searching, undeterred, "a knight without fear and without reproach." I only fall short in the physical department; Parsifal was "strong and straight and graceful", his face was "fair and pleasing and seemed to glow with an inner light". I'm grim and pasty – I need work.

I remembered something which Emma once told me.

Marie Helvin and Jerry Hall used to put mayonnaise in their hair before a photo shoot – apparently it has moisturising qualities. Emma was always doing this; giving me little tips. Teaching me, in her own loving way, how I could make myself look as good as she did. I ran a hand through my own locks. Dry, crinkly, splitting, mealy. Definitely needed some conditioner. I laid the spoon on the duvet cover, bunched my fingers into a sort of claw, and dipped my hand into the jar. It struck the thick white jelly. I giggled. I imagined Emma giggling. She would have loved this. I withdrew my hand and raised it to my head, dumping the snowy magic onto my scalp. I was laughing now, laughing with the badness of my deed. I glanced over to the end of my bed, where Emma would be sitting. She urged me on; I upended the jar and waited, smiling at her, as the mayonnaise oozed gently down the jar, descending onto my poor parched hair in reluctant globules. I tossed the jar out of the window and threw my head back until it hit the wall hard with a defiant splurge of oil and yolk.

That was Monday. I sat there for hours, in bed, mayo congealing, memories marching through like friendly forces. I can waste a day in remembering. Letting my mind jump through associations of thought, images and views and remembered feelings spinning about, darting back and forth, swimming in and out of focus. Myself, as a five-year-old, on a little cheap roundabout in the council playground, going round and round until my head spins and I'm in Ipswich, in the Novotel, being fucked by the fat man. Riding a horse for the first time, frightened, just like my first day at school, when I didn't have to go in until lunchtime and I went to my friend Laura's house and had sausages and mash, which I had with Emma on our first day at university, when I wore a pink T-shirt the same colour as the pants I'm wearing now, which suddenly makes me feel a bit turned on, which is weird. So much life, already. So much to address, before my birthday.

Sometimes strangers pop in – my divas. They remind me, when the mental going gets tough, that I am just like them, and that they'll always be there. I can be in bed chatting to Emma, to Charlie, singing to a crowd, thinking about my mum, standing at the altar at my wedding, and in will pop Ethel Merman. Just as real and vivid as the fantasies and memories of friends and family. She takes her place at the dinner table, Judy Garland enters, Liza, Barbra Streisand. We sing, harmonise, hug, and then I'm back in bed, alone, smiling, singing softly to myself, stroking the cardboard larynx. It's nice – company.

On Tuesday, I went shopping. I sensed the proximity of next Wednesday, the looming presence of my reunion with Charlie. I wanted to refresh myself, to do a little tiny something to honour the imminent glory of our meeting. A supermarket shop seemed appropriate, restorative. I've taken, lately, to using the corner shop, limiting my diet to that which is contained within the chiller cabinet and the stunted, greasy aisles around. Big bars of chocolate, huge cartons of milk, six-packs, vodka, wine, bread, beans, cheese, Bisto, wraps and pasties and Fray Bentos pies, things which have chicken tikka in them when they really shouldn't have. Trash food. I needed to explore a larger emporium. So, to Tesco. The big Tesco, where normally I only go to buy toilet roll.

I got the bus. Five hundred yards, maximum, but I'm preserving myself. If there'd been a taxi I'd have taken it. I acquired a trolley and paced the aisles. Fruit and veg. Yes.

Bananas, in they go. I'll never eat them unless they're mashed up with cream, but it's worth a try. Plums – no. Too many memories. A kiwi. Furry, nice, like an eastern European cuddly toy. I smoothed it against my cheek, gave it a quick kiss, and tossed it into my trolley. Mango. Papaya. Sharon fruit. They can all fuck off. Grapes, yes, perfect. I like grapes. You can play games, chuck them down like sweets, dip them in chocolate and sugar and turn them into sweets.

That was plenty of fruit. It rolled around the bottom of the trolley, the bananas remorselessly harassed by the brave little kiwi, the grapes making a bid for freedom, diving through the holes in the vehicle's mesh, hitting the floor below and rolling into oblivion. I progressed to the in-store bakery. Now this was more like it – rondels and wraps and torpedoes and rustic buns and unsliced loaves and pastries and happy, happy steaming things in shades of brown and cream and gold. I moved through the exhibition of yeasty joy, stroking and touching and sniffing. I eventually settled on one sliced loaf, one unsliced, two packets of wraps, some French country rolls and a packet of iced buns which looked like breasts. Then to the aisle of tins, where tomatoes were 3p a can, and only five feet away from the custard. I felt reborn. No-one takes time to enjoy the supermarket any more. This isn't a necessity, or a chore. It's a thing of absolute wonder, all that's good in life, converging in this strip-lit utopia. I took tins of rice pudding, semolina, peas, frankfurters, meatballs, pink custard, lima beans, and stew.

Then across one aisle, to the cereal. God, the rapture, the dazzling, blazing array of choice. Chocolate, strawberry, yoghurt, oats, raisins, sugar, bran. I grabbed five boxes, fast, and threw them into my trolley with a gurgle.

Confectionery next. I upped the pace through sheer excitement. A six-pack of Twixes, some marshmallow tea cakes, Dairy Milk, Hershey's, Double Deckers. A great handful of Flakes, clustered in my palm like a sheaf of corn. The best was yet to come: puddings. Chocolate and caramel in a yoghurt pot, a little spongy thing with lemon, microwave soufflé, more custard, this time with the jam mixed in. Jelly and cream, together in one pot. Why would anyone grow up, ever? Why, when there are still people who'll mix your jelly with your cream for you, for a nominal charge? I dumped armful after armful of the little tubs and cardboard sleeves and free plastic spoons into my trolley. My shopping had formed a mountain in the middle of the vessel; I reached in and rearranged things so that it became a crater. High on the promise of sugar, I stared down the aisle ahead. Long, clear, inviting. I remembered childhood, shopping with Mum at the Martlesham Heath superstore. She'd hoist me up, sit me in the little orange seat, give me an arctic roll to hold, and push me along like a princess. Sometimes she'd break into a surreptitious trot to give me a bit of an extra thrill.

I wanted that, right now. Grabbing an arctic roll, I took a quick look around, then started to push the trolley. I walked faster, began jogging. Then running, running, running. I hit top speed and hurled myself face-first into the trolley. My legs left the floor and I flowed along the aisle like a mermaid, flat-out on top of my shopping, nose pressed against a tin of macaroni cheese. God, I was going fast. I rolled over to look at the ceiling, knocking the trolley off course so that I bounced off a wall of crisps and came to rest in front of Beers, Wines, and Spirits. Still recumbent atop my mound of food, I reached out to the shelf of cheap white wine. One, two, three, four, five, six, seven bottles. That'll be plenty. I dumped them underneath me and heaved myself back onto the floor, a process which required a seal-like roll and a fair bit of twisting and juddering. I resumed my proper place behind the trolley, took a quick swing through pharmaceuticals, grabbed four or five packets of condoms, and headed to the checkout. What a marvellous outing.

On Wednesday, one week away from seeing Charlie, I remembered something. Easily excited men are advised to masturbate shortly before making love; a preventative measure to stop premature ejaculation during the main event. I felt that I should approach my meeting with Charlie in a similar spirit; I needed to get some romantic excitement out of my system, in order not to come on too strong and embarrass myself.

So, Mr Simmons. Once my teacher, now my toy. I think he's going to prove useful. He's puppyish, friendly, unthreatening, and desperate. I'm learning to use men to my advantage, like the boy in Ipswich. He may have thought that he won that particular wrestling match, that I was merely a handy fucking-doll, that he had his grubby little way with me then cast me aside. But I know better; I know that I'd been planning that fuck for longer than he had, I know that I despise him more than he could ever despise me, and I know that if he'd called me afterwards, I wouldn't have answered. So it shall be with Mr Simmons. My feelings for him extend no further than pity, now. Now that Charlie is back in the picture, young and strong and blooming, the fat little history teacher recedes. It's Darwinian, almost. But while I'm still learning, I must prey on the weak. Those in tracksuits, with patchy beards and protuberant stomachs and lowly aspirations.

I called him. He answered, a matey companionship messed up with a daft attempt at flirtation:

"Hello-oh? Miss Judy Bishop?"

"Um, hi there. How are you?"

"I'm very well, very, very well, indeed."

"Good."

"How are you?"

"I'm really well, Mr Simmons, really well. I was just wondering – well, I'm sorry that I didn't reply to your text – and I was just wondering if you fancied dinner? Rather than lunch."

"Oh, I'd love that, of course. Where shall we go?"

"I'm not sure."

I didn't want to go out. Somehow, I didn't want to be seen in public with him. Didn't want anyone, any passer-by, to think that we were any kind of an item. Odd, I know, but there it is. He butted in:

"Well, would you like to come up to my flat? I could get some food from the café, and you could see where I live."

"Oh, that would be lovely."

"When were you thinking?"

"Well, um, tomorrow?"

"Great. Meet you at Elephant and Castle tube at seven."

It's sort of a first date, I suppose. Except that I've already sucked him off, and he's been dumping horse shit on my doorstep for the last four weeks, and he bought me a pasty. Ah, well, he's only a practice boyfriend. Doesn't need to be love's young dream. I remembered, suddenly, how excited I'd been by our meeting at the party, and our encounter outside Dr Goldberg's office. I'd thought that I was in love with him. But I was lonely, then, desperate, and now I'm not. There's another man in my sights. I have hope, therefore I have power.

I considered getting dressed up. Another trip to Matalan perhaps, or back to the supermarket to cream something off the clothes rails. I decided against it; it felt disrespectful to Charlie. I needed to save the best of myself for him. I settled on jeans, my trainers, and a hoodie. As an afterthought, I cracked into my packet of condoms and shoved a couple into the pocket of my hoodie. You never know.

Mr Simmons met me at the tube. I felt a pang of almost physical sadness when I saw him – he'd dressed up. Crisp new cords, a baby-blue collared shirt above a nice red jumper. He'd trimmed his beard. Oh, the poor love. I wanted to hug him, to apologise.

"Hello, Judy! You look lovely."

I didn't. Bless him, though.

"Thanks. I like your cords. Shall we make a move?"

"Certainly. It's just a short bus ride."

It wasn't that short a bus ride. The number 253 coughed its way through the traffic for ten, fifteen minutes. Dusk, and south London was at its worst. All figures hunched, tower blocks rising above the internet cafés and dry cleaners and money transfer shops of the Old Kent Road. Both lifeless and threatening, it made Gareth's locale look like Park Avenue. Mr Simmons' outfit choice now seemed all the more heartbreaking; no Santa-jumper can bring cheer to this godforsaken interchange.

We alighted outside the Mashed Potato Café, to all intents and purposes a greasy spoon with a somewhat limited menu. The interior aped that of café sets in the cosier British sitcoms, places where a group of old friends go to be comfy with one another, to toss wisecracks and bumble on affably about their endearing personal shortcomings. Seven-thirty, peak dining-time, and it was empty. Mr Simmons opened the door, ushered me in with a solicitous hand on the small of my back, and we stood.

"Ta-dah! My fine emporium. The triumph of the Old Kent Road."

"Gosh, it's… lovely."

He breathed in, eyes closed, as if inhaling a mountain sunrise.

"Can you smell it, Judy? Can you smell the mash?"

"Yes. Amazing. Are you… are you, um, are you… open tonight?"

"Yes, but don't you worry. We'll be eating in the flat. Not many customers allowed up there. You get the royal treatment if you're a guest of the manager."

He laughed. I laughed harder, desperate.

"Gosh, what a treat. So who'll be holding the fort down here?"

"Joel."

"Joel?"

"My business partner, Joel. Actually –" he shouted. "Joel! Joel! Oh, where the fuck is he? Joel!"

He picked up a pepper-pot from one of the tables and banged it sharply against the table-top.

"Joel!"

He banged again.

"Joel!"

From behind the counter came a snort, a dry heave, an exhalation, the rustle of clothing, a sharp bang, the word "fuck" spoken in surprisingly cultured tones, and about twenty cacophonous seconds of falling metal. Then from underneath the till rose a dishevelled head, on which sat a beanie hat in skullcap position, behind a salt-marsh of wiry, tattered hair. The eyes were red-rimmed, frighteningly so, a rabbit on a crystal meth-fuelled bender. About three days of stubble. Then, bizarrely, a Ralph Lauren jersey, Levis, and expensive trainers caked in mud. Joel stood up; he was tall, over six foot, and as he stood he seemed momentarily thrown by the altitude of his own head.

He righted himself and plunged towards me, hand extended.

"Judy! You must be Judy, heard lots about you."

His handshake was firm and pumping, his tone deeply cultured, old English aristocracy, a young prince on a walk-about. He continued.

"Gosh, fuck, sorry. All went a bit tits-up back there. Had to sleep something off. Never mind, all set now, all set! Now. Right."

He shook his head as if clearing water, and stepped back behind the counter.

"Adrian, the big spoon. Have we seen the big slotted spoon? Come here, you cheeky little fucker."

Joel descended again, addressing the elusive spoon in a determined mumble. Adrian spoke.

"Joel, you know that I'm off tonight? Having dinner upstairs with Judy, and things."

"Ah, of course. 'Dinner'."

He winked at me, like a strange, cock-eyed lizard. I recoiled.

"No problem, Ade. I'm well on top of it all. Now then."

He foraged in his pocket and pulled out a packet of cig-arettes. Mr Simmons moved towards him.

"Please, Joel, you can't smoke that in here. Really."

"Oh, mate. Come the fuck on."

"It's the law. Do you remember the man who came round and told us about the law?"

"Yes, pompous little cunt. I'll show him."

He moved to light the cigarette.

"Please don't, Joel."

"Ade, if you don't let me smoke it here then I'll have to go out and smoke it. And we know what happens when I go out, don't we?"

"Oh, alright."

He lit up.

"Judy, I'm sorry, how rude. You like one?"

He offered me the packet. I took a fag; within seconds a gold Zippo appeared under my nose. I liked Joel. Mr Simmons took my free hand.

"Now, Joel, you know what to do when a customer comes in?"

"Yes, yes, for fuck's sake. Spuds. Money. Bit of banter. I invented that shit."

"Right."

We went through the back door, up a pitch-black car-peted staircase which smelt of cabbage, and into Adrian's bedsit. Once again, I wanted to cry. It was so desperately small, so desperately clean. A few Wine Society bottles on the sideboard. Just one room and a tiny bathroom leading off it, no bed apparent, but a section of the wall which sug-gested that it might fold down to produce a meagre double. A bit of furniture, a rug. So empty. The Ikea cell of the recently divorced man. There was a pleasant food smell.

He'd really made an effort. I smiled as he closed the door behind us.

"Um, Adrian – Joel?"

"Christ, yes. Sorry. Joel. He helped me start this place up. He's the money behind the operation, really. Terribly clever; Eton, then got a place at Harvard, but couldn't go because he's not allowed into America. He's OK. Really helped me through Le Divorce, as it were. I run the café, mostly, he just pumps in the funds. Lets me live here for free."

He gestured proudly round the studio, as if it were a riverside penthouse.

"Where does he live?"

"Buckinghamshire. And all around, really, when he's in London. Sometimes he crashes up here with me, sometimes behind the counter, like you saw. Wine?"

"Yes, please. Where did you meet him?"

He turned to the counter, and started to open a bottle of Wine Society red.

"At Dr Goldberg's. You meet all sorts there."

"Oh."

"Apparently he's descended from Bertrand Russell."

He handed me the glass. We clinked.

The evening was... pleasant. Passable. We sat on folding canvas chairs and ate; parsley mashed potato and bacon. He told me about his divorce, clearly his dominant thought-strand. He'd married Barbara because she was small, thin, and blonde. A bit sharky-looking, perhaps, but the nearest he felt he'd ever get to a trophy wife. She'd married him because she thought him intelligent. Once she discovered that a working knowledge of fifteenth-century corn exchanges doesn't necessarily equate to all-round mental sensitivity, things cooled off. A kettle was thrown at some-one's head, but apart from that things weren't too acrimo-nious. They separated, Adrian took none of Barbara's money and he didn't have any for her to take. He'd been unem-ployed throughout most of their marriage, the Belgium shit-fire having robbed him of what little faith he had in his teaching abilities. He'd been toying with catering for a while, idly spinning the mashed potato idea round in his head, when he met Joel. Two months later, they set up shop together. Quite simple, really. Four years of highly turbulent life, adequately reduced to an hour of chat.

I didn't tell him much about my situation. I didn't want him to know, didn't want anyone to know. Sharing my bur-dens would only add to the weight of responsibility; events themselves are bad enough without having to witness other people's reactions to them.

I talked about Cambridge, about performing, about *Gypsy*. Emma kept popping up in anecdotes, as she always does. I didn't tell him that she's dead. If someone thinks that a person is still alive, then they are, a bit. None of their iden-tity is stolen by death, stories don't have to end with a sad smile, a stoical throat-clearing, and a tactful change of subject.

The evening felt precipitous, I kept thinking about its eventual end. Not with anticipation, or dread; just wonder-ing what would happen. My fingers kept slipping down to the condoms in my pocket, feeling the thick foil wrapper, the ring, the slightly gelatinous way in which the sides of the packet moved against each other. It would be good, I think, if I had sex with him. Strike two. Practice. And I think he'd like it. I suppose it could give him the wrong idea about my feelings for him, make him imagine a level of attraction that isn't there. But he's nearly forty, he should know better. He's seen enough of the world to know that not every twenty-three-year-old is in it for the long haul, that a shag is sometimes just a shag. And if he hasn't then, well, that's his problem. We carried on drinking.

An hour or so later, we were well on the way. Slurring a little, occasionally putting words in the wrong order. About two drinks away from nausea, the perfect time to initiate sexual congress. The mood was right enough, give or take a few solitary crashes and oaths and bursts of intoxicated singing from the café downstairs. Interrupting Adrian's diatribe on the recent Elephant and Castle Renaissance Exhibition, I spoke. The topic was delicate, but the memory of sucking Turkish delight off his balls soothed my sense of formality.

"Mr Simmons, tell me something. Slight change of tack, I know, but when you've been married for a, for a while, as you were, do things tend to cool off, you know, sexually? In the bedroom. I was just wondering."

God, that was hardly aggressive. I needed to sharpen up.

"What I mean is, Adrian, did you at least get a final glory-fuck before she threw the kettle at you?"

That's more like it. The gauntlet was peeled off, ready to be thrown. He took a sip of wine and stared glumly into the middle distance.

"Well, no. Bit depressing to relate, but we never actually did that, if truth be told."

"What?"

"Well, we did things, of course. You know. Touching. But that always eluded us, biologically speaking. More her fault than mine. She just couldn't take it."

"God, I'm sorry. So you never did it?"

"No. Nearly, once. But – no."

He looked miserable. I felt sorry for him, and suddenly a bit happier with what I was about to do.

"Do you want to do it now?"

"What?"

"Do it. Sex. With me."

"Why?"

"What?"

"No, God, sorry, fuck, I didn't mean 'why', as such. God. More like – what?"

I kept my nerve.

"I'm asking you if you want to have sex with me. What's the problem?"

I held his gaze. I didn't care what he said, now. The evening had reached a plateau, and we had to move on. Either to sex, or to the disconsolate dialling of a minicab number. His choice.

"Well, it's just that people don't normally ask, you know. At least I don't think so. I never have."

"Well, I asked."

"And very politely, too."

We chuckled, and stood up. A step towards each other, ready for a duel. He leant in, went a bit to one side. I went the same way, by mistake, we weaved for a moment, then our lips met. A warm, winey tongue, two of them, his, mine, sliding round and round each other like kidneys in a jar. He increased the pressure, upped the pace, extended his fat little arm around my back and drew me closer until my breasts were pressed against his front, the toggles of my hoodie catching the buttons of his sweet blue shirt.

I didn't know what to do. When to move my hand to

his arse, or to his crotch, or to a buckle or a zip. I didn't know how long we needed to do this for, this nuzzling, grinding pointlessness. I imagine that I should have been led by some force from within, a libidinous magnet moving my hands and body to wherever they were most desired. But no, I just fumbled, made noises, stepped back and forth like a geriatric at a tea dance.

We moved towards the wall. I pressed him back against it, moved my knee between his legs, somewhere between a mugger and a whore. He took his right hand off my thigh and reached above and behind himself, grabbing a discreet handle. The bed was coming down. He gave a swift yank, then rushed me to the other side of the room as the wall descended with a juddering crash, presenting us with a sweetly made maroon double. A blank canvas. Fuck. Suddenly I wasn't sure.

Adrian was. He pushed me down onto the bed, his actions on the rougher side of sporty. His mouth twisted into a smile, joyful and determined. He wanted something, wanted something more than me. His enthusiasm transcended my desirability, and I was frightened. He pinned my arms against the duvet and ground his face against mine, kissing and licking, bashing against my nose and cheeks and chin until my face was wet with him. He reared backwards in a sort of press-up, looming over me like the horses in the fountain, the smile broadening into an epiphany. He spoke, and not to me.

"Bye, bye, Barbara."

So that was it. I had become the object. All of a sudden, this was his party. He unzipped, started grabbing at my jeans. I respected the emergency and helped, yanking them down to my ankles and handing him a condom. He vanished for a second, fiddled ineptly with himself, then launched back at me in the press-up position, entering, thrusting, slugging his way along the same dreary old path as the boy in the Novotel. I hated it. I hated him, his chest, his hair, his stomach, his heaving, snorting breath and bursts of spit and grunts and ugly noises. He should see, he should know, that he shouldn't be doing this. Sure, I initiated it. But he's seen me cry, he's sent me to therapy, he knows my parents, taught me history when I was thirteen years old. Is it too much to expect a little responsibility, the courage to be an adult, to resist the sprawled, drunken, incapable slut in front of you, and call her a taxi? Of course that's too much to expect from a forty-something man who sends bags of shit to a lonely woman, who dips five years into his own depressing past to rustle up a shag, and who mashes potatoes for a living. Weak-willed, suggestible, now huge and smothering and caked in hair, subhuman, vile, eating, drinking, fucking animal. Charlie would never do this, he'd protect me from myself, cruel to be kind, firm but fair. This can't be it. This cannot be Sex, this half-clad pig-pen, this sweat-glazed sumo-bout, this rank, heaving onslaught of desperate flesh. I have to leave, right now. If I'm not here, it won't be true.

I remembered something I once read in an SAS survival guide. When being attacked by a bear – as I effectively was at that moment – the thing to do is to play dead. That way, the bear realises that he can do little more with you, and trudges wearily off. I never thought that that information would be of practical use, but here it is. I coughed, jerked, gasped, threw my arms out and lay cruciform on the bed, my eyes closed, my breathing shallow. For a second he continued, forced on by his own desperate rhythm, then –

"Judy? Judy? Fuck! Judy!"

He withdrew. Hah. I resisted the urge to smile. He scrambled to his feet, and I relaxed, feeling that an anvil had been lifted off my chest. I stayed frozen. He ran, shouted, panicked. I heard the door open.

"Joel! JOEL! Help, please, help, Judy's unconscious."

"What? Mate, fuck."

Running up the stairs. I heard Joel enter.

"Shit. Mate. Fuck."

Someone shook me. Time to wake up, I think. I feigned bleariness, lifted my head.

"I wha – Joel – I must have…"

Two male voices, overlapping.

"Judy? Are you OK?"

"Shall I call an ambulance?"

"No, just a cab, I think. I'm sorry, Adrian, I must've passed out. From the pleasure."

I pulled up my jeans. Joel looked at Adrian.

"Simmo, you sly fucker. Always knew you had hidden talents."

Out of the sex-position, I began to relax. Adorably, Mr Simmons blushed.

"Well, I –"

"Pull your pants up, mate."

"Sorry Joel."

We had a cup of tea downstairs while we waited for my cab. That could have been worse, I thought. I'd had more of a warm-up for my drink with Charlie than I'd expected, I'd given Mr Simmons a night of company, half a shag and a nice ego-boost, and I'd met Joel. God, though. Mashed potato, flesh, Elephant and Castle... Another week gone. My cab arrived, Adrian walked me out.

"Thank you for coming."

"Thank you. I'm sorry about –"

"Not at all."

We shuffled, suddenly coy, teenagers.

"Did you – did you really pass out from my being so good?"

He looked so sweetly hopeful. Once again, a sad little man in a button-down shirt. No threat, just that sadness. I smiled.

"Yes, Adrian. Yes, I did. Thank you."

"You're welcome. Goodnight."

"Goodnight."

I sat back in the minicab, and watched Elephant and Castle recede through the patchy drizzle. Back to my flat, back under the little green duvet. Perhaps an hour or so of Merman tunes before sleep. That's not so bad. After nights like this, the little green duvet becomes a beacon of hope, the closed door a stalwart friend. Maybe I'm enough, better without other people. Just me, and my voice, and the memories. Always there. Maybe that's enough.

The Days of Judy B

THERE ARE FEW problems that can't be solved by a Night Out With The Girls. It's peculiar; I can be in a mire of confusion, torn as I am now between two men, on the cusp of ruining my love life for good, and at risk of boring my lovely readers to death about it. Things can be depressing, demanding, my family can be doing my head in as they've never done before. Yet still, the sight of four beautifully made-up faces peeping over a bottle of wine can put the spring back in my step like nothing else.

It's irrational, I know. The advice that friends offer is rarely constructive. Often quite the opposite, in fact. One chum, a trainee investment banker who drinks in the morning and describes herself as "The Sexual Terrorist", advised me to bite the bullet and stage that long-awaited threesome. Then slip quietly away in the middle and let the males of the species slug it out between themselves on the pink frilly eiderdown. One girlfriend suggested that I equip myself with two phones, like a well-heeled adulterer. Another implied that I was going to have to ditch my column, change my name, and move to Paris like the whore I am.

None of this was of practical use, and

thank God. If we want well-considered advice, we've got parents, counsellors, hotlines, and the Agony Uncle enthroned on page 6 of this esteemed supplement. These oracles function as safety valves, stopping us from poisoning our friendships with practicality. Friends are silly, friends are drunk, friends mash cheesy wotsits into the sofa, drink Sambuca, and text you at 4am because they got thrown out of a minicab. Friends don't relieve us of our burdens, they merely spray them with silly string and make us want to point and laugh.

And that's a glorious thing. Time spent chuckling into a glass of Pinot Grigio is not time wasted, as The Man might have us believe. And socialising is not something to be "built in" around work and family and going to the gym and remembering to clean out the smoothie-maker. It's as necessary as breathing. Human beings are not, essentially, "colleagues". They are not bosses, or underlings, or tradesmen. They are friends, lovers, and barmen, and the more time spent acknowledging this, the better.

So I feel no shame at having reeled home at four in the morning on a weeknight, after spending three hours drinking and the next five dancing to ABBA like a toddler at a Jungle Gym. Those hours helped me more than a whole day of sit-ups would have, or an afternoon spent with an improving book. They may have written off two days with the Hangover from Hades, but I spent most of those days texting my companions, obsessing over the silly little details of our night, and recounting the hilarious incident with the kebab.

So, readers, when things hit rock-bottom, when you're down and troubled and you need a helping hand, Gather the Troops. Hit the Pitcher and Piano. Expect nothing from them, just look at each other, and laugh at the world. And don't you dare feel guilty about it.

Judy B's Purchase of the Week: A new iPod! Naughty, naughty, naughty…!

JUDY BISHOP

9.

Charlie is now the centre of my world. I woke on Wednesday to the sight of his blushing, tousled face, peeping through the folds of the cardboard larynx on my desk. It made me want to open my heart and sing, loud and strong and joyful, until the whole city turned to look in awe at this vision of happiness and love. As I awoke, I became aware of vivid, energising sunlight slanting across the green duvet cover, making it greener than ever, as green as Charlie's Rainforest Café T-shirt: healthy, lush, human.

I got up, faster than ever before, bypassing completely the usual desperate hour of crying and sinking and closing my eyes in the pleading hope of two more hours of oblivion. I just got up, like people do. I went to the window, ready to raise the curtain on a beautiful day, a day of hope and thrill and preparation: Christmas Eve. I flipped the blind. It was raining. Worse, drizzling. The kind of drizzle which goes sideways and upwards and seeps through your body until you become mucosal, at one with the half-hearted puddles forming around the bins. Oh well. I'll just have to stay in. That's fine, I won't leave the flat until evening, until Charlie-time.

I'd done most of my preparation already. Like an athlete, I know that preparation is all, that you only get out what you put in. I had let the Wagner seep in gently for a week or so, sponged some mustard off my pretty dress, and had a good think about what I might do to my hair. Wash it, naturally, then perhaps a pretty clip. That's what women do to make themselves nice, isn't it, a pretty clip? Or a bangle? I don't know. It doesn't matter, if he's going to love me, he must love me for what I am. I won't take any shit.

Anna texted me mid-morning; "Hey guys, just checking you're all on for tonight. Half seven at the Coach and Horses, W1. Can't wait to c u! Axx" She must have sent that to everybody. Even Charlie. For one tiny moment, we were doing the same thing – reading Anna's text. Then immediately afterwards we must have both spent a minute thinking about the evening to come, about the charity, about our promises for the auction. For five, ten seconds, we were one. I held his hand.

At lunchtime, I did my vocal warm-ups. Absolutely vital, I think. It's unlikely that I'll be singing tonight, but I still need to be on peak form, just in case. Gareth has equipped me with a wide repertoire of voice exercises to strengthen and consolidate my instrument, based on a mishmash of theories: bel canto, amateur physiology, Dolly Parton, and the rudiments of yoga. Most of these exercises involve hurling oneself over a soft object and bellowing, or some variation on that theme. There's an exercise to elevate my larynx, an exercise to strengthen my tongue, a series of hacking noises to darken my tone, and a number of consonant-heavy rhymes to engage my mind and voice. I'm sceptical, sometimes, about these exercises. I wonder how many hours a day Dame Nellie Melba spent bent backwards over a worktop pounding her stomach with a ladle and shouting "hat stand", until her cheeks ached like a hamster in spring, and her tongue involuntarily protruded from her tired, swollen lips. Still, I'm dutiful. An hour a day, and, on special days like today, two hours.

At three o'clock I finished, and felt good. I didn't go to see Gareth this week; I feigned a cold and cancelled. He, in turn, feigned disappointment at my non-appearance. I couldn't face him, not right now. Not when I've got my own life to sort out, when there are going to be big things happening for me. Now I know that I've only got one song in the show, I've relaxed a bit. I can easily triumph with just one song. Minimal rehearsal, just show up and belt, a la Merman. Just you wait.

Right now, Charlie. Countdown to Charlie. Even the name, thinking that name, makes my heart warm and my toes curl in anticipation of his touch. Charlie. Charlie. I said it out loud. I tried it a bit giggly, a bit coy, laughing at his jokes. Oh, Charlie. Silly old Charlie, with his tickling and his joshing and his slightly-too-public kisses. Still, I don't mind. When I get really cross with him I call him "Charles". Charles. So stern, often genuinely angry, yet we always end up in the bedroom. It'll be years before that subsides; he brings out the animal in me. His lovemaking is tender, yet vigorous when required. I always come. He never does things like ask "do you like that"; he knows. He feels it, we're so compatible that we needn't ever speak, really. But we do, because we love each other, and his every word is a joy to me. He has only to ask if I want sugar in my tea, and

I have to touch him, running my hand through his short, scrappy curls, feeling the babyish softness of his hair overlaying his hard, defensive skull. What if something happens to him? What if he dies? Well, then at least we'll have had some time together. His life will have enriched and strengthened me beyond measure, to the extent that I'll be able to cope with his demise. Ironic, I know. Every night I close my eyes and see him, and Emma, sitting at the end of my bed. One on either side, never speaking to each other, just watching over me. Tender smiles, calm, love. I couldn't live without them.

Some might say that I'm a fantasist. They'd chalk that up as a negative, claiming that happiness must come from the actual, that it must be empirically constructed, rooted in experience and its rational response. These are the same people who eat vegetables for breakfast, pay their council tax, and tell you that you shouldn't drink alcohol when you're depressed. They're wrong, wrong, wrong. If joy must be grounded in life as we see it, then what chance do we have of being anything other than, well, a bit glum? A philosophy of exclusively rational pleasure, of glue-headed realism, curtails the possibility of revelling in the future or the past. And what hope is there for the dead, if we may not fantasise? If we can't take pleasure in their imagined touch, in the memory of them, and the hope of another meeting, then what is loss but a precursor to waste disposal? Without imagination, the dead will get deader, and the living will sink. Let the fantasies proceed, and they'll come true, or true enough.

I washed my hair at three-thirty, and briefly wished that I had a blow-dryer. I did, when I lived in Muswell Hill. But it went the same way as most of the things from that flat

– up in smoke in a wheelie-bin. The day I moved out, I bundled my possessions into five huge bin-bags, dumped them in the bin round the back of the house, and doused them in alcohol. The entire, hilarious contents of our drinks cabinet – whisky, vodka, gin, kirsch, limoncello, pitu, green Chartreuse. I then lit four matches, one after the other, one for each year that I'd known her, and chucked them in. It went up, of course, huge and blooming and brief. I made sure that I was crying when the fire brigade arrived, said that it was an accident, that I'd chucked a cigarette in the bin without realising that it was full of polyester and cheap liqueur. They put a blanket around me, took me away, gave me a cup of tea. No harm done.

I've never minded the loss of those possessions; I didn't lose anything too valuable. A few pretty outfits, photo albums, grooming appliances, bits of make-up. I'd kept my music, and my musical theatre posters, and some books. I had enough clothes safe in Suffolk, those which I now wear daily. But now, for the first time since that day, I've started to wish I still had a hairdryer. That's got to be a good sign.

By half past four, I was made up and ready to go. Dress, boots, hair artfully tousled. I'm actually proud of the effect that I achieved sans dryer, with nothing but a hard, thin towel and a bouncy minute spent back-combing with a clothes-brush. Some would say that my hair looked "flyaway". I say it looked merry, festive, bumptious. Much like me.

I had two and a half hours to fill before Charlie-time, so went to the corner shop and scanned the shelves. Food? No. Not today. Wine? That's better. I picked up a cheeky Pinot, £8.49. The most expensive wine I've ever bought. I have a magnum of champagne in the flat, tucked away at the bottom of my wardrobe. It was given to me by an uncle four years ago; I've never had occasion to open it. Perhaps I'll open it tonight, when I get back. That's a nice thought.

With an hour and a half to kill before Charlie-time, I watched *Gypsy*. Drank the wine, and watched *Gypsy*. The 1993 American TV film, starring Bette Midler as Mama Rose. It's an astonishing piece of television. Initially I was sceptical; Bette Midler is not Ethel Merman, and she's not me. Me and Merman are the only true Mama Roses. Yet she won me over – there's something so furious, so energised, so unashamedly, fist-munchingly, bum-facedly ugly about her that you can't help but look. Even when nineteen dancing boys and a vaudeville baby are singing their hearts out centre-stage, your focus is pulled five feet to the left, where Midler stands, silent, watchful, ready for Her Turn. It's nourishing and inspirational; watching *Gypsy* with alcoholic accompaniment is my equivalent of going to the gym, or for a walk, or to see friends.

The credits rolled at seven, and it was time. Time to go to Soho and rendez-vous with my future. I remember little of the journey. Just closed eyes, yogic breathing, and a mantra: "Nothing. Nothing. Nothing. Nothing. Nothing." In time with jolts of the train. "Nothing. Nothing. Nothing." That's the only word which can calm me down, "nothing". It's not comforting, it doesn't reassure me that everything's going to be fine, it's just a promise, a soft, rhythmic promise. Nothing, eventually, nothing. I opened my eyes and realised that a few people were staring; I'd been vocalizing my nothings. Well, let them look. I'm on my way to something better than them! I just needed to calm down. Nothing, nothing, nothing.

I got off the tube at Leicester Square, and walked

briskly into Soho. I remembered the last time I delved alone into the heart of Soho, just before my Ipswich trip, on the hunt for sex. I thought, with a certain degree of pride, how far I've come since then. I've been shagged by two men, my voice has come on a treat, I know a bit about Wagner, and I've done a big supermarket shop. I chuckled at the memory of myself as I then was: lonely, inexperienced, naïve. I really am getting somewhere, you know. Back then I was on the hunt for anyone, anyone at all; now I'm going to see a specific person, someone whom I've met before, who's seen my name on a list, who must remember me fondly, and who may even be looking forward to our encounter. I stopped, suddenly, in the middle of Old Compton Street, letting the early evening crowd of booze-hungry party people crash into my back and shove chippily past me. I allowed myself a broad smile, caught sight of my reflection in the window of a restaurant. Lovely. I'm lovely. I leant in and kissed myself softly on the mouth, pulling back to reveal the sticky, steamy residue of my own lips. How beautiful, what a lucky restaurant. I lit a cigarette and proceeded.

I entered the pub. Not too worried, I was ten minutes early and imagined that Charlie would be at least ten minutes late, bless him. Downstairs was full, smoky. I couldn't see Anna. A scrawled sign by the bar caught my eye – "All those for 'Old People Heating Auction' in Function Room 1, upstairs." Then there was little arrow, pointing us in the direction of "upstairs". Oh, God, she's booked a room. Of course she has. I snaffled a quick shot of Jack Daniels from the bar and trudged my way up the staircase.

I peeped round the door, gave the room a quick scan. All I saw was Anna, in skinny jeans, talking earnestly to two dumpy, middle-aged women. I entered.

"Judy!" She scurried over and scooped me up, guiding me briskly towards the two badly-suited women, who stared at me like little cows.

"Thank you for coming! Ladies, this is Judy. Beautifully on time, of course. This is Mary, and Alison, who work for the company which will eventually be supplying the solar heating equipment for distribution. So they're really the stars of the night, ha!"

"Hello."

They each shuffled forward, and we shook hands. I didn't know which was which. Bugger. Oh well, I'm sure they're pretty much interchangeable. One of them – slightly older, with a slightly more circular haircut and a slightly dowdier suit – spoke.

"I really enjoy your column, We're so happy that you've volunteered your time to the cause."

"Oh, no, not at all. I don't mind."

The other one spoke.

"Well, we think it's very brave that you're going to be allowing someone to watch you work. Letting them in on your secrets, and things."

That made me nervous. Reminded me that I hadn't really thought this through.

"I wonder what kind of person will 'buy' you."

"Well, I'm rather tempted to put a bid or two in for myself. I'm quite a prize!"

They laughed.

"She's so funny. Isn't she funny?"

"Just like your column. I've got a daughter about your age. She's moving to the city next year and she reads you every week. I just hope she has as much fun as you seem to be having."

"Well, I wish her all the best. It's a wonderful city."

Where the fuck was Anna? I wanted to walk away. Actually, I wanted to headbutt them both briskly and rhythmically to the floor, then run shrieking into the night. I thought of Charlie. He'll be here soon, and I'm sure he'd like to see me being polite. I cracked on.

"Tell me a bit about your involvement with the charity. You actually make the heating equipment, is that right? How did you get hooked up with this project?"

"Well, actually, they approached us, and…"

I heard no more; within seconds I crunched into a great wall of boredom, her words all mashed together into a vast, charitable, eco-friendly drone. Fiscal considerations. The value of material goods weighed up against ethical capital. The unprecedented versatility of solar power. NASA. Sending old people into space to make their houses warmer. Insulating people with love. Oh, I don't give a fuck. Shut up, shut up, shut up you dull, squashy little woman with your daft shoes and your flat hair and your wet piggy mouth. I nodded politely, smiled. Wouldn't it be funny if I leant in and gave her a massive snog, just like that? I wonder what she'd do, if I said, "shh, darling", cupped her saggy bulldog face in my hands, drew her to me and rammed my tongue down her throat, perhaps shoved a hand up her beige pencil skirt and ripped a hole in her M&S control-top tights. She'd love it, I bet she would. I came to and realised that I was snorting. The woman had started to look a touch uncomfortable. I spoke, tried to justify my sudden merriment.

"Gosh, that's just so fascinating and inspirational. It just… it just makes me so happy."

I flashed her a massive grin, and peeled off.

"Excuse me."

"Of course."

I circled the room. It had started to fill up, about fifteen people now. No Charlie, still. I took a couple of glasses of wine and headed off into the corner. I stood for a bit, watching people trying to introduce themselves to one another, hunting for common ground, smiling, nodding, chuckling, desperation just millimetres beneath the mascara. None of these people knew each other, yet it seemed that they all knew Anna. So she floated from body to body, smoothing the cracks, pushing people together, spouting names and interests and occupations. Every conversation dipped periodically back to the subject of old people, and how to keep them warm whilst protecting the environment. Someone would bring it up when their own chat began to falter, their interlocutor would look serious, uncomfortable; they'd make a comment involving the word "worthy", then one of them would scamper off to get another drink.

I must have stood there for twenty minutes or so, trying to stay out of Anna's eyeline lest she hurl me once more into conversational prison. I began to get cross, tense, quietly irritable.

Where was he? He has to come, Anna said so. I became aware of my own sticky, blushing face, I felt every smear of make-up sitting reluctantly against my skin. I looked stupid, like a bad clown. My hair was a wig, my clothes were stolen, my body doubled in size, and everything I'd said that evening rushed back into me, clawed at my chest and scratched and mocked me until nausea began to rise. All the conversations around me grew shriller and more pointless, each word, each noise from every other person was an act of aggression. He wasn't coming. He was never going to come.

I'll never see him again and now there's no hope, no marriage, no life ahead that I want to live. I felt my throat grow hard and my eyes blur, a toddler about to fall to the floor and scream and scream and scream until my body went slack and I slipped fretfully into unconsciousness. I had to go. No goodbyes. Time to go.

I picked up my bag and moved towards the door. Coat? Did I have a coat? Oh, fuck it, give it to the charity. Down the stairs. Halfway down the stairs, then it all gave up. Legs, face, body. I sat down hard, and made noises. Loud, initially, a wrenching howl, which I muffled when I remembered the proximity of a party, the proximity of Anna, whose healing touch couldn't have been less welcome than it was at this moment.

I closed my mouth, and sorrow set up shop in my nasal passages, blocking out air as I snorted and sniffed. I sat, waited, snuffled, and things quietened. My chest remained clogged with something cold, wet and heavy: leaf mulch, or Swarfega. But I was composed, nearer to silence. I found my legs and stood. Moved, as I'd planned, down the stairs.

The next thing I knew, I'd fallen over again. This time the impact was physical rather than emotional; something like a head had struck me in the stomach as I rounded the steep, narrow corner. I wobbled, shrieked, and fell, hitting some shirt, a bit of trouser, a knee, and the tip of a well-scuffed lace-up. I landed at a forty-five-degree angle, my feet a good seven steps higher than my nose.

"Holy fuck, are you OK?"

I knew that voice. Knew it better than my own mother's, better than Ethel Merman's. I mumbled, involuntarily, into the fag-stinking stair carpet.

"Charlie Rogers?"

"Who is tha – Judy? Judy Bishop? My God, Judy, are you alright?"

Still on the floor. I might stay here, I think. Let's keep it breezy. Speak into the stair carpet.

"Yes! Hi! How are you?"

"I'm very well. Look, here, let me help you up."

He extended a hand. I took it, and a jet of ice water shot through my body, lifting me, coaxing me back to life, electro-shock therapy. I looked at his face. Unchanged, perfect. A lovely blue T-shirt, cord jacket, black trousers, and those amiably scuffed shoes. Donnish yet youthful, smart yet breezy, boyish yet – dear God – all man. So perfect, so ready to lure me back into the mainstream, back to cricket and tea and meeting the parents. I want to meet his parents, I think they'd like me. I stood, and allowed myself to look at him straight on. As I looked, I believed it all. Everything I'd thought, all true. I wanted my hello kiss. I didn't want my fall to deprive me of this delicious little courtesy.

"Well, hi there. Shall we say hello properly?"

He laughed, not a wry chuckle, but a moment of genuine amusement at something I'd said. He remembers me, you see, he knew me before I went wrong, before London, before the column. I was peripheral to his life, sure, but we had bouts of fun. We joked in the dressing room. I was funnier than anyone else, that much I know. I remember one moment in particular; he was in the middle of a dull conversation with a pretty, earnest girl who was in *Guys and Dolls*. I walked in to catch the last line of this chat; her saying "You see, it's really the gift that keeps on giving." I caught this as I entered and replied, sharp as a whip, "What, a vending machine?" How we laughed. How he laughed. The fun girl had saved him from the boring one. And back in the days of *Guys and Dolls*, first year of university, I was Fun Judy. During the intense times with Emma, during *Gypsy*, I became Too-Much-Fun Judy: too drunk, too loud, too merry, too desperate. He never saw that, of course. He just saw wit, and curves, and ambition. That's all he knows of me, and he can't fail to love it.

I gave him a kiss on the cheek, lingering briefly to sniff the area around his ear, searching for the scent of aftershave, shampoo, gel, a little clue.

"Well, Judy, lovely to see you! It's been too long."

"It has."

I smiled. He looked at me, closer, different.

"Are you – are you alright?"

"From the fall? Yes."

"No, I mean, you just look as if you might have been… well, crying."

Shit. Actually, not necessarily shit. Crying is quite good, quite womanly. It shows vulnerability and soul. And he's an actor. Actors love crying.

"Well, um – not really. Actually, yeah. I've just been having a, well, a bit of a tough time lately."

"I know. I was so sorry to hear about… about Emma. You became quite close, the two of you, I heard?"

I was astonished. No-one says that any more. Nearly a year has passed since the event. The expressions of sympathy have faded, or were never there at all. Not for me, someone who was "just a friend", one of a gang, not a sister or a parent or a boyfriend. Yet Charlie had come in and said the one thing that helps, the one thing that can touch me and sustain me and give me hope. An acknowledgement of Her, of Us. I looked at the floor, and shuffled.

"Yes, we did. Thank you, Charlie."

"No, no. It's just that I only heard a few weeks ago. Weird, how you just don't hear things when you've been busy. I bumped into Seb – you remember Seb? – and asked after her… and then… shit. And Seb said that the two of you had become really good mates, I was hoping I'd run into you tonight."

He might as well have recited the sonnets to me, there and then. God, the love I felt, the hope, the sheer, unadulterated pleasure such as I haven't felt for months, years even. I couldn't speak. He continued.

"You must have had a shit year. I know I would have, in your situation."

"Yeah, yeah, I have."

"Listen, I ought to go up in a moment, but do you fancy a quick drink down here? Before I enter Charity Hell?"

"I'd love that."

We drank together, propped up against the bar, for about fifteen minutes, the best fifteen minutes of my life. He had a pint of Hoegaarden, I had white wine. As it should be. We chatted, we talked about work. I decided to be honest.

"Well, I'm still pursuing the singing, really, that's my main thing. I'm doing a show, actually, before the auction. But I'm sort of writing this column, for a newspaper, to fund it all."

"Oh? Which paper?"

I told him.

"God, I'm afraid I've never seen it. I tend to turn straight to the arts pages. Self-obsessed, I know."

"Ha! Well, I wouldn't bother. It's a bit hacky. I don't really like doing it, to be honest."

"Ah, well, all the great ones had to, at some stage or another. Pays the rent."

"Where are you living?"

"Belsize Park. Eton Avenue."

"How lovely."

Or at least I assume so. I've never actually been. I've heard it's leafy, cultured, salubrious, the best of north London. Just like him. We chatted on, came back to Emma. He brought her up.

"God, Judy, I hope you don't mind my coming back to it, but... I was just really so, so sorry to hear about Emma."

"I know. She was amazing. So many people miss her so much."

"Absolutely. She was so... so central. And so much fun! So much fun."

He stared ambiguously into the middle distance, letting the word "fun" hang in the air. He was calling her a slut. Again, elements of truth in that. A moment of wistful naughtiness, then he came back.

"Actually, I must say I always had a bit of a crush on her. I'm sure she wouldn't mind my saying that."

No, I'm sure she wouldn't. I'm sure she'd fucking love it. I'm sure she is loving it, somewhere. Still he went on, turned to me, got a bit coy, a little smirk clouding his beautiful face.

"You know, I actually – we – well, we had a bit of a snog once, Emma and I. A party in college. I felt a bit weird; I was a third-year and she was a first-year. It's funny how these things matter so much at the time, isn't it?"

Yes, hilarious.

"But she was great. So much fun."

I felt malice; vicious, sharpened flint. I heard her laugh.

She was back in the room, loud and vibrant, sapping everything from everyone around her, drawing their energy into her own. I needed to regain my status.

"You know, I kissed her."

Oh, now he was interested. Now that we were pooled together in an agar plate of Emma's saliva. He gave me the naughty look I always dreamed he'd give me.

"Yeah. We toured Europe together in *Gypsy*. Had a bit of a snog in a youth hostel in Nuremburg. Not the most romantic of venues, I know."

"God, I didn't know she was that way inclined. I should have guessed. Fun girl like her."

"Well, she was."

"And you…?"

"Well, no, not really. But, I mean, it was Emma. Who could say no?"

I finished with a chuckle, but became aware of the truth in what I'd just said. Emma was magnetic – as Charlie said, central. And when she invited you up onto the plinth, took you with her, you never turned her down. No-one ever did. Perhaps that was the problem. I shoved the thought aside, let my revelation be what Charlie thought it was: an amusing nuance in a tragically terminated friendship. He smiled in response to my comment.

"Too true, too true."

We talked more, mostly little Emma-memories. Still, she pulled focus. It was OK. Mostly I was glad to chat, interested to hear another perspective on her life, however ill-informed and wrong. I felt as if Charlie and I were in a play or a film, a sentimental comedy where old college-mates meet up, reminisce about the good times, and eventually are left standing together on common ground, realising that they only ever had eyes for each other.

"It was a car crash, wasn't it?"

That was a brutal way to yank me out of my reverie.

"Um... yes. It was. Killed on impact."

"Fucking hell, was she driving?"

"No."

"Who was driving?"

"I don't know."

It was time to go. He drained his pint. Gave me a kiss, and headed upstairs.

"Time to face the gaping maw of charity, methinks. Lovely to see you, Judy. I suppose we'll meet again at the auction. Can't wait to see which mad fucker's going to buy me."

I laughed.

"I'm sure it'll be fine. Bye, Charlie. Good to see you."

"You too. Stay well."

Oh, I will, I really will. That was above and beyond anything. I floated out into the night. He liked me. He was pleased to see me. The conversation had been sentimental, companionable, and momentarily erotic. There's hope, there's so much hope, hope that softens me, opens me, makes the streets of Soho look warm, clean, vibrant. I went home, via Belsize Park. It added about an hour to my journey, but was worth it. I got off the tube and had a look around. I was right; it was nice. I got out my A-Z and found Eton Avenue. I breathed him in.

Then back to my flat, back to my life, which has never seemed fuller, or happier, or more real, than it does right now. I opened the champagne.

The Days of Judy B

I MENTIONED a couple of weeks ago that I was going to have a haircut. Well, I've had it – I didn't bottle out and insist on a mere wash and blow-dry like last time – and I am delighted. When my lovely editors finally fork out for a new byline pic, you'll see me in all my golden-haired glory. That's right, Golden Haired. I am now blonde, or blondish.

I had no plans to go blonde, and if I had done, you would have been the first to know. Essentially, I was attacked by a persuasive homosexual with a tubful of peroxide. I didn't really notice what he was doing; I was enjoying my complimentary apple and lemongrass smoothie, tucking into a copy of *Marie Claire*, and engaging in light banter about Celebrity Breast Implants.

We exchanged a few words, sure; he asked me if I wanted a "little bit of a lift", and I said yes. Who wouldn't? He said that he fancied playing around with a little colour, and who was I to deny him his sport?

Only when I came out from under the dryer, looked in the mirror and saw what appeared to be a dark-browed Midwich Cuckoo did I grasp the enormity of the situation. I was blonde. Brassy, glossy, Marilyn. And you know what? I wasn't cross. I could have been, sure. But as Antoine rocked back on his heels, crossed his gym-pumped arms over his exposed, pierced navel, and let out a wolf-whistle, joy coursed through my newly-tarty heart.

Nevertheless, I asked him to explain himself. He responded as I would, hope; "Well, my little sugar-plum, I've been reading your fabulous column, and it seems that you're needing a bit of disguise from all those naughty, naughty men. So I thought I'd swing to the rescue! And it's fabulous!" "Yes, Antoine, yes, it is." I replied. And I meant it. So we went for a cocktail, he told me about his man-troubles, and I told him about mine.

That's the brilliant thing about homosexuals; they always cheer you up. Even when you don't know you need it, they'll beam in with some hair straighteners, a feather boa, and a fruity cocktail, ready to blast the cobwebs from your dull, tiring, heterosexual existence. The conversation is always a bit naughty, a bit sexy, with a slight magazine edge to it, adopting and dismissing topics with the gleeful flippancy of a 30p glossy. You never really find out anything about their life, and they tend not to listen to the less interesting aspects of yours. You just look at life through a pink, swirling kaleidoscope, air-kissing the serious issues, then sending them on their way.

So Go Forth, ladies, and find yourself a

Gay. Spend two hours with him, drink a cocktail, tell him your problems, then let him scamper off to Soho and do the dirty things that you don't want to know about. And if he wants to dye you blonde, let him.

Judy B's Purchase of the Week: A big hat, just in case I change my mind.

JUDY BISHOP

10.

5th November, 2006

I've spent the last week exploring my sexuality, and am decidedly alarmed by my findings. It would seem that I'm a passive bi-curious snob, fearful of nudity, with male-centered homophiliac tendencies and a slight fear of regional accents. Add to that a Broadway fetish and an overwhelming lust for a vocally ball-breaking New Yorker who died in 1984, and it seems wildly unlikely that I'll ever conceive children. No bad thing, perhaps. Given my tendency to trade down sexually, to target those in a state of more acute longing even than myself, their father would probably have to be on death row, or in a zoo, or so obese that I would have to be lowered onto him in order to extract his seed. Unless things work out with Charlie, of course. That's always a possibility. And this week, however grubby and morally questionable, has moved me a week closer to bed-bound happiness with the man of my dreams.

It was the conversation with Charlie that got me thinking, properly, about my sexuality. Emma, obviously, sat at the centre of things. That kiss, what followed, what it meant. But aside from the knowledge of Emma's centrality, I was puzzled. I turned, as ever, to musical theatre for my answers. I think I've found them, and they all come back to Jaqueline Susann. Ethel Merman, my forerunner, and Jaqueline Susann, vampish author of *Valley of the Dolls*. During the original Broadway run of *Gypsy*, Susann heard that Merman was having a little trouble negotiating the physical bump 'n' grind of the role. So Susann went to Merman's hotel room, and performed – unbidden, I imagine – a private striptease. Thus began what was perhaps the definitive, ongoing affair of Merman's life: her and Susann, together, in secret. Perhaps, I thought, Emma had provided me with a similar service. She'd taught me something which I hadn't known about myself, taken a chubby, brash, frightened virgin and show her that she could be touched, that her body was as much a playground as anyone else's. But now Emma is gone, where do I stand? She made me – however briefly – happy, and there must be someone else who can do the same, someone on this planet who can make me feel that way again. Men haven't, so far, been all that brilliant. So I'm left with women. I must find myself a woman.

My decision to employ a prostitute began, oddly enough, with Gareth. I went to see him on Tuesday, as usual, for my lesson. I packed a bottle of water, some Vocalzone, the Jerome Kern songbook, and my knife. I'm keeping the knife. The feeling of specialness, of security, that it gives me is incomparable. It's a secret, a happy secret, the grown-up equivalent of the troll doll I used to carry with me to exams, when I was at school. I patted my bag, felt the rigid steel lying safely against the music folder, and headed on out.

I arrived at Gareth's, and began to retrieve my music. As I did so, the strap caught against my elbow, causing the bag to flip over and the contents to slide out onto the floor. The knife skied across the smooth cover of a songbook, and came to rest a few inches away, on the dirty kilim rug. Gareth stopped, halfway through his weekly, tentative descent onto the piano stool. He hovered there for a second, eyes fixed on the knife. I remained nonchalant. I had to ride this out – no explanation needed; I haven't done anything wrong. Just happened to have a knife with me. None of his business. I carried on humming scales and flicking through the book, made a quick comment about one of the lyrics of "My Bill", wondered aloud if it might be a suitable audition song, went back to humming, took a sip of water. All as it should be, just with a knife on the carpet. I put the songbook to one side, bent down, and looked through the rest of my music. I wasn't in the mood for Jerome Kern. I'm in love, and those lyrics have become too deep, too meaningful to waste on Gareth. Now, *The Sound of Music* for piano and voice. That's more like it. Number five: "The Lonely Goatherd", I think. I suggested it.

"Gareth? 'The Lonely Goatherd'? Are you up for that? The yodelling will be good for my middle range."

His eyes remained fixed on the rug.

"Judy, dear, why is there a serrated kitchen knife on my rug?"

I drew myself up to my full height, looked him directly in the eye, and spoke.

"In case of danger, Gareth."

"Right. Any particular danger?"

"No. Nothing I can think of. Just danger. Lurking."

"OK."

"Can we get on with the lesson, now, Gareth? We're on the clock."

"Of course. Shall we just leave the knife there, on the floor, for the time being? Would that suit?"

"That would suit me very well, Gareth."

"Good."

All hour, he was tenser than usual. Watchful, serious, overly accommodating of my vocal faults. For once, there was no digression, nothing from him, nothing from me. I just yodelled, strong and pure and lovely, and he sat, quiet and professional, playing the piano.

Then, a nosebleed. Another fucking nosebleed. That's twice, now, in front of Gareth. He must think that I have a brain tumour. Maybe I do have a brain tumour. Shit. Maybe in a minute I'm going to fall over, "The Lonely Goatherd" forever unfinished, as the cancerous bun warming in my skull finally pushes what's left of my brain to one side and fills my head with malignancy, sending me screaming and dribbling to the floor, the piano accompaniment bashing on beneath me. There'll always be a lapse, however tiny, between a death and its acknowledgement. Those inappropriate seconds of normality before the catastrophe is made official by another's knowledge: the moments when Mr Simmons continued fucking me as I lay dead – the heart attack in front of the telly, the wife in the next chair, still enjoying the costume drama. I imagined dying in front of Gareth, just Gareth. Him not knowing who to ring, Mum and Dad and Clare going about their lives in different parts of the country with no idea that I had died of a brain tumour, in a bedsit in Archway whilst singing "The Lonely Goatherd". The thought of them, carrying on, made hot tears spring out and roll down the sides of my upturned face, trickling into my ears as I rammed the tissue against my streaming bloody nose. I really ought to phone home more often.

"Judy?"

"Hm?"

"Are you alright?"

"Fine."

"OK."

"Just my nose."

"OK."

Silence. Gareth stood up, moved to the rug, and lean- tover to pick up the knife. My knife, he couldn't take my knife, my comforter. I need it, and he doesn't. Fear rose, and I threw down the tissue and hurled myself forward, my body splayed out across the rug, the knife, danger. I felt Gareth's hand, holding the weapon, trapped beneath my stomach. It would take nothing for him to rotate his wrist, flick it upwards, and slice my body open through the fabric of my hoodie. He could then put the knife in my hand and claim that I'd done it to myself. We stayed still, face to face on the floor, eyes locked, noses almost touching. I looked at his eyes. Big, brown, sad. A teddy bear. I giggled, despite myself. His face softened, we relaxed. The moment had passed. We scrambled to our feet, changed, relieved, like actors after someone's yelled 'cut'. The knife stayed where it was.

"I think we should probably call it a day."

"We probably should."

I picked up my bag, shoved my music in it, took a sip of water, and reclaimed the bloody tissue from the floor of the kitchenette, where it had fallen.

"Will I see you next week, Judy?"

"I hope so."

"So Tuesday, twelve o'clock."

His tone was gentle, measured, calm. I appreciated it; he was calming me, him and singing, all things good.

"Let's write that down."

I wanted to remain noncommittal, yet positive. I couldn't vouch for my own likely whereabouts; next Tuesday suddenly seemed a long way off. But I wanted him to know that I was still around, that I was having a few problems at the moment, but that I was still a professional, I could still be in his show. In fact, this business with the knife would only make me more suitable for the musical stage. All the great performers had their quirks and problems. None of them ever turned up to work happy, with a flask of honey and lemon and a larynx full of constructive arpeggios. All of the great ones were messy. Elaine Stritch – drunk. Judy and Liza – off their mash on barbiturates and gin. Merman – romping nightly in the sack with Jacqueline Susann. I spoke.

"How's everything going with the show, Gareth? You do still, still… want me?"

He smiled.

"Of course I do, Judy. I'm still deciding on your song."

"Good. Thank you."

"What are you up to for the rest of the week, Judy?"

"Um, I don't know."

As I said it, I realised how frightening it was, that little scrap of honesty popping up when I least expected it.

I really, really don't know what I'm doing for the rest of the week. It's going to involve more sex, that much I know.

Something exploratory with a woman, or a transsexual, or, if possible, a hermaphrodite. Something off-centre and new. Gareth spoke.

"Judy, I don't want to pry, but… are you seeing anyone at the moment?"

"What?"

Is he coming on to me? That's the last thing I need right now. God.

"I think, I think it might not be a bad idea to, you know, call up a professional."

"What the fuck are you suggesting?"

"It's nothing to be ashamed of. I've done it. Lots of people have, good people, successful people, famous people. Singers, even. Just talking to someone, having them cast an eye over you."

Oh, he means therapy. Well, I've done that, and look where it got me. Legs akimbo underneath a fat stalker, above a mashed potato café in Elephant and Castle.

"Gareth, really? You've done that?"

"Once a week for three years. It helped. Took me out of myself. Look, I'm sorry, perhaps I've crossed a line. But when things are a bit, well, barren, and you can't take it, you call in the pros. Just think about it."

"Thank you, Gareth, I will. See you next week. Not long before the show now."

"Absolutely. Bye bye."

"Bye."

I left, and thought about it. Therapy – obviously not. There's a rush on, and I don't have time to be retracing my steps. But, in the abstract, maybe professional help is no bad thing. I heard him again: "When things are a bit, well, barren… call in the pros." What I need in this instance is not a supportive ear, but a willing female body on which I can experiment. I could go to a gay club; look one up in

Time Out, put on my party dress, do my hair, throw some shapes, drink Lambrini, and find myself a lovely lady for the night. But that would involve a degree of emotion, a couple of lies, the accepted mutual callousness of the One Night Stand. Two drunk people trying to pretend that they're not just using each other as a masturbatory aid, exchanging false numbers, spitting out false promises of a reunion. I'm not up for that; there's no time. I need to be clinical, honest, and proactive. Things are barren. Call in the pros.

I stepped into a phone box, and surveyed the sexual buffet on the wall before me. There were what seemed like hundreds of cards: bright colours, neon, legs and breasts and waxed, glossy patches where pubic hair should be. Leather and buckles and plastic lace. I had an image of myself, at age eight, standing in front of a rack of greetings cards, trying to pick something out for Mother's Day. A crippling wave of sorrow, which I suppressed. This is business; I am my own managing director, working to improve the company's prospects through creative development. It's nothing to be ashamed of. Now then, "Miss Titty". Aptly named. She looks fun, but atypical of the female form. No use. "Genevieve Spank". Too frightening. "The Sex-Tuplets". No thank you, I'm only after one of you. Oh, maybe this isn't going to work. They were all strange, distorted, their erogenous zones magnified until they ceased to be women and became reflections in the Hall of Mirrors, magnetic yet perverse. I turned to leave, then a small card, to the left of the others, caught my eye.

"Gemma". Unlike the rest, she was smiling. Coy, flirtatious, but still the identifiable ghost of a real smile. She wore a white strappy top, breasts full but real, a little curve outwards at the hip. Sandy blonde hair. A bit like Emma.

Gemma. Emma. Gemma. Emma. I dialled.

"Hello?"

Oh, shit, she answered. What now, what?

"Hi… um. I saw your ad. I'm looking for, um, well… actually, are you Gemma?"

"Yeah, I'm Gemma. Which ad did you see?"

She sounded just like every other operator I've ever spoken to: gas, water, BT, Chinese Takeaway. Brisk. This was OK.

"Archway. Just opposite the tube."

"Alright. It's seventy-five pounds for full sex. Oral, anal, hand-jobs and S&M, forty quid a whack. And don't even think about asking if you can shit on my face, because I don't do that and I never will."

I held the phone slightly away from my ear. How crude.

"Um, I'm a woman."

"Yeah, I got that."

"I don't know what I want."

Her tone softened a touch, or at least so I thought.

"Where do you want to meet? I'm in Dalston, but for thirty pounds extra I'll come to your place."

"I'd like that. Thank you."

"Where are you, love?"

I gave her my address.

"And what's your name?"

"Emma."

"OK, Emma. I'll see you at nine-thirty, for an hour. Would you like me to wear a costume?"

I thought for a minute.

"Uh, no thanks."

We hung up.

● ● ●

How does one prepare a flat for the arrival of a prostitute? Do you tidy? Or mess it up a bit to make her feel at home? Do you lay on a bottle of wine, some candles, soft music, clean sheets? I suppose it's up to you, really. This is your party, no-one else's desires need be considered. I'd taken five hundred pounds out of the cash machine; I wasn't sure quite which services I'd require, or what they'd cost. Best to be safe. I ordered a pizza, I suppose as a sort of warm-up for the evening's big delivery. I paced around the flat, munching, getting excited. Honestly, excited. She was coming, she was mine, I could touch her wherever I wanted, and she wouldn't judge me. She'll have seen bodies worse than mine, she'll have seen men, and perverts, and hateful, hurtful people. I'm a soft, clean woman, who's pleased to see her. I have very few profound sexual kinks. I reached for the last slice of pizza, then thought better of it and withdrew my hand. I should leave some pizza for the hooker, she might be hungry. I really want her to like me. I'm sure she will.

I tried to keep women in my mind; why I loved them, why I wanted to touch them, I stared out of the window at a couple walking past, holding hands. Which one of them do I fancy most? Him – denim jacket, nice T-shirt, jeans, tight little arse and a bit of a strut. Or her – shift dress, jacket, breasts nicely rising out of a slim, concave torso. If I were allowed just one shag, only one more for the rest of my life, would it be him, or her? Pounding or stroking? Perfume or stubble? I closed the curtains and let them walk on in peace.

Tonight was about a woman, one woman, Gemma. Waist, hair, skin, tits, thighs. Come on, Judy. Be aroused. Not excited in the abstract, not intellectually delighted by the idea of sex, but horny, like generations of sluts before you. I was angry now. Why wasn't I turned on? I went into the bedroom and knelt up on my desk, until my face was level with Ethel Merman's. I leant in and kissed her mouth, already open in song. Cold, flat, two-dimensional. I went back into the kitchen, found a screwdriver underneath the sink, and drove it into Ethel's gaping mouth, ripping a hole in the poster and cracking into the wall beneath. I gouged and gouged and chunks of wall came loose, falling from Merman's lips until there was a little cave, mouth-sized, inviting. I went back into the kitchen, replaced the screwdriver, and got a little pot of jelly and cream from the fridge. I took the pot back into my bedroom and emptied its contents into Ethel's wall-mouth-cave. That's more like it. I leant in and kissed her, licking and sucking and stroking, the sweet, soft jelly moving from my mouth to hers.

Things changed; I felt energy, energy between my legs such as I haven't felt since Emma. I kissed harder, moved my body up to the wall, grinding, touching, noises, lights, sensations. I was damp, hot, furious, every nerve in my body firing as I plunged my tongue deeper and deeper into the wall, into Merman, until I could taste only plaster and could imagine no better taste. I was Jacqueline Susann now, the seductress. I ripped open my cardigan and threw my naked torso at the poster. I had to be touched, there, right now. Still kneeling, I yanked down my skirt until it bunched around my knees, and drove a hand into myself, the other moving between my own breasts and Ethel's as I pounded my pelvis into the wall, one two, three, then my stomach clenched, an unbearable ball of sensation and colour which spread in waves through my chest and limbs and pelvis, and

I fell, plunged backwards into the orchestra pit, with a gasp and a crash and a pain which I could not feel. I lay on the floor, panting, exhausted, a leg on the desk and my vision still swimming with violins and Merman and Emma. A final twitch, a jolt of acute sensation, then my body slackened, and I was done. Broadway.

Slack, I remained there. A minute, perhaps two. Incapable of motion, of thought. I needed sleep, wanted to melt into the carpet and stay there for ever, crotch pounding, Merman smiling down. I closed my eyes. The buzzer. The buzzer? Ah, the door. The prostitute. Shit, what can I say? Thanks but no thanks, I just had sex with the wall; but please do help yourself to a slice of pizza? Bugger. I pulled on my skirt and cardie and stuffed a sock in Ethel's mouth as the buzzer went again.

"Hello?"

"Hi, it's Gemma."

"Come on up."

Gemma came in – skinny jeans, halter top, heels, make-up, and a slightly incongruous puffa jacket. I'd never seen a prostitute before, in real life. She was so normal. No attitude, no wisecracks, no leopard-print sack full of sex toys. Just… normal. A touch wary, perhaps, a touch brittle, but not too far to the side of the girls I grew up with. Actually, she reminded me of my old dance teacher, Donna. Donna taught a beginners jazz class in Suffolk, which I went to when I was about fourteen. She was sharp, tense, physical, kind, with a penchant for slutty tops and a slight Essex twang. Just like Gemma. Weird.

"So, Emma, what are you after?"

"I… I don't know yet. Would you like a glass of wine?"

"Oh, thanks, babe."

I poured a glass and handed it to her. She sipped politely, and put it on the sideboard. That shocked me. I'd imagined her downing it crudely in one, like the Julia Roberts character in *Pretty Woman*. But where I gulped, she sipped. She's classier than me. I should have known that. Who isn't?

She repeated herself.

"So, what are you up for?"

I thought for a minute.

"Could you – could you just stand there, just for a moment?"

"Sure."

"May I touch you?"

She laughed, not unkindly.

"Of course."

I crossed the room, and put a hand on her waist. I trembled, fearful, if anything. She stood still, looking down at me as I explored her, ran my shaking fingers over her hips, down and round, up her inner thigh, down to her ankles, around her back and up to the nape of her neck, through her hair; thin, wisped, slightly greasy. Like a child playing on a statue, I got to know her shape. Feet, sinews, a slight bulge of fat over the waistband of her jeans. Was this what I wanted? She stood still, her eyes following me as I touched, only occasionally moving an arm to sip her wine. I arrived at her face. It wasn't the face I wanted, that much I knew. But it was a face, a face which was letting me move at my own pace, devoid of any desire of its own.

"May I kiss you?"

"Of course."

Again, not like *Pretty Woman*. I cupped her cheeks, and kissed her mouth; small, tight, too wet, teeth slightly too evident. I pulled away.

"I – I want to do something. But I don't know what."

I continued, as if ordering a winter-flowering shrub at a garden centre, or a good wine to go with a casserole.

"Is there anything you can suggest?"

"How much do you have?"

"What?"

"Money?"

"Oh, right, of course. Sorry. Five hundred."

"Well then. Bedroom?"

I led her into the bedroom, through the detritus of my previous escapade; broken chairs, music everywhere, my cardboard larynx strewn across the floor, in pieces. I'll have to deal with that in the morning. I sat on the bed. She gave me orders. Lie back. Skirt off. Hitch up your top. Legs apart. Herself fully clothed, she pulled my pants off with her teeth, and began to do what I imagine a lot of women do in bed, something I once read about in *More* magazine, something that's always frightened and enthralled me, something that had nearly happened to me once before, in the dark in Muswell Hill.

It was peculiar. I'd always imagined sex with another woman as being somewhat… floral. Two equals, unexpectedly and magically soft to one another's touch. Hints of chrysanthemum would waft through the air as we sensed each other's desires; our identical bodies melting together in mutual need and trust, building gracefully to an explosion of satisfied femininity and a passion that could write an opera.

This, on the other hand, was turning out to be more of a veterinary experience. I stared at the ceiling, looking for cracks, fissures, wishing that I had a Monet print up there, like at the dentist's. I was vaguely aware that I was being interfered with, but other than a slight bewilderment I felt very little. No aggression, at least, or fear. Just nothing. Oh, maybe I'm not gay. Not even bisexual. And if I'd wanted to be, then perhaps I should have put in a bit more effort when I was at university. Joined one of those societies, gone on marches. I can't expect to enjoy this if I'm not willing to get to know the lesbian community. Where is the lesbian community? Brighton? No, Hastings. Well, I could go to Hastings. I'll go tomorrow. I could get a day return on the train for twenty pounds, fifteen if I use my railcard. Then I'll come back and have another crack at this whole Sapphic business.

I felt a light tap on my thigh.

"Hello?"

I did a little sit-up.

"Hello."

"Everything alright up there?"

Oh, dear, she sounds cross. I must make it up to her.

"Yes, no, that's fantastic. Thank you. You're really really good at it. Lovely. I think I've just… just had enough."

"Alright then."

She stood up, drained her wine, and handed me back my pants.

"How much?"

"Two hundred and fifty."

"No, look, take the whole five hundred. I feel dreadful about not being more responsive. It really was lovely, I promise. I just got a bit carried away before you arrived. That's all."

She pocketed the money, and smiled.

"Happens all the time. Bye, love."

"Bye."

She left. I ran to the toilet, collapsed over the bowl. How, how, how, how could that have happened? Both things? Both bits of sex, both lonely, vile moments of abandon. Horrible, horrible bodies; my own, Ethel Merman's, Gemma's. I finished vomiting, turned off the bathroom light, and lay down, watching the crack of dusky light peering round the door. I imagined the door opening, and Emma coming in, as she once did, in our flat. One night, a month or two after we moved in, she came to my room. A soft knock, the shaft of light, and there she was. Padding across the floor, tucking herself in with me, putting a silencing finger over my mouth, and playing. Her hands skimmed over the soft cotton of my pyjamas, then inside, coming to rest down there, stroking, touching, loving me. Then she plunged inside me, hurting me, but I couldn't make a sound. The silencing finger remained, as restrictive as a gag; her tiny little arms were chains around me. She finished, removed the finger, and kissed me softly, padding back to her own bed, satisfied. We never talked about it, never in daylight. It was her thing that she'd done, that she could do because she was so beautiful, because I loved her so much. Every night I'd lie there in the dark, staring at the door, conscious of her body only ten feet away, wondering if she'd come again, hoping that she wouldn't, curious to know what would happen if she did. I still wait for her. I lowered my head to the cracked tile, and wept.

I slept there, and woke late the next morning, about eleven. I showered urgently, and felt an overwhelming desire to do something normal, something everyday, some business. I dressed, sat down at the desk next to the kitchen, and I checked my e-mails. Spam, spam, spam, a circular about the Auction of Promises – dress smart casual – and one from Gareth, about the revue. Brilliant. We're going to have an hour's rehearsal on the day, learn our cues, and get the feel of the theatre. There are about four or five of us involved – I didn't recognise any of their names. Other pupils of Gareth's, I imagined. But most exciting was the song list. My solo number – "Everything's Coming Up Roses", from, of course, *Gypsy*. I smiled, som so happy. I will be Mama Rose again, Gareth trusts me to be Mama Rose. It's fine, it's all going to be fine.

There was also, to my surprise, an e-mail from my editor. Huh. Unusual. It's not their day for communicating with me. I opened it.

TO: Judy Bishop
FROM: Olivia Gee
SUBJECT: Congratulations!

Dearest Judy,
You may have heard this already, but a new set of media awards, entitled "What Women Think", has been established this year, in order to honour and encourage premier contributors to national discussion. I'm happy to tell you that you have been awarded "Lifestyle Columnist of the Year" for your wry and witty take on the life of a young urban professional. SO, congratulations, my dear, you deserve it! There'll be a reception next Thursday, 9th November, at Bar 197 on Great Portland Street, where we'll give you a little trophy. Really hope you can make it! It'd be great to see you in the flesh again, it's been far too long!

Lots and lots of love,
Olivia xxxxx

Wow. I'm an award-winner. Officially an archetypal Young Woman of the Media. I picked up the prostitute's card, threw it into the dried-up window-box, and lit a cigarette. Donald Crowhurst popped up and gave me a quick high five. I'm officially giving him a run for his money. Nice one. Better write a speech, I suppose.

The Days of Judy B

PARTIES, PARTIES, parties. That's my life. At the moment, certainly. It comes and goes, of course. Sociability rushes at you in waves, sparkly and giggling, when you least expect it. Sometimes there are so many parties that you start to resent them, hangovers creep in, suede shoes get scuffed, conversation gets more and more hysterical until you find yourself telling a straight-laced colleague about the time you had one too many Kir Royales and pinched a bishop's arse, or the time you dropped a kebab on a new boyfriend's cashmere sweater.

But when a celebration is, at least partly, in your honour, everything changes. You spend the extra hour on your hair. You splash out on those new mules, and the toenail polish to make them marvellous. You swing by Jo Malone and treat yourself to that lime, basil and mandarin cologne. I recently experienced the pleasure of being at the eye of the social storm, and I'll tell you now that there's nothing quite like it. For I, I am pleased to announce, am an award-winner. "Lifestyle Columnist of the Year", as decided by the judging panel of the What Women Think awards. I was presented with a lovely trophy, made a pithy yet moving speech – in which I, of course, thanked You, The Reader, then drank a lifetime's worth of free white wine and danced my little socks off until well beyond home-time. It was marvellous.

I must say, I hadn't been looking forward to the experience. Because of the surfeit of parties in the last week – an engagement, two birthdays and a housewarming – I was All Partied Out. Yet still I loved this one. Why? I've figured it out. Because I was the Centre of Attention. That points to a low impulse in humankind: the desire to be looked at. The desire to be a demi-god for a night, to conjure up chicken satay on a whim, to steer all conversations back in the direction of You, You, You. I will happily get drunk in honour of a friend's birthday, engagement, or new house. I will turn up and be polite, of course. I'm a well-brought up young lady. But unless I, Judy Bishop, am allowed to sparkle, the pleasure will always be decidedly second-rate.

I think that's true of all of us. Why, for example, do women dance on tables? Not because they're a convenient place to dance. No, because we want to get all eyes on us, everyone looking our way, albeit at the expense of the girl being Bat Mitzvah-ed. We needn't do this, we needn't rush ourselves, drown out our friends. We ought just to wait our turn. Because everyone will have Their Moment. It's a rare person who goes through life without a single party being thrown in their honour. A party where there's food you like, glorious people flown in to entertain you. Friends, clowns, magicians or, as time goes by, strippers. Not everyone will have the unique pleasure of being voted one of the most insightful women in the papers today, but everyone will, at some point or other, get Their Turn.

Right now, it's my turn, my moment. It remains my moment until both the rosy glow and the hangover have subsided. This could take a while, particularly in the case of the latter. So kiss my feet. Photograph me to death. I am Judy Bishop.

Judy B's Purchase of the Week: A tiara, because I'm worth it.

JUDY BISHOP

11.

12th November, 2006

Have you ever been chucked out of an Angus Steak House?
If you had, you'd remember it. No matter how detached you
were from the experience, no matter how addled your mind,
how far removed from sentient existence the surfeit of meat
had rendered you, you would remember being chucked out
of an Angus. The cool, controlling hand of the waiter on
your shoulder, the firm stare of the doorman, the wild hostility in the pit of your stomach, the hot, wet T-bone clasped
between your blistering fingers as you run screaming into
the crisp city night.

It's liberating. When the lowest common denominator
of modern cuisine deems you unfit to rest on one of its fag-
reeking velour banquettes, there's only so much further you
can fall. As rock-bottom recedes, you start to enjoy the trajectory, admire the ever-darkening colours, watch layer after
layer of humanity swishing past you and above you as you
hurtle towards no particular kind of oblivion.

I was, of course, drunk. This week has been defined by

drunkenness. An odd kind of cumulative drunkenness, the kind where the first drink after waking somehow reignites the last seven, and full-body toxicity becomes an acceptable state, perhaps even a desirable one. For once, your body is driving your mind, like lust, like death, like yoga. Heavy drinking is a sport, a physical activity which forces you to engage with your own living self and, for once, listen. Now that I've given up sex, drinking is my expression of physicality; every wave of nausea is a vital sign, and I am glad of it.

Everything is speeding up. Encounters are blurring into one, the auction and the show are looming, time's flying, and I have a sense of an end. The party was on Thursday. The party for the What Women Think awards, where my contribution to the LifeStyle Review section – indeed to humanity itself – was honoured by a panel of fun-loving ladies who've earned themselves modest yet admirable success in their chosen fields. The foundress of a lingerie company, a newsreader, and the editor of a monthly glossy. They all, apparently, turn to me once a week for light relief. As they said in an e-mail, forwarded to me by Olivia, I "remind the world that life is fun, and that young, well-educated women aren't necessarily 'above' such things as shoes, make-up and silly dancing. However, Judy's columns also have a more serious undertone, and she doesn't shy away from more heartfelt issues". They drew the panel's attention to my column dated 10th September, in which I recounted an incident involving the redemption of an unhappy transsexual through the purchase of a sleeveless wrap dress.

So I'm good, very good apparently, at the thing I despise. My editors believe that I am earning my money, doing them proud, justifying their early faith in me. And my readership, the very demographic which would find the real me so unpalatable, are cheerfully consuming every hateful column I spew out, blithely dunking me in their skinny cappuccinos and chewing vapidly away, smiles playing across their artfully conditioned lips.

And then I had to meet them. I had to go to a party, and show myself in all my mendacious glory. Worse, I had to be blonde. A sly postscript to one of Olivia's e-mails. "PS Can't wait to see your new blonde look." Right. They wanted blonde, they'd get blonde. Platinum, if possible. Marilyn, just like the Judy in the column.

I went to the chemist, scanned the hair products. "Home Bleaching Kit." Eight pounds ninety-nine. I don't think so. I looked for a cheaper alternative. A wig? Extensions? Paint? Flour? No, implausible. I remembered an old beauty hint, one of Emma's. Hair can be lightened by the application of lemon juice and direct sun. I went home to attend to the matter. An old plastic bottle of ready-squeezed lemon juice, from concentrate. I held the green, translucent plastic up to the light. It appeared to have curdled, possibly some time ago, possibly through coming into contact with milk. I opened the bottle. A gelatinous white lump had formed in the bottom, around which flowed a revoltingly thin, evil-smelling acid: curds and whey. No, that wouldn't do. I replaced it and headed for the cupboards.

Cleaning products, all there when I arrived, left for me by a sweetly hopeful landlord. Not used, not as far as I can remember. Ajax, Windolene, Brillo Pads, dishcloths, Domestos. Why would I need these things? I'd never use them. I suddenly had a sense that I wasn't going to be living in this flat for much longer, that it had to be cleared for my departure. Where was I going? It didn't matter. The cleaning products had to go; if I am to fly I must jettison dead weight. Domestos, Brillo Pads, ugly things. I picked up each item, one by one, and slung them out of the kitchen window into the alley beneath. I found a rhythm, accelerated, ceased my slinging and began to hurl, angry, furious, seething with rage at the fuckers, all the fuckers. Bottles exploded, scouring pads bounced off into oblivion, dishwasher tablets dissolved on impact and dusted the pavement until I'd created the first frost: beautiful, peaceful, Dickensian. I calmed down as the contents of the cupboard dwindled and I was left, red-faced and panting, holding a large bottle of domestic bleach. Perfect. If that wasn't fate, then I don't know what is.

I went to the bathroom, put the plug in the sink, and upended the bottle. The smell spurred a flashback to the nursery. Which nursery? Surely not my own. Perhaps my own. Perhaps I'm seeing things I've never seen before, perhaps my whole life is easing into focus and it won't be long before I can see it all, a slideshow, and be able coldly to judge its worth, as I would a film or a play. I leant forwards and pushed my hair over my face, head upside down. When I was little my sister and I would upend our heads like this, then backcomb our hair, spray it, and pretend that we were troll dolls. The memory sparked the intention to smile, but in the end sadness won and I calmly lowered the tips of my hair into the waiting liquid. I really must call my sister. We hadn't spoken since the party. A shame, I think.

As I lowered my head my eyes began to water and sting; I caught a reflection in the clear fluid and briefly noticed the rims redden, before I closed them in pain, screwed up my face, dove deeper. The tips of my hair grew wet, I moved further in, the smell suffocating, violent, savagely antiseptic. Was this grooming? I had to groom. I had to do this, had to be blonde. I had to look nice. Like a Rhinemaiden. A Rhinemaiden! This was for Charlie: me, blonde, Wagnerian. The next day, I'd go to my singing lesson, sing Wagner with my blonde hair, and become a Valkyrie, the woman of his dreams. Soon my hair was submerged; bleach splashed my scalp with such chemical power that I threw my wet head back, a shampoo commercial, backlit, by a fountain. Toxicity slapped against my naked back, lashing, burning, and I screamed, stumbled backwards, until the pressure of the upcoming wall once again forced bleach into my skin with its porcelain chill, and I screamed again, forward this time, so that my foot hit some water and I fell, bashing my jaw against the lip of the shower tray, screaming and screaming like a woman on fire as the smell of bleach rocked my head and closed my throat. I reached up, each move generating a yelp, a shriek, a whimper, and turned on the shower. Water sprayed over the room, over me, cooling the pain and dispersing the fumes. I let it run, run over my body, over the bathroom floor.

Within twenty-four hours, approximately a third of my hair had fallen out. Not so much fallen out – that implies an involuntary yet peaceful self-extraction by the roots – as frizzled. Frizzled and crisped up, the tiniest touch turning it to dust. I played for a while, cracking off strands of my hair, watching them turn to a coarse powder as I rolled the dehydrated clumps between my fingers. Soon there was a little heap of dessicated hair sitting on the worktop. I shuffled the heap until it became a line, rolled up a stray Chinese takeaway flyer, and snorted it. There was a little kick, a spin, a headrush. Must have been the bleach.

The remainder of my hair was a grim, dead, orange.

Patchy, with variations of virility and tone, but mostly just orange. Across my forehead fell the one lock of hair as I knew it, soft and brown. Quite nice, actually, I realised. I took the kitchen scissors and tenderly, lovingly sliced off the sweet brown curl. I gave it a quick kiss, wrapped it in a tissue, took it into the bedroom, and pinned it to my photo of Charlie, right between his eyes, where he could see it. I wandered back through and had a look in the mirror. Orange, bald patches, moments of vivid, stinging redness where the bleach had seared my skin. A little light blistering, but nothing that a few days of R&R won't cure. Right now, I thought, I'm probably the only woman in London with this exact hairstyle. Perhaps the only woman in England, in Europe, in the world. I'm bucking a trend. Maybe even starting one.

Hence my decision to go to my singing lesson without a hat: this is me, now; I am what I am, and the world must learn to love it. That includes Gareth. This week, I went without a weapon. I am enough. I could take him, if necessary. I trudged up the dank staircase and knocked at his door. He opened it, and jumped backwards with a little cry.

"Oh, holy fuck."

He didn't like my new look, apparently. Well, fuck him. I'm restyling myself. He'd see, when I got up on stage, just how fabulous I could be with my new hair. I drew myself up to my full height, and looked him in the face.

"What?"

Nonchalant. Airy.

"What do you mean?"

"Your… your head. Fuck!"

He put his hands over his eyes and flinched away for a second, as if in pain.

"I bleached my hair."

"Please, please sit down. Here."

I didn't want to sit on his crappy sofa-bed. It looked dusty. I stood still.

"Please. Sit down. Water?"

I did want some water.

"Yes, please."

He fetched me a glass, then sat on the stool opposite, staring.

"Judy, are you OK?"

"I'm fine. I'm going to a party. I won."

"What did you win, Judy?"

"A prize. For being good. They think I'm blonde, so I am. Can we sing now? Can we rehearse? 'Everything's Coming Up Roses'?"

He looked at me with a weird intensity, almost an appraisal. He seemed to make a small decision, and spoke.

"Judy. Can I tell you a story?"

"Aren't we going to sing?"

He was firm. The campness faded, pushed aside by an unexpected authority and focus. His voice was low, coaxing, altered.

"When I was at music college –"

I exhaled sharply, and started to make a move. I didn't have time for this. He shifted forward and pressed a hand against my arm, firm. I sat back down.

"No, Judy, listen. When I was at music college, I had this friend. Jerome. One of the finest young baritones I'd ever heard, and one of the nicest men. We were close. I was his best friend. More, even, than that. He was astonishing. He was driven, intelligent, ambitious, committed to his music like nothing I'd ever heard. Then, halfway through our second year, he started to have some problems. No-one of us knew what kind of problems, not even me. All we knew was that he'd started missing classes, turned up late, mid-afternoon, sat in the corner. His voice disintegrated. He left the course, never said goodbye. We kept in touch for a bit, then he drifted. Or I did. As we moved into our final year, we came as near to forgetting him as humans can, we were so busy thinking about our careers, about our concerts, voices, agents. Then, one day, I stayed in late in college to practise. Really late, eleven o'clock, maybe. I was walking along the corridor, all little practice rooms off it like cells, and I heard something. I walked towards the noise, and..."

Gareth slowed, swallowed. I seized the opportunity. I couldn't take this parable, this bollocks, this irrelevance. I am a diva, and he is my minion. He's lucky to have me. I got up.

"If we're not going to sing, I'm leaving."

"Will I see you next week, Judy? For the show? "

"Yes, yes you will. Of course you will."

"Well, let me know if you'd like to rehearse any more before then. I know you know the song, but, do let me know if you'd like a last bash through it."

"I will. Though I'm busy at the moment. Lots of public appearances. I won an award."

He looked sad. Envious, probably.

"I know, Judy, you said. I'll see you next week, in Sydenham."

"Bye bye, Gareth, see you then."

• • •

I left, music tucked under my arm. Apparently, I need to

buy a hat. My new hair is too surprising, even for the diamond-jumpered Gareth. I went into the street. Hat, hat, hat. A trendy evening hat, for the party. That man's wearing a hat. A trilby. He'd never give it to me, though – people are selfish. I scanned the street – a baseball cap, a beanie, an old lady in a rain bonnet. I lowered my head, and saw it. My hat. A peaked denim number, with subtle ornamentation on the front. A pearly queen's hat, attached to the head of a tramp, sitting in a doorway. I went over and stood in front of him, looming. He didn't look up. A good sign.

"Hello."

"Spare any change?"

"Yes, actually."

I groped around my handbag. A pound, two, three, three pounds fifty. I placed three of the coins on his grubby, upturned palm, and let the fourth roll away, just a couple of feet. The tramp leant over to rescue the shiny silver fifty, turning his back on me. It was time. I darted forward, snatched the hat from his head, whacked it firmly on my own, and gave the tramp a sharp push so that he rolled alcoholically onto his side, flailing. I heard a few cries, a few oaths from the mouldering heap, and beat a sharp retreat, darting nimbly into the tube station, merry as hell. I glanced at myself in a pane of glass. I love my new hat.

For the party, I coupled it with my nice dress, my boots, and some artfully distressed tights. I tucked the remainder of my orange fuzz up under the denim, and tried a little make-up. Fine. That should satisfy them. I think I looked quite cool, actually, having made the best of my own possessions, and patronising what was effectively an open-air thrift shop on the Holloway Road. My hat still smells slightly of tramp, and everything else carries the vague scent of bleach, but it's nothing that won't be drowned out by the perfume of fifty overdressed women and a mountain of Thai-themed canapés.

I started drinking. I'd been drinking, on-and-off, since just after the great bleaching. Pain medication, then, now just a bare necessity. I'd had a couple before my aborted singing lesson – just an experiment. I needed to regain my love for my voice, for my music, and what better fuel for passionate love than a little bottle of maraschino, mixed into some chocolate mousse and microwaved until it became a nourishing soup? The smooth, nursery flavour of marasca cherries and cocoa, with the kick of a truculent donkey. I'd continued after the lesson; mixing, sampling, swallowing. Darting in and out of pubs, a quick shot here and there, cider, Aftershock, a slice of pizza to settle the stomach. Then home for a relaxed, civilised bottle of wine. It's a happy thing, when you lower your barriers and allow yourself to do whatever's necessary, whatever gets you through the day.

The only thing that could get me through the party, however, was kirsch. A colourless brandy made from the fermented juice of the small black cherry. God. God. Actually, who needs God, when there's kirsch? Ninety-per-ent proof. Ninety-per-cent proof that life is worth living. Game on. I tucked it into my handbag and got on the tube.

As I arrived, the What Women Think awards were just warming up. The room was about a third full, full of honed, exposed flesh, intermittently draped in black and chocolate brown, little sparkles here and there. And the chatter. So much chatter. A yammering birdcage. Each lift in pitch, each staccato rattle of feminine mirth lunged at me and bit – bit harder than the kirsch, or the bleach, or the hooker. I slipped in, moved along the wall to the unattended drinks table, grabbed two glasses of champagne, and tucked myself under the clean white cloth. There I crouched, panting and sipping, like a hired assassin preparing for the kill.

"Judy? Judy Bishop?"

My name. A high, posh voice. A voice so female that you could pickle it in Stella and still have enough high notes left to crack a window. I whacked on a smile, put the empty glasses on the floor, and stood.

"Olivia! Hi! Just sorting out a shoe problem, sorry if it looked suspicious."

"Ha ha! No problem."

She dived in for a kiss. I pretended not to notice and turned my head away, still conscious of the scent of tramp and bleach that lingered about me.

"Great hat, love. Where's it from?"

"It's vintage."

"Oh, my God, that's amazing! Good for you! I just never have time to trawl the boutiques, what with editing – amongst other things – your marvellous award-winning column!"

She said all this, it seemed, without moving her mouth. The words just seeped out from behind a fixed smile: a hysterical, well-meaning expulsion of air shaped into conversation by goodwill alone.

"Yes. It's all very exciting."

"Certainly is. Shall we get you a drink?"

"Lovely."

I clutched the glass, and circulated as best I could. I nodded as I absorbed the congratulations of people who shouldn't be strangers, people who expressed their regret at never having seen me before. I met the editor-in-chief of my paper, a small, dour man in his early sixties who nodded courteously and thanked me for my contribution to the paper. I nodded back, again, turned and nodded at someone else, placid, like a dog in the back of a car. I got used to the up-and-down motion of my chin, liked it, established a rhythm, found new people to nod at. Everyone admired my hat. Some said that they were sorry not to be seeing my new, widely publicised blonde hair.

"Well, in this life I'm afraid there's not always time for a proper blow-dry! Ha!"

I watched the mass of people in the centre of the room growing larger and stronger by the minute, like a tumour. Louder and louder and happier, women chatting back and forth like toddlers throwing foam at one another in the bath. Easy, uninhibited, recreational. Did I want to be one of these women? Did I want to fit in, shape up, become Judy B rather than Judy Bishop? You know, I thought I did. The realisation spawned another great wave of sorrow, coursing through me, illuminating my insides like a barium meal. I yearned to be one of these women. They couldn't all be wrong. They're what people are supposed to be, they're mainstream, media, lovely. They're not bad, or bland, or unwelcoming. There's a reason for their eminent acceptability. Could I join them? Or had I gone too far in the wrong direction? I don't know what my direction is, but I knew, surveying this scene, that it was wrong. I was wrong. I sipped my champagne.

The ceremony began. About three awards – polemicist, humanitarian, broadcaster. Then me. "Lifestyle Columnist of the Year – Judy Bishop!" I walked onto the podium, unable to avoid a kiss in this situation, and headed to the microphone. I took a moment, couldn't have been longer than a second, to scan the room. Hopeful faces, upturned, clapping. For once listening to me, to me, in the flesh. It was time. I held the microphone.

"Do you like my new hat?"

Cheery responses. A few cries of "yes!" Some laughter.

"Well, I stole it from a tramp. On the Holloway Road. I couldn't be arsed to go to a shop, so I approached a homeless person. I gave him three pounds fifty, pushed him over, and stole his hat. Nevertheless, I'm glad you all like it."

Laughter. Gusty, shrieky laughter. Whoa. I need to say more. They must listen.

"Furthermore, the reason that I'm wearing it is as follows. In an attempt to live up to a recent lie I told in my column, I dyed my hair. Bleached it, in fact. At home, in my sink, with a bottle of domestic bleach. It is now bright orange and tufty. My scalp is blistered. I hope you're all happy."

Gales of laughter. Hoots and shrieks, a smattering of applause.

"Alright then."

I took off my hat. A collective gasp, then silence. Stunned faces. I felt my head smart, and tears begin to come.

"You see?"

I left. I parted the crowds like Moses, and left.

Outside, I swigged unhappily from a bottle of kirsch. Things spun, I felt my stomach begin to lurch horribly. I needed to eat something. I walked towards the West End. I needed lights, energy, food, humans. I crossed Oxford Street and hung a right, back into Soho, back to the last place where I was truly hopeful, where I saw Charlie. I was crying, mostly from the pain on my head. I stopped, and looked around. Why wasn't anyone else crying? Why couldn't they see how awful it all is, how unbearably dead and remote everyone, everything, has turned out to be? I wanted to hit them, steal their hats, make all of them cry, too. Perhaps I'm just hungry. As a child, whenever I was low, or grumpy, or sad, it was always attributed to a sugar deficit, hunger anger. Food, that's the ticket.

Hence the Angus Steak House. Most of all, I needed to sit down. I walked in. I didn't Wait to be Seated, I wanted to find my own seat. The place was about half empty, as ever. I don't know who eats here. No-one does, really, but we all share a vague assumption that the clientele must be transatlantic or, at the very least, provincial. For a Londoner to come in here at the end of an evening is a joke, an excellent, self-deprecating joke to be mulled over for years to come, exaggerated in the retelling, the lowest point in an otherwise restrained and erudite life. Well, I'm here, and it's not a joke. I'm here because there's nowhere else that's as miserable and incongruous as me, and I want a steak. Put that on your poster, Angus Steak House.

I wandered in, hair blazing. Still, I think, unobserved, I moved between the empty tables, taking a little something from each. Slipping it in my handbag, or tucking it neatly down the front of my dress. Hoarding, like a squirrel. Pepper pots, ketchup, side plates, and steak knives. One steak knife from each table, into the handbag. I deserve some prizes, I realised I'd never taken my trophy from the What Women Think awards; I'd left it on the podium when I ran out. No problem, the Angus Steak House will provide.

A tap on my shoulder. Another horrible official, like the man who chucked me out of the fountain. Another uniform. "Angus Steak House" emblazoned across the front pocket. The meat police. Well, they won't catch me.

"Miss, I think you should leave."

Fuck him, fuck him. I'm happy, doing this. Wandering, looting, taking in the ambience. If I leave then I'll be outside again, in the cold with all the lights and the noise and the people who should be crying when they're not. Can't this man see that by some glorious fluke I've found somewhere comfortable, I've found something to get me through the next ten minutes, a little oasis of bearable activity? And he's trying to take it away from me. Well, as I say, fuck him.

I glanced down and to the side, twisted, stuck out my arm and plunged my knife into a nearby steak. Like a Samurai warrior, I extended my arm violently and jammed the hovering steak into the face of my aggressor.

"Meat! I've got meat!"

"Miss, please, calm down."

"No! I came for meat, and I got it, and I'm happy! You should be pleased, you little fucker! Meat!"

The restaurant hushed, everyone looked my way. This was my party, my moment, my turn. The waiter was frozen, his nose only a fraction away from my weapon. For all he knew I was going to jam the burning meat still harder into his face until the knife fully penetrated the hunk of cow, going on to tear through his own skin, piercing the place between his eyes as the surrounding hot protein burnt the skin around. I was the master, and it was time to show mercy. I withdrew the steak, turned, and ran, scrambling over banquettes with astonishing agility, darting round and grabbing steaks from every table, shoving them in my handbag before running, running, running, towards the tube station, heavy with meat and salt and pepper and ketchup and knives, just as one should be after a good meal out.

I went to Belsize Park. To Charlie. I didn't go to his

road, didn't try to see him. I just sat on a bench by the tube station, eating my steaks, sometimes singing a little. After a difficult night, it's good to be near the ones you love. I'll see him next week, of course, for the auction. I wonder how much I'll be worth. Ah, well, I'll find out soon enough. For now, there's steak, and kirsch, and a nice sturdy bench. That'll do.

The Days of Judy B

THIS WILL BE my penultimate column. Not my final column – no, that will be an infinitely more monumental and heartfelt affair – but my penultimate column. A warm-up to The Last Blast, if you will, a little appetiser, the cocking of the gun. The imminence of my columnar demise may shock you. In fact, it most definitely will shock you. The last thing you knew I was bouncing along, happy as a sandboy and revelling in my new haircut. Now I'm leaving you. I'm sorry.

It's not you, it's me. Actually, it's neither of us. It's my paper. They're remodelling, giving the décor of the supplement an overhaul. And, as we home-lovers know, that involves stripping down a fair deal of the old paint to make things nice for the shiny new coat. Who knows where or when I'll pop up again? Wait and see, and scour the newsstands for my beaming, bumptious face.

In the meantime, we have some loose ends to tie up. I know that we have two weeks in which to do this, but we may as well start now. We've been together for so long, shared so many shoes and haircuts and nights out that we're practically flatmates, and I feel I owe you a little honesty and closure. First of all, my hair. Some of you may have seen the pictures of me receiving my trophy at the What Women Think awards, and noticed that I wasn't looking quite as – ahem – glossy as I may have led you to believe. I know it looks suspicious. But there's a simple explanation. In preparation for the awards ceremony, I planned to top up my roots a little in an attempt to eliminate a slight hint of raddled porn-star that was creeping in, as my hair grew. I couldn't get an appointment with my Gay Best Friend; he's gone to South America for Mardi Gras. So I used a home bleach kit, and dozed off in front of *Ugly Betty* with the treatment still on. You can guess the rest. The GBF is furious, and I'm going to see him next week to get it sorted.

Secondly, and most crucially, the Two Men. The Big Dilemma. Well, they're both dangling. I have now visited both of their houses, I've only – shockingly – slept with one of them, it's going very well with both, and a decision is imminent. In fact, out of respect for You, I've resolved to sort it out this week. Next week, I shall report back. You will know my happy ending. As I say, I owe you that much.

Judy B's Purchase of the Week: Tissues, of course. I suggest you get some as well. We're going to be needing them.

JUDY BISHOP

12.

I got fired. Two days after the party, the editor called. Not Olivia, not the editor of the LifeStyle Review, but the editor-in-chief. The small, dour man at whom I nodded. He told me that, due to budgetary constraints, considerable restructuring and a general change of tone, my final column would be published on the 26th of November. He expressed regret at the situation, and wished me all the best for the future. Also, as a goodwill gesture, he's going to put a small plug for Anna's Auction of Promises in the "Other News" section of the paper, emphasising that the winning bidder will have the opportunity to witness Judy Bishop write her last ever column for the LifeStyle Review. I could hear his cheeks squeezing into a magnanimous smile as he said this; he told me that I would always be a part of the "LifeStyle Review family", and that he felt himself privileged to be able to help the charity in question. We said our farewells, and hung up.

I felt disappointed. Bitterly, savagely disappointed.

This reaction goes against the facts; I've finally been released from my column, I've achieved another of my three aims – effortlessly, I might add – and I'm going to be paid until my contract expires, a good three months from now. I should have been jubilant, liberated, dancing round the room with a bottle of Lambrini, treating myself to an hour of show-tunes and a huge iced bun.

As it was, I wanted to cut myself. I felt, as I hung up the phone, a near-overwhelming urge to go to the kitchen, pick out a knife, and draw it hard across my forearm, focus-ing all problems on that one red line. When a burden has been lifted from your shoulders and you feel no relief, when you're given a gift and see no way to hold it, life begins to flatline. Like someone allergic to sunlight, you're damaged by that which is nourishing and pleasurable, out of sync, angry with yourself, with the world, with anyone who dares question your misery and tell you how fortunate you are.

Like Anna. I am furious with Anna. She called me on Tuesday, to give me details of the auction on Saturday night. She asked how I was. I said that I'd just been sacked.

"Oh, Judy, of course, I read your column! What bad luck. But that was sort of what you wanted, wasn't it?"

"Mmph."

"I mean, it was. You said so."

No, Anna, what I really want is to take all my columns, crumple them into a big newsprinty ball, and smash it in your charity-fucking little face.

"Yeah, I suppose."

"Are you at least getting some kind of pay-off?"

"Three months."

"Well, that's wonderful. And it's great for the auction, the plug I mean. Your final column."

"Yeah, it's great."

"Well, then. Now, Saturday night –"

And she yammered on. Big excitement, couple of celebrities in the offing, nice podium for us all to stand on, lots of fun, canapés, smart-casual, after-party, delivery of cheques, contracts... all I could see was another clump of undulating flesh, me standing on the periphery, staring, like a veal-calf on a truck. I could see the bottom of an empty glass, some faces of concern, my mouth saying things my brain hasn't yet processed. I could see enemies raising their hands, bidding, paying, then bursting into my life for a week, hanging around like mildew asking me questions that I'll no longer have the facility to answer. And I could see myself at the end of the evening, once again drunk, once again humiliated, staring into the mirror at a puffy, red-eyed vision of toxicity, one-up from a bloated corpse. I jerked back to the present. Anna was being loud.

"So? Judy? Are you?"

"What?"

"Excited?"

"Yes, very."

"That's amazing, love. Also... now, this was going to be a surprise, but I thought I'd let you know – a few of us have booked tickets to see your show on Friday, as a sort of warm-up for the big event. So we're coming to hear you sing! Isn't that amazing?"

"Yes, amazing."

"OK, see you then. Bye-ee!"

"Bye."

I hung up, and lay down. On the floor; a little on the carpet, a little on the rug. Just lay. Stared. I'd forgotten about the show, almost. Or, if not forgotten, then forgotten to be excited. The bleach, the party, my dates and deadline, everything had pushed it out. I looked at my flat, at the mess, food from my big supermarket trip beginning to rot, the number 15 scrawled in odd little places – cigarette packets, walls, surfaces. Crowhurst had a number, as well – 243. That was his deadline. He'd planned to finish the trip in 243 days, recorded a false distance of 243 nautical miles in one day's sailing, and ended his life on the 243rd day. Now my fake log, my transmitted log, the newspaper column, has been taken away from me, all I have is the madness, the memories, Emma, the grief. And one last chance to show a positive, impressive public face; next weekend, the revue and auction. I had to make it, that would get me up to my fifteenth week, my deadline.

I lay on the floor, thoughts swirling. Memories growing only more vivid and consuming as time passed. I stayed still, felt nothing now but an occasional throbbing in my scalp, the remains of the bleach. I thought of my sister, how vital it was that I should call my sister. Or my mum, or dad. They're all still there. I can't speak to them. Can't speak to anyone. My phone rang, three feet away on the sofa. I didn't pick it up. It rang again and again, perhaps ten, fifteen times. I just lay. Occasionally lifted a hand and examined it, pondering the miracle of fingers, the evolutionary glory of opposable thumbs, small, manageable thoughts. Then down again, quiet, staring.

It's odd, I thought, how loss recedes in the minds of everyone except yourself. Initially, there are people. So many people that you don't know what to do. Vats of coronation chicken. Dangerous amounts of tea. Five hundred people to occupy the space of one, all there in a spirit of love, sharing in a pain which you yourself can't yet feel. You get a bit cross with them, want them to go away. Soon enough, your wish comes true. They dissipate. The subject which, for those glorious few weeks, was all they could talk about, becomes a bit embarrassing. People fear your tears as much as they once encouraged them. They assume, hope, demand that, almost a year on, you will be well. So you start to hate them for expecting the impossible. Soon enough, that's all there is: envy, resentment, hate, the cold, hard fact that others are living well when you cannot. The weak will fall victim to themselves, I realised, and some things do change you for the worse, for ever.

I wondered how many millions of people were carrying something around with them, how many were living in a place of loss, of trauma, of confusion. And how well they hid it. This prompted me to go to the window, look out at the weekday afternoon people. They all look fine. At least I don't look fine any more, all orange and tufty. I crossed the room and picked up my phone. Twelve missed calls, all from Mr Simmons. A text message, again from Mr Simmons. I deleted it without reading it. Then another, from Gareth, telling me to arrive at the theatre at 3pm on Friday. That one I will obey.

I sang through the song a couple of times during the week. That was all I did, really: sat, hummed, sang. Thought about what to do with my hair, or lack thereof. I texted Gareth about it. No problem, apparently, he'd arranged me a wig. Not a costume wig – it was a concert production, we were all wearing our own clothes – but a "high street" wig. The mind boggles. It was kind of Gareth, to still let me be a part of this, I thought, after the shocks I'd been giving him recently. The knife, the bleached head, the nosebleeds. Maybe he really does have faith in my ability as a performer.

That's the only possible explanation; he really thinks I'm good. Perhaps I am.

I held onto that thought, as I travelled down to Sydenham on Friday afternoon. It was difficult, two tubes and an overground train. Hard, suddenly, to get my head around. I got lost a few times, went the wrong way up the Victoria Line, north instead of south, ended up in a suburb. Then back down again, missed a few trains, sat on the platform in Sydenham, went to a pub, called Gareth up. He sounded stressed. And rightly so. I was missing, his star, "Everything's Coming Up Roses". I arrived at seven, four hours late, half an hour before curtain up. I thought, numbly, that I might be told off – no chance. If you're late enough for something, then panic will overtake fury. And so it was at the Sydenham Bull. I arrived at the pub, was directed to the theatre upstairs, and grabbed by Gareth as soon as I arrived. The tiny dressing room was full: about ten people. Gareth, in black tie, looking rather sweet, if a little peaky. A few fellow Musical Theatre performers, milling around, humming. Tiny, dancey little women, light-stepping men. One chubbier man, my male equivalent, clearly about to sing a comedy number of some kind. Gareth manhandled me towards an older gentleman in a brown suit.

"Judy – Roger. Roger's the accompanist. Judy's Mama Rose. One song. Judy, you're on fourth, after Barry –" He indicated the chubby man. "No time to rehearse. Now, Judy, doff your hat and don this, asap. Curtain in five. Break a leg."

He handed me a curly brown wig, a Merman wig, and bustled off. I took a seat backstage, and breathed. OK. Fine, this was fine. I know this song, I know this part. I squeezed a dollop of adhesive onto my head, rubbed it in like moisturiser or sun cream, and laid the wig over the top. I felt the glue begin to harden, tighten on my scalp. It was painful – I didn't mind. I've done worse to my dear old head in this past few weeks than a bit of glue could do.

Through the door, I heard the piano play a few opening chords, heard a smattering of applause. A dozen or so people, not too scary. Gareth began to speak, clearly reading his script, giving a warm, full-throated welcome to the assembled few, telling them his reasons for wishing to mount this "little chocolate-box of my favourite pieces, performed by my very favourite singers". He is brave, Gareth, no doubt about that. This is a terrible show, in a terrible venue, performed by quasi-amateur stragglers and, in all probability, paid for on credit. But it got a listing in *Time Out*, and the thought of it made me happy, for a time. I hope that it's making Gareth happy, now. It probably isn't. Ah well, that's life.

A small blonde woman had passed through the door – again, the smattering of applause – and was singing a Rogers and Hammerstein song in a glassy soprano. She finished, someone sang something from *Company*, then it was me. I stood, breathed, focused, and stepped out. My applause was louder than anyone else's, someone gave a little whoop. I wondered why. Then I remembered. Anna. Auction people. Fuck. I looked up. The auditorium – twenty four chairs in a little room above a pub – was fully visible; only when I looked directly into the spotlight was the audience in any way obscured. I peered out, wondered who Anna had managed to rustle up for the night.

There she was, sitting neatly in the middle. On either side of her sat the two women, the two square, besuited, dumpy middle-aged heating women from the party, looking

a bit confused. Ugh. And then, next to one of the women –
fuck. Charlie. How? How did Anna persuade him to come,
to come to Sydenham, to a tenth-rate musical revue, just
because I was singing? Perhaps it's because he loves me. Or
at least fancies me. The wig shifted, my scalp burnt harder,
a sharp reminder that this could not possibly be the case.

I can't sing, can't sing any more in front of him. It's all
gone. The words, the tune, the spirit of Mama Rose. Too
late. He's watching politely, the opening chord has been,
played, I have to belt. I paused. No, nothing. Roger the
pianist looked up at me, paused. Played the note again, a
touch more emphatically, as if I hadn't heard. Again, nothing. The same from Roger, again.

This was the moment, surely, when it should all come
together. I was aware of that, as I stood there. Had I been
watching myself in a film, I would see the two false starts,
fear that all was lost, but know deep down that, any
moment, my heroine was going to have something of an
epiphany, the clouds would lift, and she would sing, loud
and strong and true. She'd bring the house down; in fact, all
the strands of her life would be melded together by the
white heat of her bravura performance.

I smiled, momentarily, at the idea that this was supposed to be happening now. It was implausible, miles away.
The smile helped me, and I began to sing. A moment of
eye contact with Gareth, who smiled; nervous, encouraging.
Then into the song, a song I knew well. I got through
it. It was weakish, unexpressive. I felt, as I sang, disappointment. Mild, drizzly disappointment. Nothing special.
Nothing unique. Mama Rose had left the building. I finished, still competent. A smattering of applause. Then off
the stage, everybody underwhelmed.

I left. No hellos for Anna, certainly nothing for Charlie. Just left. Slunk away into Sydenham, south London. I'd speak to Gareth later. I walked, again, past bins and tramps and the gloomy, threatening detritus of an outer London evening. Saddish, coldish, numbish. Nothing, nothing, nothing, nothing, nothing.

Then, something. A quick punch in my back, and my collar tightened as someone grabbed the back of my jacket. I turned my head. A man, Caucasian, young, tall, carrying a knife. Everything in me snapped open, all the positive faculties that had been shutting down, one by one, over the past weeks sprang into life, and I was alive. I looked into the man's face. Glanced down at the knife, felt the emptiness of the streets around, and knew the ease with which he could hurt me.

And so I sang. I pinned my feet to the floor, moved my face to his, and felt Mama Rose spring into action, inhabit my body and my voice. "Everything's Coming Up Roses". Loud, loud, loud – triumphant, majestic, admirable, in the face of adversity, I sang. I gave the number everything that it could ever want, I know – I know – that in those moments, as I sang, I was taking my place among the greats. I spun round, releasing myself, and grabbed his collar, forcing myself into his face, still belting. As the song reached its climax, I pushed him back onto the pavement, went down with him, until I was on all fours atop him, hurling the greatest showtune ever written into the anonymous face of a felon.

I finished, and the mugger ran. Took nothing from me – except, obviously, the most glorious fucking performance you've ever seen in your life – and ran. I turned and walked calmly off into the night, safe as houses. I didn't care now.

In the nicest possible way, I no longer cared whether I lived or died. That was my swansong, and it was all I'd ever hoped for. I floated home, as if from Sardi's, back to the flat.

I slept until 4pm, and woke just in time to get ready for the auction. Back into the dress, the boots, the make-up. I found a beanie hat, soft black wool, to cover my head. Not really evening-wear, but near enough. The party clothes felt like chainmail, the application of make-up was as effective as painting a face on a potato, my handbag was full of faintly rotting meat and my head – now with a few lumps of wig-glue adhering to the carroty tufts – was already beginning to react with the wool of my hat. It was time to commit some Acts of Charity.

I trudged along Piccadilly, ducked into the relevant ornate and opulent sidestreet, and came to a halt outside the Union of Words. I realised, with a jolt, that I was sober. Why? I'm several notches below suicidal, I'm carrying a sack of old steak, and I'm about to be auctioned off for a small sum to stop old people using up excess fuel. How am I still sober?

I dived into a pub, and ordered two pints of Guinness and a Sambuca. Nutritionally punchy and substantial, with an exotic twist. The alcoholic equivalent of Pad Thai, or a chicken tikka wrap. Perfect. As my drinks hit the bar, a short, chubby arm extended over my shoulder, proffering a ten-pound note.

"That's on me."

I looked round. It was Mr Simmons. I turned back to the barman, thinking that I might as well make the most of the tenner.

"And a packet of crisps, and some peanuts."

Mr Simmons spoke.

"Right. Yes. I'll get those too."

"Thanks."

"So, what brings you to this drinking-den, Miss Judy Bishop? Shouldn't you be being groomed for auction?"

He laughed, a horrible little gurgle. He looked incredibly happy; better, I suppose since having had sex with someone other than Barbara. Ah well, I'm glad that one of us benefited from the encounter.

"Don't have to be there for half an hour. What are you doing in this neck of the woods?"

"Coming to bid for you, of course! Always liked the idea of owning you for a week."

The horrible little gurgle. Oh, God, he's going to buy me. He's going to spend all his meagre mashed potato money on having me installed as his whore, and he's going to sit in the corner of my flat talking bollocks about steam rallies, and the First World War, and the history of the E2 postcode. Oh God, I really am fucked.

"That's... nice."

"Are you expecting someone?"

He nodded at the Guinness.

"No no, all for me. I just haven't... eaten today."

"Well, better get cracking on the peanuts, then. Pint of Stella, please."

I found a table, sitting with my back to the room. Mr Simmons bumbled over with the crisps and peanuts, ramming himself between the table and the wall like a squat pig. Merrily, industriously, he opened the two salty little packets, tipped the crisps into the empty ashtray, added the peanuts, and mixed the two together with his ungainly little sausage-fingers, massaging one salty snack into the other until the crisps cracked and the mixture took on the aspect of an evil pot pourri.

"Why the fuck did you do that?"

Now he's arsed up the crisps and the peanuts. He really is a contemptible little man.

"Ooh, bit testy, are we? Nervous about being auctioned off? No, I've always done this. For the last couple of years, anyway. I call it "Wedding Mix". It's what Barbara and I had on our big day. Try some."

I did. It was shit. I was just about to tell him so when I heard an unearthly crash, and an oath, such as could only herald the arrival of Joel. He rocked between the tables, a glorious, narcotic column, and sat down hard on a chair, backwards, like a warped Christine Keeler in a trenchcoat. An unlit fag dangled from his mouth.

"Lighter, lighter... Hello, Judy, have you recovered from your knock-out orgasm? Has anybody got a fucking lighter?"

He weaved his head from side to side, up and down, searching, like a twitchy racehorse in a stall. Adrian offered a match.

"Cheers, Adey. Now then. Auction time, yes. Judy, I shall be bidding. Oh, yes."

"Not as high as me, Joel."

"Don't bet on it, Mister."

Joel stopped, and stared suddenly at Adrian's gut.

"Have you put on weight?"

"No."

"Have you always been that fat? Christ, you're going to die. Isn't he going to die, Judy, the little fat fucker, stealing all the mashed potatoes?"

Joel leant over the table and prodded Adrian's midriff, stopping on the way back to steal one of my pints. He downed half in a gulp. I didn't mind. I was starting to like Joel. Adrian looked awkward.

"I have to go to the little boys' room."

He got up, miraculously squeezed himself free, and tottered off. Joel was lighting his second cigarette from his first, twitching a little, mumbling, an amiable presence. He spoke to me, his attentions still focused on the delicate exchange of embers.

"He has put on weight. You know he's getting back together with his wife? Probably."

I didn't know this.

"No."

"Well, he is. She's spent the last fortnight in the flat above the mashed potatoes. Horrendous woman, looks like a glockenspiel. Eats a lot of mackerel. In a back-brace. She fell off a massage table in the Azores, Adey sprung to the rescue, and Love Has Bloomed once more. Curtains for the business, I think."

"Really?"

"Yes. Christ, yes. I'm not going to spend the rest of my life wallowing in glutinous shit which no-one eats. Fucking stupid idea. Do you have a lighter?"

"Sure."

I gave it to him. Mr Simmons was remarrying. I felt strange; I should have been happy, and I wasn't. I was, to my credit, happy for him. The thought of him plodding though life in that Elephant and Castle studio, serving mashed potato to no-one, with no company except a slightly bilious entrepreneur of mysterious provenance, was too much to bear. It's good that he has someone, anyone, to team up with. But I should have been happy for myself, too; I didn't really like him and his attentions were unwelcome. I would now be relieved of the burden of his affection. But, as with the loss of the column, I couldn't bear the removal of that unsolicited appreciation. Even appreciation from those who I look down upon, appreciation which seemed to make my life harder rather than more pleasant.

I realise, now it's going, how very welcome it was. And now tonight looks even grimmer, knowing that Mr Simmons will be bidding out of sympathy, or support, and that anyone else will be seeking the car-crash fascination of witnessing a columnist on the way out. Well, they'll be satisfied, at least. I drained my pint, knocked back the Sambuca, and made to leave.

"Better be going, Joel, bit late as it is. Give Adrian my congratulations."

"Will do, see you in there. Is it just me, or can you smell meat?"

I grabbed my handbag sharply, and scurried out.

And so to the auction. Charlie. Breathe, and think of Charlie. He's all I have left. He's there, still waiting, still the same, still fond of me. And I've worked to fulfil that promise I made to him, of my bisexuality. He needn't know what I've been doing, but it's still good that I've done it.

He was there when I arrived; there was a podium, about two hundred chairs, auctioneer and auctionees aimlessly milling about. Suits, dresses, drinks, smart-casual. There was some bunting across the top of the stage, the only appropriate response to which was a sad smile. I adjusted my hat, and went up to Charlie. My last chance.

"Hi!"

"Judy, hello! Lovely song last night. Sweet little show, I thought."

I secured my kiss, thanked him, then stepped back.

Suddenly I didn't know what to say.

"How – how are you?"

"I'm really well. Really well. Actually –"

He extended an arm, and touched the shoulder of a small redhead, deep in conversation with Anna. A quick "darling", and he turned the redhead to face me.

"This is Juliet. She's a big fan of yours."

Juliet extended a pretty little hand. Who the fuck was she? Girlfriend? Fiancee? I lost my peripheral vision, and sensed my feet going numb.

"Hi, Judy, I really enjoy your column. Lovely to meet you in the flesh."

I spoke, as if from the bottom of a lake.

"You're welcome. Thank you. Excuse me."

I turned slowly, stiffly, a trawler being navigated by a tug, towards the drinks table. About a hundred glasses of fizzy white wine, all in pretty little rows. I suddenly wanted to launch myself onto the table, spreadeagled, facedown, shattering the glass and spilling the nectar, lacerating my body with shards of cheap champagne flute. Instead, I took a drink. And another. And another. Neatly picking up the glasses, draining them, putting them back in their place. About three seconds for each glass. I'd got through about five, six, seven, when Anna came over.

"Judy."

I didn't look up. Carried on downing the beautiful fizzy things. Mmm, lovely. Anna, louder.

"Judy!"

"Fuck off, Anna."

"Judy!"

She grabbed my shoulder, a little more roughly than a lady should. I turned round and gave her a look of raw fury which I hadn't employed since I was seven, when Mum wouldn't let me take an icecream into the sandpit.

"What?"

"I'd like you to meet our auctioneer. Christopher. He's from Sotheby's."

I turned back to the drinks table. I didn't want to meet an auctioneer.

"Hello, Christopher."

Anna leant over and hissed in my ear.

"Judy, you look at someone when you're talking to them. What the fuck is wrong with you?"

"Ooh, swearing. That's not very ladylike. What will the old people think of that, eh, Anna?"

I took another drink.

"Judy, this is one of the biggest nights of my career. Why are you trying so hard to fuck it up? Stop drinking!"

"No, I won't. And you don't have a career. It's pretend."

Ooh, she was very cross now. This was fun. Clearly about to launch into a little-girl temper-tantrum, she breathed, calmed, clicked back into affected adulthood.

"I was just about to say that I thought you sang very well last night. Now I'm not going to. So. I will speak to you later."

She moved to leave.

"No, you won't. I'll be dead later."

"You will be if you keep drinking like that."

"That's the plan."

I took another. That was really going to mess with her head. For all she knows, I've got a gun in my bag. I might do it up on the podium, fire it into my head just as the idle rich start bidding for a three-hour consultation with a celebrity florist. That'd really shift the tone of the evening, wouldn't it? Still, I'm sure that Anna would find a way to keep it light.

I started to feel a bit sick, and stepped away from the table. I wanted to sit down.

"Anna, which is my chair?"

She wordlessly indicated one on the podium, near the centre of the row. I flashed her a huge grin, and sat. I felt a certain lightness. I really was fucked, and that sudden knowledge was liberating. The floor had been pulled from under me, tile by tile, over the last eleven weeks. Often I hadn't noticed it, so slight were the disasters, so potent was my energy. I'd just shifted my weight accordingly, found a way to stand on the new terrain, positive, determined. Now, suddenly, everything solid had gone, and I was sinking. Mr Simmons, Charlie, Gareth, singing, sex, the column, my hair. All gone. I sat again, just sat. The seats on either side of me filled up, an audience trickled in, the hum of conversation became a roar, agonising, infuriating, but nothing to do with me.

Christopher the auctioneer approached me. What a polite man. Something of a bedside manner, I thought.

"Judy, I was wondering. Would you mind taking off your hat?"

"Sure."

I took off my hat. Christopher rocked backwards, stumbled a bit, a faint vibe of nausea.

"Oh, my God….you can leave it on if you want. I'm so sorry, I didn't realise."

"No, it's fine."

I put the hat under my seat. Charlie looked over, jumped a little, then approached.

"Judy… your head? What happened?"

This felt like my last chance. My last crack at levity, wit, charm. I made a smile, feeling as if my face might split in two.

"Oh, this… ha ha. Bit of a bleaching accident. I was aiming for blonde, you know, *Wagnerian*, and left it on a bit too long. My mistake. Should heal in a week or so. I may have to live with a boyish crop for a bit, though. Ha!"

"Christ, well, I'm sorry. I hope… I hope it… gets better soon."

Pass or fail? How did I do? It was fine. I didn't cry, I wasn't rude, I may even have given the impression of being a bit charming. That was… OK. Neither triumph nor despair. Fine. Keep breathing. Drunk, really drunk now. It's all kicking in at once. Is my chair still? Moving a bit, I think, like the sea. Someone would tell me if it was moving. Christopher would tell me. I like Christopher, he's a nice man. Oh, I do want another drink.

I watched Charlie showing little ginger Juliet to her seat, giving her a kiss on the cheek. Leaving his hand on her shoulder for a bit too long, smiling, walking up onto the podium. He really likes her. Of course he does. She's small, light-voiced, polite, sweet. Her hair is the good kind of orange. I closed my eyes, trying to stop the spinning. I had to leave, but couldn't. I was pinned to the seat by the weight of alcohol, sudden immobility, and my obligation to Anna. The auction started. Shouts and cheers, people steeping forward, the crash of the hammer. Christopher speaking, burbling fast, too fast, confusing. I closed my eyes again, more spinning, violent and noisy and real. Thoughts spun, too, faster, angrier.

And then the one thought that I've suppressed for the last year, the one that's required superhuman mental energy to shut out. It came back in, without warning, storming and looting and pillaging the last of my happiness. The crash. Emma. Spinning and screaming, blood and glass. I was there. I was driving. We were in Suffolk, she was coming to meet my parents. The radio, Radio 1, music which she liked and which I never understood. I asked her to put on a CD, change the music. I'll always remember her response.

"No. I like this."

Just that, a cold little "no". No discussion, no consideration. As she said that, fury boiled, a fury which I'd never felt before. "No. I like this." I thought of how many other things she did simply because she liked them. No thought of others. I thought of her mocking, smug little face as she played to the audience after kissing me, I thought of her cold hand inside me, stroking and scratching and ripping, and I thought how much I loved her, and how stupid she made me look, and how she always had to have sex with someone else to get over having had sex with me. I thought of all that she'd taken away from me; other relationships, other crushes, other thoughts. I thought how all my hope, all my joy, was invested in her, and I thought how little she cared.

I thought of her wit, her charm, her body, her voice, and how I could never measure up to her, never be as full and alive and beautiful as she was. I thought of our future, and realised that it didn't exist. I thought all of this, and I wanted her to die.

Then a scream, spinning, light, and darkness. I woke to a windscreen devoid of glass, and a cool, pale, body, marbled with red. Apparently, it was a truck. Rounding the blind corner at speed, careering into us, sending the little car over and over into a ditch, upside down, then the right way up again, the damage done. It was no-one's fault. Unavoidable, people told me, said more about rural roads than it did about either of the drivers.

But I knew better. I knew that the moment of Emma's death had coincided with my intention to wipe her out, that from somewhere in the cosmos, a wish had been granted. I killed her.

Another crash of the hammer jolted me back into the room. I sat up as best I could. I was being announced. My turn.

"… LifeStyle Review section… star columnist… bear witness to the creation of the final column… insight… discussion. Journalistic *enfant terrible* in recovery from a severe peroxide-related incident – Judy Bishop!"

They applauded. I think I may have burped, I don't remember.

Christopher started the bidding at two hundred pounds. Mr Simmons stuck his hand up. Two fifty. It went up and up Mr. Simmons, two strangers, a couple of bids from sweet little Juliet with her red hair. Around the five hundred pound mark, now. The field was thinning, Mr Simmons was the frontrunner. Just as I was resigning myself to his company, another voice chimed in. Joel? I refocused my eyes and looked out at the audience. It was Joel. He was standing up.

"Four hundred thousand pounds."

"Excuse me? Sir?"

"I'd like to bid four hundred thousand pounds for Judy Bishop."

"Sir?"

"You heard. I'm an entrepreneur."

Joel looked completely off his face. I was alarmed, but

bizarrely flattered. Christopher regained his professionalism.

"Well, it seems we have a surprise bidder. Would anyone like to go higher than four hundred thousand pounds for the privilege of a day with Judy Bishop?"

Unsurprisingly, no offers. The room froze. No-one breathed for fear of their movement being construed as a bid.

"Going, Going – Gone! To the gentleman in the trenchcoat, for four hundred thousand pounds. Congratulations, sir. Now, to our final lot of the evening –"

It was Charlie. He went to a middle-aged lady for three hundred and twenty-five pounds. No-one really cared, attention was still focused on Joel's astonishing bid. A hoax? A cruel joke? Or perhaps he really thought I was worth it.

As ever, I was too tired to care. Charlie came over, congratulated me briefly, then went back to his ginger bit of stuff. She expressed regret at not having won me. I thanked her nicely. I said goodnight to a completely banjaxed Christopher, and accosted Joel, writing a cheque, unlit cigarette hanging from his jaws.

"Joel?"

"Judy, hello, hello, just sorting out the payment. Good stuff all round, I say. Your friend Anna's a bit of a tit, isn't she? Seemed suspicious. Still, some people will never trust, the poor fuckers."

He handed over the cheque.

"Ta-ra, see you next week."

"Bye, Joel."

I left, not particularly fancying a chat with Mr Simmons. I wouldn't be able to stop myself bringing up the subject of Barbara. I made for the door. I heard heels behind me, trotting and clicking, a sharp little voice.

"Judy!"

I stopped, sighed, turned round.

"Hi, Anna."

"Do you know that man?"

"Which man, Anna?"

"You know perfectly well which man. The one who bought you for an implausible sum. Is this your sick little idea of a joke?"

"It's got nothing to do with me."

"Yeah. Right. Well, if his cheque bounces, you're going to be making up the difference."

I've never seen a face so nasty, so twisted with bile and malice and humiliation.

"I don't think I am, Anna."

She sniffed.

"How much have you had to drink tonight, Judy?"

"A lot."

"Well, I hope you get home safely, because I will not be at the end of a phone if you run into trouble."

"What a shame."

"You reek of alcohol. It's disgusting."

I'd had enough.

"No, Anna, you know what's disgusting?"

"What?"

"Meat. Week-old, half-chewed meat."

"Eh?"

I reached into my handbag, gathered up the remnants of the steak, and heaved them at her sneering little face, hard, at point-blank range. Ha. She responded vocally, I'm sure. I didn't wait to hear it. I turned and strode out into the night, four hundred thousand pounds' worth of woman. The most expensive contract-killer in the kingdom, the meat-slinging doyenne of the Union of Words, home-hair-bleacher extraordinaire, vocally assured mugger-repellent, star of the musical theatre, and winner of the 2006 Lifestyle Columnist of the Year award, as decided by the What Women Think panel. I am all of these things. For how much longer, I don't know. But all that, I think, will be enough to see me through the night. And that's not to be sniffed at.

The Days of Judy B

Judy Bishop is away.

13.

The presence of Joel, I think, somewhat diminished the gravity of my suicide attempt. Although not in attendance at the actual moment of annihilation, he managed to insert himself pretty firmly into this momentous week. He turned up at five o'clock on Tuesday morning. I'd woken early, as has been my habit for the last week or so, and was lying in the dark, staring. The misty silence was suddenly interrupted by the unique sound of a wheelie-bin capsizing, an unmistakable boomed profanity ("minge", I think), and a furious, prolonged percussive interlude on the front door, as if the cast of *Stomp* had gone on an all-night bender through east London.

I lay there as the banging continued, waiting for him to find the buzzer. I was told by the landlord when I moved in: "unless you're expecting a guest, always use the entryphone". So I lay there, obediently, waiting for the buzz.

Soon enough, it came.

"Hello?"

"Hi, Judy. Joel."

I let him up. He steamed in, lurching, twitching, fag in mouth.

"Judy, yes, hi. Touch early, I know. Sorry about that. Got a glass of water?"

I fetched him one. He gulped it down, Adam's apple bobbing up and down like a frog in a tank, gasping. He handed me back the glass. I refilled it. He downed it, handed it back. We repeated this little dumb-show about four times, then Joel collapsed on the sofa.

"Lovely."

He looked as if he'd been pulled out of a river. Dark, greasy hair falling over a face of wet chalk, the eyes of an albino rabbit.

"Everything alright, Joel?"

"Yes. Hunkydory. Had a bit of a night of it, actually. Good fun."

Joel really is an excellent human being. I rather wished he was my flatmate. He stared madly into the middle distance, transfixed, as if looking at the northern lights, or a blazing array of jugglers. Still staring, he spoke.

"Judy?"

"Mm?"

"That four hundred grand."

"Yes."

"Fucking cheeky, I know, but I was wondering if I could have it back."

"What?"

"Obviously keep a tenner or so for yourself, for your trouble and all that, but I was rather hoping to repocket the remainder, as it were. Alright if I smoke?"

"Yes, fine. But, Joel —"

God, how could I tell him? The poor man. Is there any way that I could scrape together four hundred grand to give him? Sell the flat? I don't own the flat. Oh dear.

"But, Joel, I don't have that money. It went to the charity."

"What charity?"

"The charity that the auction was in aid of. Funded eco-friendly heating for the elderly."

"Oh, I wondered why that Anna girl kept banging on about some shrivelled harpy called Ada. So she's got all my money?"

"Not just her. Lots of old people."

He seemed quite calm. Bullish, even.

"Christ. So what are you getting out of this?"

"Well, nothing. I'm doing it for free."

"Awfully nice of you."

"Thanks."

We were both silent for a moment, brooding on the situation from our different perspectives.

"Joel, is everything going to be alright?"

"Well, fuck it all, really. See, I needed somewhere to put that money for a little while, thought perhaps I could snaffle it back within the week. You seem like a nice girl, happy to help. Didn't really think it through, perhaps."

"No."

Another pause.

"Alright if I stay here for a bit, Judy?"

"Yes, of course. You can have the bed, actually. I'm just getting up."

"Oh, cheers."

I led him into the bedroom. He climbed into bed, coat still on, and pulled the covers round himself. He suddenly sat up, looking at the wall opposite.

"What happened to that?"

He was pointing at my Ethel Merman poster. The screwdriver mouth-cave was still very much in evidence, a light ring of spit glazing the edge. I felt self-conscious; I could have sworn that the imprint of my naked, sweating body was visible, smudging the gloss of the poster.

"That. I – I – had to do a home repair. On the wall. Trying to put a picture up. Needed to dig a bit of a hole."

"Oh, right."

He curled up on his side, drawing the covers over his head, and mumbled.

"Well, Merman's fucking ugly, anyway. Always preferred Mary Martin, myself. Night night."

"Night, Joel."

I crept out, picking up the crumpled, broken cardboard larynx from the floor. I must fix it, I thought. I didn't want it to be alone with Joel; it's too precious, somehow.

I pulled on some tracksuit bottoms and a hoodie, and went for a walk. Halfway out of the door, I stopped, and turned. I picked up the crumpled larynx from the worktop, and took it with me. Like a gypsy woman and her lucky rabbit's foot, or a child and her teddy, I needed it.

I walked, probably further than I've ever walked before. Through Bethnal Green, along Brick Lane, through Shoreditch, Spitalfields, Bishopsgate; vibrant, mercantile east London. Cold, dark, not yet awake. The odd office light was on, the odd early-morning banker trudged through the slush to work. Past Liverpool Street station, which made me feel a bit sad. Liverpool Street was always the conduit to Suffolk, to home, to my family. I need to phone home. I need to sort things out with Clare. Maybe this week I'll do that.

I walked south, and west, to the river. I sat on a bench, suddenly freezing. I wasn't wearing a coat, I hadn't noticed. I strolled over to a bin, grabbed a couple of pieces of old cardboard, unfolded them and arranged them round myself on the bench. A happy little igloo, shielding me from the worst of the November wind. I stared out at the choppy water, at the South Bank beyond. Dawn was beginning to spread. I examined the battered little larynx in my hand. It was beyond repair, no better than the refuse cardboard wedged around me for warmth.

It was a year, a year tomorrow, since the crash. I looked at the back of my hand, at a thin pink scar, the only physical reminder of that day. I'd been concussed, of course, a bit of whiplash. But I'd walked away. Just like they say on the news, walked away from the scene. Quite a long way away, actually. I'd taken one look at Emma, red and white, unbuckled my seatbelt, and walked. No desire to shake her, scream at her, sob over her dying body. Just the need to walk, fast, across a field, away from what I'd done. The paramedics had to chase me, guide me back to the ambulance, wrap me in a blanket and tell me that Emma had been declared dead. They didn't need to tell me; I already knew. Even if I'd been five hundred miles away, I would have known, instantly. You can sense an absence, sense when someone you love is leaving, feel the dreadful, sucking vacuum in your stomach the second they've gone.

I wonder, now, if people know that I am leaving. I am. I have been for a while. Nearly a year. But I've been denying it. In September, I decided that enough was enough. It was time to move forward, put the past behind me. I've only succeeded in moving down, inexorably down, into a primeval sludge of food and wine and shagging and hookers and baldness and pain and humiliation. I've taken all the steps that should be taken when stepping into adult life for the first time; I've been out, I've met men and women, I've had sex, I've worked on my skills, I've helped a charity. And all the while, I've chronicled the life of a young urban professional to an award-winning standard. I've done all I should, and I remain in poor condition. I've taken stock, and the cupboard is bare. No love, no friends, no joy, just a suppurating welt of life experience, which can surely only grow deeper and more painful as I continue to live.

But there's always singing. That's what I've said to myself, that's been my mantra for as long as I can remember. There's always singing. But is there, really? I auditioned to train at college, nearly a year ago. Two weeks after the crash – my face was bruised and my jaw stiff, my mind still tossing up images of blood and glass and cold, distorted flesh. I was doing it in Emma's honour, hoping that she'd look after me, help me to do my best. She didn't. Of course she didn't. I'm no singer, and I never will be. Once I sang, alone with a mugger, and once I was mediocre on a pub stage in Sydenham. I should be thankful for that, and leave it there. I stood up, walked to the water's edge, took one last look at the poor, sad, cardboard larynx, kissed it, and heaved it into the river. The grey foam pulled it away, sucked it under. I turned my back, and commenced the trudge back to Bethnal Green.

I arrived, about mid-morning I suppose, to find Joel

cooking bacon. An awful lot of bacon, actually. Must have been about twenty rashers, arranged three-deep in my diminutive frying pan. The air was rich with bacon, steam, and what smelt like marijuana. He greeted me warmly, if distractedly.

"Judy! Bacon?"

"Erm... sure."

"Great. Here we go."

He pulled three rashers from the pan with his bare hand, folded them, stuffed them on the end of a fork, and handed it to me. Quite a nice idea, actually, like a hot savoury toffee-apple.

"Thanks."

I munched. It was good. Joel decanted the remainder of the bacon onto a side plate, and set to it with vigour.

"Now, Judy. Nice walk?"

"Great."

"Good stuff. Quick housekeeping point, felt I ought to bring it up. If anyone comes to the door, we're not answering. They shouldn't. Only Ade knows I'm here, and he's in Windsor. But if they do –"

He brandished a forkful of bacon at me, I can only assume for effect.

"If they do, we're going to tell them to fuck off. What are we going to tell them?"

"To fuck off."

"That's right. D'you have any ketchup?"

"Sure."

I fetched him the bottle. He took a huge bite of meat, tipped his head back, and squirted the sauce directly into his mouth. He chewed, swallowed, and exhaled.

"That's fucking lovely."

"Good. I'm going out again, Joel, in a minute."

"Christ, you get about. Don't you have to write that column-thing? That's what I'm here to witness."

He squirted in some more ketchup

"Not until Saturday. You can stay for as long as you like."

I went into the bedroom, and gathered my things for my lesson. I have to go, have to honour this final commitment. I got out my chequebook, as usual, to write the cheque for Gareth. As I picked up the pen, I changed my mind. I made the cheque out to Michael and Lillian Bishop, my parents. I wrote in the amount: one thousand, five hundred and fifty pounds. The entire contents of my bank account, give or take a few pence. I put the cheque in an envelope, addressed it, stamped it, and tucked it in my bag. I also added the *Gypsy* songbook, and the hat I stole from the tramp. Tying up loose ends.

"Joel, will you look after the flat for me?"

"Sure thing."

"Cheers."

I arrived at Gareth's a touch early, stopping only to post the cheque to my parents. I wasn't sure what to say to him. I didn't want to sing, that much I knew. I suppose, in a strange way, that I wanted to say goodbye. Not directly, and not in a spirit of sadness or regret. I just wanted one last look, a chance to silently offer my thanks for what pleasure he's given me. And it had been pleasurable, for all its faults. For all his oddness, for all my problems, we've made music. No-one heard it, and no-one ever will. But we tried.

He wasn't in. The final door, shut in my face. Gareth was not there. I called him. No answer. I called him again. Still nothing. I felt tears, choked them back. This was more than tears could mean. I pulled the vocal score of *Gypsy* from my bag, and leant it up against his door for him to find on his return. He'll know what I meant.

And so back along the Archway Road, back to the doorway where I found the homeless man. It was unoccupied. Perhaps he'd moved on, perhaps only feet away. Perhaps he'd died, or found a home, or made a friend. No matter. I pulled the hat out of my bag, and set it down in the place where he'd once sat. I found a scrap of paper and a pencil amongst the handbag-mulch, and scribbled a note: "Sorry." I tucked it under the hat and added, as an afterthought, a five-pound note and my Hello Kitty ruler. Then onto the tube. Only three pounds left on my travelcard. Probably all I'll need.

Last stop, Belsize Park. I emerged from the station, wandered through the quiet streets, past the shops, nice shops, nicer than where I live. Bare trees, the promise of shade, of sun, of pleasure. I strolled onto Eton Avenue, Charlie's home. I didn't know the number of his house. It didn't matter; the whole road was suffused with him, elegance and leisure and well-used education. A boulevard of opulence and civilisation. It was beautiful, and right now, it was my catwalk. I advanced. It was time for one last song, a classic. "On the Street Where You Live", the melodious battle-cry of the hopeful stalker. I sang, to let him know that I was here. That I was here for him, that if he chose to twitch a curtain or cast a glance my way, right now, then I would always be here for him.

My voice rose and twisted, I had to convey the urgency of the situation with the gentlest of melodies, and the only way to do this was through volume. Louder, brighter, faster, until it became a scream, unrecognisable as music. I started to run, I called his name, over and over again until it ripped my throat apart and every breath began to sting. I ran until I stumbled, ran down the centre of the road, stopping traffic, halting pedestrians, giving the citizens of north London an afternoon to remember.

He must be here. He must respond. He must know that he's my last chance at life, that one kind word from him would stop me doing what I'm about to do, what I'm not really sure that I want to do. I kept running, wondering what he was doing inside one of these big red houses. Playing the piano, reading Greek, dandling the redhead on his lap and singing her Art Songs. Whatever it was, it didn't involve me. It never would. He wasn't mine, he was the ultimate false hope. I couldn't expect him to save me. No-one could save me. I became aware of something inside me, a kernel of energy, energy that had only two possible applications. Life, or death. Something paused for a moment; I was suspended, waiting for a decision. It came.

To make oneself die requires more vitality than any other act. It's not a case of surrender; it's a final uprising, a last stand. You have to summon everything within yourself, good and bad, and put the force of your entire life behind you as you fly forward into death. In those moments, you acknowledge and dismiss everything you've ever been. I slowed my pace, walked along the centre of the road, focused, shielded. How do I go about this? It must be instant. I reached the top of Eton Avenue, saw a busy intersection, a fast road, cars, buses. But also, children and old people and drivers and those who must continue living. If I were to step into the road, my death wouldn't be certain, but their distress would be. No. I turned to the left, and saw a building, odd-shaped, concrete and glass. The glass appealed to me. It's fair that I should die by glass, just as she did, a year ago tomorrow. No tomorrow, I can't do tomorrow.

It was a swimming pool. To be fair, a swimming pool complex: a gym, a crèche, a sauna, and the fifteen-metre pool. And a café, one side of which was glass, a window overlooking the pool. Blue and inviting, seemingly far, far beneath. I entered the café. I could see, even from my vantage-point, that it was lovely. Different coffees, an array of cake. I imagined my mother taking me here, me, as a child, after swimming, and us having some cake. I felt tears streaming down my face. I must have been crying. Well, it's sad. From the outside, it's very, very sad. People having tea and cake, and me dying. Well. There you are.

A waitress approached, anxious.

"Can I help you?"

"Yes, I'd like a large cappuccino, please, and some chocolate cake."

"Sure. Have a seat"

She moved away. It had to be now. I took the breath, the long, deep, final breath which I thought I'd never take, and ran. Speed and nerves and lights and flashes, and a blessed, final relief from the memories. Now there was just my voice, high and potent, screaming out a year of pain and a life of wasted hope. Then an impact, and some give, and an inexorable forward momentum as I tumbled into the water, shards of glass raining savagely around as the blue advanced, and receded, and turned to black. As Crowhurst said, It is the Mercy.

14.

3rd December, 2006

I didn't die. Not even nearly. Apparently, it was a five-foot drop; the suicidal equivalent of trying to slit your wrists with the gummy edge of an envelope. What's more, it was safety glass. Of course it was; it was a floor-to-ceiling window in a mother-and-toddler-friendly area. The glass-storm I generated with the impact of my hurtling body was composed not of shards, but of attractive, smooth-edged rounds, such as you might string onto a necklace and sell for two pounds at a craft fair. Certainly, there was an explosion. Safety glass tends to explode rather than shatter, covering up its shameful innocuousness with a dramatic display of translucent chutzpah. So, essentially, I fell five feet through some safety glass into a well-chlorinated pool. Far from being the insufferably noble and courageous end of a life, it was a hilarious mishap, which wouldn't have looked out of place on *You've Been Framed*. Bollocks.

There were repercussions, of course. The waitress who had attempted to serve me suffered mild shock and had to take the rest of the afternoon off. A man's Black Forest gateau was all but ruined. And I lost consciousness, probably because I was so convinced that I would do so. There were some injuries. Mild concussion, a few cuts. Shock, but probably no worse than the waitress suffered. The overwhelming feeling, looking back, is one of mild embarrassment. Even as I was dragged, unseeing, from the pool, I felt a little twinge of ridicule, a sense of someone, somewhere, shaking their head with a wry smile. This was compounded when I realised that, had I died, my last words would have been a demand for chocolate cake and cappuccino, a far cry from Tallulah Bankhead's dying wish for codeine and bourbon.

Still, very little of this knowledge sank in until later. My rescue was baffling, and the hours afterwards, days even, remain cloudy. I came to, halfway out of the water, with a male hand in each of my armpits. One belonged to a lifeguard, undoubtedly, and the other to a civilian, someone familiar, someone whom I knew and was glad to see. I remember plunging and splashing and swearing and dragging, angry farmers heaving a stranded cow from a river. I remember smiling at the familiar face, scowling at the lifeguard. Then back to sleep, back under, halfway to where I wanted to be.

Then the hospital. I woke up again in the hospital. I had a splitting headache, wondered if I'd been drinking, realised that I hadn't. Nurses came in and out, their faces suggesting, I thought, reproach. Or compassion, or pity or, most likely, ambivalence. That was when I started to feel shame; before I knew the facts of my attempt, before embarrassment began to set in, I felt shame. Then, relief. Relief at being alive, a potent sensation, one I remember feeling once before, when I was five, when I got lost in a theme park and had to be taken to the lost property office. I thought then that I'd seen my mother for the last time, and wept bitter tears for the end of my life as I knew it. When my mother reappeared, I had a sensation of a second chance, a new beginning. That was what I felt then, in the hospital bed, with the little curtains pulled around me. Each breath generated a tiny, unthinking burst of pleasure. Like it used to, perhaps, when I sang. A little smile, then sleep.

I woke again, and primal relief gave way to more rational thought. Where was I? Hospital, but where? Was it even hospital? It could be a secure psychiatric unit, or a clinic, or some kind of home. How long had I been here? I began to panic. A nurse came in, checked a little chart at the foot of my bed. I didn't know that they really did that, I thought it was just on telly. Another little smile. I wondered if they'd given me a pill, causing all these little smiles and dozes and thoughts of nothing. I spoke, a bit hoarse.

"Excuse me, where am I?"

She smiled, indulgent.

"Hospital. The Royal Free."

"Oh."

I paused, remembering what traditionally happens in these sorts of conversations.

"Have I had a lucky escape?"

She smiled again, this time on the verge of a chuckle.

"Um… yes. Yes, Judy. You've had a lucky escape. You're going to be fine. Someone will be here to collect you soon. I've got your clothes."

She put my hoodie and tracksuit bottoms on the end of the bed, clean, dry and folded. I must have been here a while.

"How long have I been here?"

"About an hour and a half."

"Oh."

She began to leave.

"You can get dressed if you like."

"Thank you."

I got out of bed. A bit sore, persistent headache, nothing worse than that. I tried to pick up my clothes, and couldn't. My hands were muffled. I looked down, and saw that the fingers of each hand were bandaged tightly together, a little blood seeping round the edges of the white elastic. That made sense. I remembered my posture as I went through the glass. Arms up, in front, each at a forty-five-degree angle. I dressed carefully, and sat back down on the bed. "Someone will be here to collect you soon." Who was coming to collect me? Mum? Dad? They wouldn't have been able to get here yet. Joel? Not a hope. He's in Bethnal Green, uncontactable, stewing in a fug of soft drugs and bacon. Mr Simmons? In Windsor, Joel had said. I wonder why.

What if no-one was coming to get me? What if that had just been a turn of phrase on the nurse's part, and I was going to have to leave on my own, go back to my flat, explain to Joel what had happened, then carry on as if it hadn't? I started to cry, climbed back under the covers, shaking, whatever veneer of calm I'd had dissolving. I'd just tried to kill myself. Not very well, but I'd tried. What if I tried again? I might, I don't know. Now that I'm the sort of person who does these things, who knows what might happen? What if I kill someone else? Another person? What then? More than ever before, I saw my own terrible potential. I realised how young I was, how many years I had left. All the hateful, desperate things I could fill them with, now that there was no more music, no more effort, no more hope. I fell asleep again.

I woke, curled up on my side, to find a hand on my shoulder. I opened my eyes, twisted my head, saw some fingers, and raised my own hand to swat them away. A short, sharp smack to ward off the intruder. I began to drift off again. The hand returned. I wanted to pick it up and bite it, hard, so that it wouldn't come back. I kept my eyes closed, mumbled.

"What?"

The soft, pleasant voice of a middle-aged woman.

"Judy?"

"Hmmph."

"My name's Diana Rogers. You're friends with my son, Charlie."

Charlie's Mum? Why? Perhaps Charlie had died. Perhaps I'd killed Charlie. I opened my eyes. She was pretty, groomed, in pearls and a cosy jumper.

"We're going to take you back to our house for a little while, OK?"

I was in no state to resist.

"OK."

I got up. Stood by the bed. I needed to be taken, carried, looked after. Suddenly I wanted the cake, the cake that I'd ordered before I went through the glass. I saw a trolley standing by, loaded with tea and cups and saucers. I grabbed a few little packets of sugar, held them together, ripped the tops off in one motion, and emptied them into my mouth. Just like Joel had done with the ketchup. That seemed an awfully long time ago.

I followed Charlie's mum through the corridors.

Imagined my own parents walking through those corridors, on the way to see my body. I was suddenly struck by how perverse that would be, how revolting, inappropriate, out of time. My being here, dead, twenty-three. My having chosen to be here.

Who would choose this? I'd chosen this. And now I had the choice to leave, with Diana, in this nice blue car. I wanted to look at myself, and watch myself leaving. I wanted to take a photo; this was a far more seminal and interesting day than the hundreds of birthdays, holidays, outings, and graduations which do get photographed. As Diana started the car I leant out of the window, and glanced at myself in the wing mirror.

The head of a vast, malevolent baby stared back at me, round and smooth and shrimp-pink. I was bald. Some fucker had balded me. There's a huge, huge difference, I now see, between hair and no hair. Even if the hair in question is orange and wounded and tufty, it's far, far better to have it. I looked absolutely terrifying, denuded yet savage. Why had they made me bald? Perhaps they've given me a lobotomy on the sly. Or perhaps it was a shaming device; perhaps this woman wasn't nice, gentle Diana, but some kind of medieval enforcer who was going to put me in the stocks on Hampstead Heath, or make me go back to the leisure centre and clean up all the broken glass with my mouth. I touched my head, laid my hand flat on top of my scalp, and felt the bones of my skull shift as I experimentally moved my jaw.

"Bald."

Diana looked nervously towards me.

"Yes, darling. I'm sorry. They had to. It'll grow back."

Yeah, right. I know what's going to happen. I'll look

like Mr Potato Head for a bit, then it'll blossom into a crew cut, then when it finally starts to grow, it will advance vertically before fastening itself to my head in tight little curls, and I'll spend the next two years looking like David Hasselhoff circa 1985. Marvellous.

"Oh."

Now that the channels of communication had been opened between us, I thought I might as well glean some information from Diana.

"Where are we going?"

"To my house, on Eton Avenue. Just for a little while."

I couldn't help but smile. Charlie still lives with his mother. Hadn't realised that. I felt a little burst of superiority. I may have just thrown myself through a plate-glass window, but Charlie still lives at home. I know who wins.

"How did – when did you –?"

She spoke very slowly, very quietly.

"We saw you running up our road. Charlie noticed you, and was worried, and called the police. Then we followed them to the leisure centre, and... well... went with you to the hospital."

I'm sorry, Charlie called the police? He called the police? Because he was "worried". Worried, my arse. If someone you know is fifteen feet away from you and you're worried about them, you go over and talk. You don't call the police when you're worried, you call the police when you're absolutely shit-scared. Well, at least he didn't get his mummy to do it for him. I felt myself toughening, rising above him. I sat up a little straighter, squared my shoulders. He'd called the police, because he was scared of me. Me, little Judy. I suppressed a chuckle.

"Thank you. That was very kind of you."

"You're welcome. I'm just glad you're OK. Here we are."

She led me into the house, through a beautiful porch. Wellies lined up by the door, coats on hooks, pictures of children and familes and houses in the country. Through to the living room, book-lined, grand piano in the corner. A large television, discreetly covered by a throw. Stacks of music littered the floor by the piano stool, everything from Grade 1 to Rachmaninoff. I imagined five generations of the Rogers family sitting around the piano, applauding each other's talent, singing funny songs, then finishing off the evening with something more reflective and sentimental. "Keep the Home Fires Burning" or some Vera Lynn, perhaps a little Elgar. Then they'd kiss each other goodnight and pad off to their downy beds, tucking the hot-water bottle underneath the goose feathers and looking forward to their next spontaneously cultured day. I wonder if I could build a life like this for my own family, if I ever have one. I doubt it. Someone would spill Vimto in the piano and there'd be a massive fight, then big bald Mummy would come home with a family bucket and we'd all smear each other with chicken skin while we watched *Wife Swap*.

Diana came up behind me with some slippers.

"I thought you might like to wear these."

I realised that my feet were bare and dirty, and the bottoms of my trousers were dusted with the residue of the hospital car park.

"Thank you."

The slippers were lovely, purple velvet with gold piping round the edges. I felt like a maharajah. Diana handed me a cup of tea.

"Thank you."

She sat down in an armchair. I took the sofa. Her manner was calm, still, caring, a housemistress demonstrating the highest standards of pastoral care. She smiled, to show that it was fine that I was bald, that she didn't mind, that I shouldn't worry, that we've all hurled ourselves through one window or another at some point in our lives. I smiled back. Maybe she was going to let me live here. I'd like that. Charlie could be my brother, he could introduce me to all his lovely, posh friends. I could marry one of them, and then he could give me away at the altar. That would be lovely.

"Charlie's just upstairs. He's making a few phone calls. He'll be down in a minute."

"OK."

"I hear that you're a singer."

"I used to be. Or I used to want to be. I was never very good."

"But I heard you've got a lovely voice."

"No."

A pause.

"Do you want to take it up again?"

"No."

"That's a shame. I hope that you do, one day."

"I might."

"How are you feeling?"

"Weird."

"Of course."

A little smile. A sad smile, this time.

"You're going to be fine."

I was tempted to believe her.

• • •

Charlie had done the rounds. He'd called everyone he could, let them know what had happened. It must have been hard, initially; we have no network of friends in common. I have no network of friends, full stop. He'd started with Anna, he said. I asked him what she'd said. He told me that she'd been "deeply practical", and that she sent her love. Of course. I imagine that I'll get back to my flat to find a "Get Well Soon" card and a vat of stew. It would serve her right if I tried to drown myself in it.

Anna had then called my parents, happily taking on the role of ringmaster to the suicide-circus. Delighted, I imagine, to be playing a pivotal yet supporting role in some-one else's drama. She told them – calmly, I imagine – that there'd been an accident, but that I was fine. I was at a friend's house in north London, and they weren't to worry. She gave them the number of Charlie's house.

Soon enough, the phone rang. Diana took it into the next room to answer, speaking in a low tone, for quite a long time. I didn't like that. I was perfectly capable of telling them myself what had happened. "It's quite simple, Mum, I realised that I couldn't live another day – tomorrow being the anniversary of that day that I killed someone. But it's only to be expected, really; I've spent the last thirteen weeks in postures of unwilling submission, variously employing hookers, eating pizza, drinking spirits, and being pounded hard by unsuitable men, one of whom you used to pay to teach my little sister history. I just thought, really, that enough is enough, so I chucked myself through a plate-glass window into a swimming pool. But then you always urged me to be proactive, didn't you? So it's all to the good. And, while I have you, could I borrow some money for Christmas shopping?"

Eventually Diana came in and handed me the phone.

"It's your mother."

"Thank you."

She left, softly closing the door. I didn't want her to go. I took the handset. Deep breath.

"Hello, Mum."

She sounded frightened. Frightened of me? Her own daughter.

"Judy?"

"Hi."

"Are you OK?

"I'm fine. I'm going to be fine."

"OK."

I heard her voice crack and twist. I'd never heard that before. It was horrible. I held the phone momentarily away from my ear, then replaced it.

She spoke again.

"But you're not fine, you're not, you're..."

Sobbing. I was bit cross. I'd said that I was fine. I ought to know.

Why can't she pull herself together? I'm a grown-up, and I'm fine. I just sat there, like a Samaritan at the end of a hotline, listening to her cry. Getting crosser and crosser. She spoke again.

"Your dad would like to speak to you."

"OK."

The sound of the phone being handed over, a whispered word of comfort, then –

"Judy?"

He was so calm, so steady. I could imagine his big, solid hand clasping the phone, other arm around Mum's shoulder, dealing with the family tragedy. Oh, God, I was the family tragedy. My throat tightened. I tried not to cry, and failed, bit by bit.

"Dad?"

"Oh, Judy."

"I'm sorry. I didn't mean it."

I'd said those words to him so many times before, before I was a grown-up, whenever I was trying to make up for doing something nasty. Putting a rat in Clare's shoe, stealing her hairband, killing her puppies.

"I know. We're just glad you're OK."

"I am. I am OK, really."

A silence.

"Would you like us to come and get you, love?"

"Yes, please."

"We're on our way."

• • •

They came. Soon enough, the Volvo pulled up outside, adorably out of place amongst the well-heeled city cars. I said goodbye to Charlie and Diana and climbed into my place, my old place, in the back seat. Next to the dog blanket, and the inexplicable board game, and the donkey's headcollar. I sat quietly, and felt London recede. I didn't know if I'd ever see it again. Was this rescue or was it kidnap? All I knew was that I was being forcibly taken away from adult life, while I was too weak to resist. Too weak, too many thoughts, too much accomplished. I watched the rain drifting down the windows of the car, liquefying the orange light of the city, melting the view until my eyelids grew heavy and I greeted, once again, the restorative dark.

15.

10th December, 2006

It was towards the end of my second week in Suffolk that I became aware of my growing celebrity. Anyone who attempts suicide is, to a degree, the fulcrum around which life must spin. For a while, anyway, and amongst those who care about you. No-one can pass without offering you a hot beverage. The world goes silent when you speak, people believe in the importance of your words, suspect that every audible intake of breath may be the prelude to an outpouring of profundity. People are fearful of you, even those closest to you. You have a secret; you've been to a place which they can't even countenance, and they fear your knowledge. But most of all, they're afraid that you'll try again, that you'll succeed, and that they'll be the one who has to find your grisly husk. So they tiptoe around you, nervously acknowledging the fact that you, for once, are the star of the show.

To be frank, I made the most of the situation. Clare has always been the diva of this particular company, and however dreadful the circumstances, the chance to upstage her was not to be sniffed at. She, apparently, was devastated by the news of my escapade; her first thought was that my guilt at ruining her birthday party had finally tipped me over the edge. She, of course, blamed herself. She said as much to me, the morning after I arrived home. I thought for a minute, then magnanimously forgave her and accepted the offer of a turkey sandwich. She brought me the sandwich. No cranberry sauce, I couldn't help but notice. She got in the car to go and fetch some. By the time she returned, the sandwich had become a little flaccid. She apologised, and made me another one, which I accepted graciously.

I've got a bit of a history of malingering. As a child, I never had flu that didn't mutate into something more sinister, something that required a week and a half of telly and vast quantities of hot Ribena. Every time someone observed an improvement in my condition, I'd stage a coughing fit of the sort traditionally associated with TB wards in the late nineteenth century. That would buy me another day or two at home, at least. And if it didn't, then I'd do something more dramatic, something that couldn't be argued with, like breaking my fingers with a brick when I didn't want to go to a clarinet lesson. I've always gone to great lengths to avoid getting out into the world, inflicting unenviable injuries on my poor little body just so I can stay in, stay sitting, stay safe. Perhaps that's what I was doing at the leisure centre; I didn't really want to die, I just wanted a little holiday, a rest, some positive attention.

And that's what I'm getting. At home, at least. The Bishop family, is pulling together in the face of adversity. Adversity, in this case, being me. We've had lots of dinners, just the four of us, chatting as pleasantly as we've ever been able to. We've been for walks, fed the animals, watched telly.

We go to bed early, and get up at a reasonable hour. None of us are drinking much. There's vague talk of Christmas, of guests, of food. It's nice, the four of us in the house together. I'm woken daily with a cup of tea and a smile, and when I come down to breakfast there are three beaming faces at the table, asking me what I want to do today, beaming harder when I suggest anything at all, my wish is their command. So far, we've been to the indoor boating lake, the otter sanctuary, three cinemas and a farmers' market. I've watched approximately forty hours of television, all in the company of at least one member of my family.

I'd been home almost a week before I realised that this was a little odd. Both of my parents have jobs, and Clare is living, for the most part, in Durham. How convenient, I thought, that my having a little bit of a wobble has coincided with their choosing to take some time off from work. Then I grew unsure; I overheard conversations, Mum asking Clare whether she wanted to go back to Durham to collect her things, Dad on the phone to work, telling them that he needed a few more days off, the three of them, in the next room, talking in a brief and hushed manner about "the situation".

"The situation." What was the situation? A family emergency, I suppose. But a family emergency that could only be solved by drinking tea and taking their twenty-three-year-old daughter to the wildlife sanctuary three times a week. After about ten days, I overheard Dad, on the phone in the hall. The door to the living room was slightly ajar. I'd moved over to close it, when I heard the words, in that infernally hushed tone;

"No, completely bald."

He must have been talking about me. No-one else he

knew was completely bald. Except for Uncle Jack, and that isn't really news. I stepped behind him. Seeing me in the mirror, he brought the phone call to an abrupt and nervous end, and turned to face me.

"Judy."

"Dad, why aren't you and Mum at work? And why is Clare home?"

His tone was measured, cautious, as if he'd been dreading this question.

"Well, darling, we just thought that it would be nice to have the four of us all together, for a change."

"Really, Dad?"

"Well, yes. Just nice, you know. All of us here."

I began to tense up, what I'd said making me realise that other things were wrong.

"You know I'm fine, Dad. You don't need to do this. You can leave me on my own, and I'll be fine. I've just been tired, and I'm having a rest, and it's OK."

"I know, love. I know. You're fine. But you're having a bit of a drama at the moment, and it's best if you're here, away from it all, with us."

What did he mean? Surely any "drama" had been happening inside my own head, so how could I hope to get away from it? What did he mean? It occurred to me that I hadn't seen a newspaper since I got here. Was there something there, something that they didn't want me to see?

"Dad, why haven't we had any newspapers in the house?"

He looked panicked, hunted. I felt a bit guilty.

"Please, Dad. Whatever it is, I can take it."

He stared at me, unsure.

"Please."

"Alright."

He went into the kitchen, took a key from the bundle on his belt, and unlocked the drawer underneath the fruit bowl, the secret drawer where him and Mum used to hide the chocolate when I was going through my pre-school kleptomaniac phase. He took out a decent sheaf of press-cuttings, contained in an elastic band, and put them on the kitchen table.

"We weren't going to show these to you, not for a little while. But if you really want to have a look, then –"

"Yes. I do. Please."

"Alright, well, let's have a cup of tea, and look though them together. And remember, it's tomorrow's chip paper, so don't you worry."

His concern was touching, but I could handle this. I know the press. Newspapers, like it or not, are my field of expertise. I wondered what they'd done, what they'd covered, what, in fact, had happened. I wanted to be alone with the cuttings.

"No, Dad, honestly. I'd like to see them by myself."

"Really?"

"Yes. You go and deal with the animals or something. I'll be out in a bit."

"OK."

He started out of the door. Stopped, turned, paused for a moment, and spoke.

"Judy?"

"Yes, Dad?"

"You know that we all love you very much."

I smiled.

"Yes, Dad."

"And you know that you look alright, you know, without your hair."

I love my Dad.

"Go and feed the animals, you sad old fool. I'm fine."

He left.

I turned to the heap of cuttings. They were arranged chronologically, the oldest on top. So typical of my mother. I imagined all three of them getting up an hour before me, trawling the newspapers, cutting out anything potentially alarming, hiding it, and stuffing the rest of the papers in the incinerator. Them rushing back and arranging themselves at the breakfast table with a smile, some boiled eggs, nothing to worry about. God, it must be bad for them to have gone to all that trouble.

It was. Well, I can see how my family thought it was. The first coverage of my incident was last Thursday. A small factual piece, in my paper, actually: "Judy Bishop, former columnist for the LifeStyle Review section of this newspaper, was yesterday involved in an incident at a north London leisure centre. Police stated that Miss Bishop, 23, suffered minor injuries after falling through a window into the shallow end of the swimming pool area, following an altercation with a waitress. Miss Bishop's contract with the paper was recently terminated, following the restyling of the section to which she contributed. She has since been discharged from hospital and is recuperating at the home of a friend nearby." Nothing wrong with that.

The next day, apparently, a tabloid picked up on it. "JUDY B'S SPLASHY SUICIDE BID." "Chubby pundit Judy Bishop, 23, yesterday flung herself through a sheet of plate glass into a north London swimming pool, in a frantic bid to end her life. The usually uptempo Judy had recently been fired from her highly paid job on a broadsheet after she appeared at the glamorous What Women Think awards looking somewhat worse for wear, having had a cosmetic 'accident' with a bottle of domestic bleach. An onlooker described her as 'deranged and dangerous', and 'clearly on the edge'. Judy was unavailable for comment, but a spokesperson from her old paper described her as 'a much-loved member of the LifeStyle Review family, and we all hope she gets better soon'. The next day, a slew of little articles, news, gossip, sly pokes in the diary columns: "Judy B goes to town", "Nearly a grisly end for unloved singleton", "My Judy B terror in the Angus Steak House". There were photos; my byline picture, shots of me at the awards ceremony and at the Auction of Promises, flame-haired and gurning, shouting, frightened. Holding a glass, always holding a glass.

Within days, the broadsheets had picked up on it. Big, serious articles about the pressures on young women today, and the negative impact of the Media, all citing my "dramatic collapse" as a potent example of failing womanhood. I smiled as I read all this. Silly fuckers. They don't know me, they don't know what happened to me. It should be painful, unbearably painful, reading about myself like this. It should be the most terrible of shocks, having my life held up as a national disaster, a harbinger of doom for an entire gender. But they're all writing about Judy B the columnist. She's not me, and she never was. I can see very well how her breakdown and attempted suicide is a damn fine news story. I, for one, am enjoying reading it. And I, Judy Bishop, am sitting here thinking, "I got away with it." There's nothing, nothing in this coverage that says anything about me. Not really. Nothing about death, or Emma, or music, or singing, or anything that I love or have loved. They got their story, and I don't begrudge them it. Long may their dinner tables resound with the woeful tale of Judy B, the Modern Urban Woman. I won.

There was one rather alarming element, though. About a week after my big crash, just as the comment seemed to be thinning, something else emerged. A news piece, page 6 or 7 of a rival broadsheet. My byline picture, again. "Fire in flat of ex-columnist Judy Bishop." "A fire yesterday swept through a flat in Bethnal Green, believed to be the home of recently sacked columnist Judy Bishop. No-one was in the property at the time of the fire, but the last known occupant is believed to have been entrepreneur Joel Rylance, 29. Mr Rylance recently 'purchased' Miss Bishop for four hundred thousand pounds in an Auction of Promises, in aid of the charity Eco-Heating for the Elderly. He is currently under investigation by the Serious Fraud Squad, following allegations of money laundering surrounding one of his business ventures, a café in Elephant and Castle, south London. He and his business partner, Adrian Simmons, 41, have been remanded in custody. If anyone has any information regarding the property fire please contact etc etc."

Huh. Well, apparently my flat has burnt down. Better deal with that, in the fullness of time. I really should have guessed, about Joel. I hope he's alright. I would happily testify on his behalf in court, possibly wearing a black veil and velveteen elbow-gloves. And I'm not entirely sure that Mr Simmons would thrive in prison. Oh dear. I hadn't wanted that to happen.

I put down the cutting, and sipped my tea. I couldn't help but smile. I'd been exposed, mocked, analysed, humiliated in a series of national newspapers, and yet I felt as if I'd escaped scot-free. They hadn't got me, hadn't understood. My breakdown was still my own, an experience to be held close to me and treasured as time goes by. And now I have a few cuttings for a scrapbook. Not many people can say that. A little memento of my peculiar few weeks, as well as a testament to the idiocy of the press. Did they really, really think that I'd hurled myself through a window because I'd lost my column? Did serious pundits, intelligent women, really imagine that I'd decided to end my life following the early termination of a short-term contract with a mediocre glossy? I thought of them all, all the idiots, and laughed, loud and solitary, genuine and merry.

I put the kettle on, and saw my family creep back in. Their faces were questioning, concerned, braced for tears. I smiled.

"I'm fine. It's all fine."

Clare's bottom lip wobbled.

"But, Judy… they were so mean."

Poor kid. I went over and gave her a hug, affectionate and voluntary.

"It's alright. It could have been worse. And I did make a bit of a tit of myself, didn't I? Falling into a swimming pool, all bald?"

I released her. She sniffed, wiped her nose, and tried a little smile.

"Yeah, you did."

She rubbed my head.

"Baldy."

"Not for long, Scraps, give me three months and it'll be longer than yours. And it won't have as many split ends."

We laughed. A tiny joke, but nice. We were on our way. Dad stepped in.

"Tea, everyone?"

I had a thought.

"In a sec, Dad. I just have to make a call."

I went upstairs to my room, and rummaged through a drawer. I'd lost my phone in the pool, all my numbers, but I remembered writing this one down. Over a year ago, on the back of an old diary, in a spirit of positivity. I found it, went into the hall, and dialled. A few rings, then:

"Hello?"

"Hi, Gareth, it's Judy. Judy Bishop."

We chatted for a bit. He'd been worried, tried to phone me many times, tried to phone my paper, to find out how I was doing. Wanted to thank me for doing his show, to tell me that it made a little profit and that he'd be delighted to give me fifty quid or so for my services. I can believe that. He's a good man. I'm lucky to have known him. A sad man, a worried man, but good. I remembered something that I ought to ask him about, a little reciprocal care.

"How's your granny?"

"Oh, Judy, she – she died. A few days ago."

"I'm so sorry."

"Thank you. I was there when she went, you know. That's why I wasn't there, for your lesson. I'm sorry about that."

"It's fine. And I really am sorry. I know how much you cared about her."

"Thanks."

"When's the funeral going to be?"

"Next week."

A pause.

"Can I come?"

He said yes. I'm going to Wales.

301

16.

17th December, 2006

It was an odd drive, down to Gareth's home town. I met him in Archway, outside his flat. Going back there, even after so little time had elapsed, felt peculiar, nostalgic, like going back to my old college, knowing that I'm now a different person. He met me outside and walked me to his car, three streets away. I find it odd that he has a car. I imagined perhaps a rickety bicycle, or an old pram, or a junk shop sedan chair with no-one to carry it. It was, to be fair, something of a comedy car. A Renault Five, probably built at least three French governments ago, which let out a low growl of resistance every time it was politely asked to change gear.

The radio didn't work, which made things stranger. We talked little on the journey. There was a mutual acceptance that my presence was deeply odd, but somehow necessary. We neither of us really knew what I was doing there, only that it had to be done. Even small talk seemed to peter out after we left London. It was one of the most amiable silences I've ever experienced, almost compassionate in its comfort.

We stopped once, at a large motorway service area near the Severn Bridge. Gareth put petrol in the car, refused to take any money for it, and took me inside to get some food. I had a salad wrap and some fruit juice; Gareth ate one of the most peculiar combinations of food I've ever seen. A lamb chop, black pudding, a gelatinous brick of lasagne, red kidney beans, a slice of pizza, fruit salad, and about three pints of Dr Pepper. It was very much the hunter-gatherer approach to buffet wrangling. He fell upon it like a cheetah. I looked away politely as he smeared lasagne on the lamb chop and then licked it off again. Grief wants what it wants. He clearly has an extraordinary metabolism, to say the least.

We continued, eventually left the motorway and dived deep into the rolling green of Gareth's valleys. As the little Renault sped us further and further from what I know to be civilisation, further from streets and flats and fast food and crowds and concentrated human energy, I began to feel safe. The vitality of the surroundings fed me, in some strange way, and freed me, and I began to feel things that I should have felt a long time ago. Youth, energy, and a potent, overwhelming sorrow for those who've been denied that for ever. If I were to take off all my clothes and run, singing, up that hill, no-one would judge me. Perhaps a farmer would applaud, perhaps I'd catch a cold. But no-one would mind, and few would know. I was happy in that thought, but sensed somehow that I hadn't found a solution, that I couldn't expect to, yet. If I moved to Wales, I'd probably be really miserable. For all the pleasure in the idea of it, I know that within three days I'd be trying to buy kebabs on the internet, and curling up nostalgically alongside wheelie-bins. It isn't, as I say, the answer. But for today, it's a start.

We arrived in a small village. Not too pretty, one

attractive street, then quiet little rows of houses, detached bungalows, two or three little shops. Not a historic community, but a community, nonetheless. Everything seemed slow and leisured, and everyone walked gently in the direction of the church. A lovely old church, far from flashy, but big enough for the community which it served. I pulled on my long black coat, donned the trilby which I'd borrowed from my father, and stepped into the drizzle. I walked into the churchyard with Gareth, and he was immediately accosted by a group of old ladies, cooing and clucking and pinching his cheeks. I realised that he was their little star, that he was the boy from the village who went to London, who went to music college, who's a singer. I felt proud to know him, proud to be here in his company. It's so easy to mock, but what these women believe to be an achievement on his part, is. It really, really is. That they think that he's a star makes him one. I tacitly released him from the task of introducing me, accounting for me, and wandered off to look at the graves.

I had the usual graveyard thoughts – read the inscriptions, clucked sadly at youth, thought of the stories behind the stones, little Welsh lives. I remembered doing the same after Emma's funeral. Her body was taken away to be cremated. I was glad, perversely relieved that I wouldn't have to imagine her decomposition, wouldn't have to lie awake at night thinking of one of the most beautiful, complex, lively, intelligent, cruel women that I could ever know being reduced to a simpler state of matter by the inexorable processes of biology. She'd just go up, she'd burn, she'd twist, she'd crumble, and then that would be that. But still, I looked at the headstones, imagined hers, thought about what shape would best convey her, what words could summon up her spirit and shout her out to passers-by. Nothing, nothing could do it.

I remember, back then, seeing a stone. In the middle of the gravel path leading up to the church, a small smooth stone amongst the hustling gravel, nestled away, doing its own thing, oblivious to the prods and kicks of the units around. I leant over and picked it up, turned it over and over, ran my fingers over it, held it up against my cheek and felt its cold pressure, leaving a violent red mark on my already wind-whipped face. I clutched my stone fiercely, like a child with a toy, and wandered back towards the church, saw the milling post-service clumps of people, already beginning the horrible process of forgetting her. "We have to go on." That's a euphemism if ever there was one. What you mean is that you want to go on, that this is all deeply embarrassing, and, if she has to die, then right now we'd rather she'd never lived. Young people, my age, not really wanting to be wearing black against a grey sky, facing something so huge and violent that it can only be ignored.

I'd walked up to the church, dry-eyed, blank-faced, and found myself standing in front of her parents. I didn't know what to say, what to say in the face of such a terrible, terrible loss. Emma may have been growing into a troubled adult, hurting her contemporaries, hardening, souring, causing as much pain as she did pleasure. But that didn't matter to her mum and dad, and nor should it. She was their little girl, their only child, frozen in a bubble of perfection, which should never, ever be burst. They'd lost their baby, the product of their love, that which should continue, the thing that confirmed them as a couple, as humans. I stood, a foot away, witnessing two people in the face of an unfathomable absence. Her father smiled gently, softly, through his tears, and spoke:

"Hello, Judy."

I couldn't speak. Not for fear that I'd cry, and not because I didn't know what to say. I just couldn't speak. No words, no sounds. I held out my hand, and offered Emma's father the stone. He took it, bemused, and I turned away, walked away. I wonder if he still has that stone, I wonder if he knows that it meant something.

I stood and remembered all this, until Gareth came and stood by my side.

"Shall we go in now?"

"Sure."

He took his place at the front of the church, and I stood at the back. The service began. An introduction, a prayer, a few brief words from the vicar. He was amiable, perhaps a touch dim, clearly well loved by his congregation.

"It is right that advent was the season of her going. It was a sign of magnanimity on her part to withdraw just as we begin to celebrate the coming of Christ, to leave us at the time when we become aware of a sure and certain hope of a resurrection to come. And she knew, she knows, that we'll all be celebrating Christmas. And she'd want that, even though she left because she knew that she was too poorly to have a drink with us all, but she'd never have begrudged us one, is that right?"

A murmur of "right", from the congregation, noises of approval.

"And we're going to sing a hymn, now, an advent hymn, because she loved it. And her grandson, Gareth, is going to sing the first verse on his own, because he's a proper singer. And then we can all join in. Alright?"

That seemed to be the cue to stand. The hymn was one

I vaguely remember, sang a few times at school, the one that begins "Lo, he comes with clouds descending", Couldn't be less appropriate for a funeral. It was the sort of roaring, drunken hymn that has about eighteen notes to each word, apparent key-shifts in the middle of each line, a Victorian religious bravado to which a modern, civilian congregation couldn't hope to do justice. Gareth stood, moved to the centre, in front of the coffin, facing down the aisle, breathed, and sang. His voice was ragged, his pitch imperfect, his knowledge of the lyrics sketchy at best. But he sang, sang bravely and hopefully, for his granny.

As I listened, I felt weak, floored, knocked sideways by the nobility of this man, this voice. He was singing, as he had been asked, and he was doing it with every fibre of his soul, because he was alive. No-one would pay to hear this performance, this performance of a weird hymn in a cold church, but it was magic. I cried, with pleasure and sorrow in equal measure. It was tragic, tragic, that Gareth's granny wasn't here to see him do this for her. It was unbearably, staggeringly sad that she was dead. I don't care if she was old, I don't care if she was ill and wanted to die, the fact that she had to die, the fact that anyone has to die; ever, is cruel and wicked and beastly. We can erect all the civility we want around the fact, we can shroud it in mystery, redeem it through faith, adorn it in poetry. But it's still there, it still hurts, and there are no words. Just loud, racking, cathartic sobs, ripping through my body and joining Gareth in song, the only expression of anything. No words, just noises. Just make a noise.

On cue, the congregation joined in. I blew my nose, breathed, focused, and sang. I sang as I've never sung before, wild and unshackled and real. Fuck London, fuck music

307

college, fuck lessons and professions and rejections and hope and shows. This is me, and my body, saying something.

The hymn ended, and I sat. Shattered. The rest of the service passed. I cried more, sang more, let my body take over, uninhibited in this crowd of Welsh grannies. Soon enough, we were filing out. I saw Gareth, gave him a hug. Congratulated him on his performance. It didn't seem inappropriate. The boy had done well. A lady came over, homely, about fifty. She indicated me, and spoke.

"I thought we must have had one of Gareth's friends down from London. Cracking little voice, that girl."

Gareth spoke.

"You're right about that, if only she knew it."

"She from your music college, then?"

He smiled, glanced at me.

"She will be. Give her time."

I was happy. Tired, confused, but happy. Soon enough, Gareth and I drove back to London. I approached the city not with fear, but with relief. Perhaps that was what I'd been searching for, for the last fifteen weeks. Perhaps it hadn't been in London at all. Perhaps I'd just found it, there in the church with the old ladies, somewhere within me. Who knows.

Gareth and I parted ways near his flat. I was going back to Suffolk.

"Thank you, Gareth."

He smiled.

"You're welcome."

There was something else, something I'd been toying with for a couple of weeks.

"Gareth?"

"Mmm."

"That friend of yours, Jerome. Did he die?"

Gareth nodded.

"So was that what you found, in the music room? Him, dead?"

"Yes."

Another pause.

"Did you think that I was going to die?"

"Yes, Judy. Yes, I did, a bit. But I'm glad you didn't."

We shared a smile.

"So I'll see you soon, Gareth, for a lesson?"

"I – I don't think so. After today's performance I think you're ready for someone better."

"Oh, Gareth!"

"No, really, Judy. Move on. You're good. Get better."

"OK. Goodbye, Gareth."

He turned and walked away into the drizzle. I stood and watched him, striding on, back to the bedsit, back to the hat-stand and Rosa Ponselle and bread-and-butter-pudding in a tin. Twenty-eight going on sixty. I thought again that I've never known such nobility, such courage, to keep on living his life when all sense points in the other direction, to keep on singing and collecting and eating and sleeping and washing and smiling. And trying, in his way, to save another's life when his own must be such a disappointment. I'll miss him.

17.

It was my birthday this week. The 20th of December. Mum and Dad always said that I was their best present ever, until Claire. I know better. I know that I will always be The Child Who Fucked Up Christmas by her premature arrival. And now I pay my penance by never getting any decent presents. Or only ever getting one decent present, one for "birthday and Christmas combined". My arse. They're never that good. Last year, my twenty-third, I got a chemistry set. I'm not kidding. A "University of Cambridge Chemistry Set". It was meant to be a joke present. All I knew was that I'd been saddled with a polystyrene box of graduated beakers and pipettes and litmus paper and crappy little test tubes of copper sulphate and tartaric acid and potassium hexacyanoferrate. I can't remember what Clare got. Probably a three-week holiday in Mustique, or a racehorse.

Actually, this year, I didn't do too badly. Probably one of the ongoing positive repercussions of my suicide attempt. Good presents for six months, at least. Clare gave me some make-up brushes, really nice ones, the perfect gift from one sister to another. I accepted it with pleasure, and gave her a hug. We're on our way, Clare and I. Soon we'll be going on double-dates and chatting about boys and stealing each other's underwear. She thinks that I'm terribly complicated, and I have no desire to disabuse her of this notion. My grandad gave me a large autographed poster of Ethel Merman which he'd bought off eBay. If only he knew. Anna sent me the *Little Book of Calm*. I dunked it in some copper sulphate left over from the chemistry set and chucked it on the fire. It went up beautifully, and I shall tell her as much in my thank-you note.

Mum and Dad gave me a beautiful hat, and the promise to help with a rental deposit on a new flat in London. I thanked them for the present, and for understanding that I need to go back to London, to try again, to remeet old friends and engage with new. Even if I wasn't the Young Urban Madam of the Judy B column, I still deserve another crack at the Big Smoke. If I leave, it should be because I want to, not because I feel that I have to.

I went back to Bethnal Green to look at my old flat. It was, indeed, absolutely trashed. Clothes, furniture, posters, wallpaper. All gone. Just a black, reeking husk. That seemed appropriate, somehow. I felt no sorrow, no regret. My little green duvet cover was still tragically recognisable, a few bits of what I believe to be indestructible kebab meat floated around on the window sill. There was still a discernible dent in the wall, where Ethel Merman's mouth had been. I looked on the floor, under the desk, and saw a cracked photo in a frame. I pulled my sleeve down over my hand and rubbed off the soot. It was me, playing Mama Rose in *Gypsy*. I smiled, stood it up on the desk, took one last look around, and left.

It was Joel that started the fire. He wrote to me before he left the country, thanking me for his visit and the ketchup, and apologising politely for the trouble. No real explanation. I imagine that he just thought he should start a fire, because that's what people do when they're sort of on the run. It turns out that he was the most inept money-launderer in the history of that noble practice. He only got away with it for so long by pretending that he was paying Adrian a salary of £80,000 a year to cook mashed potatoes. Adrian has since been released on bail. Apparently he broke down under questioning and confessed everything, everything, from the time he stole a KitKat from the corner shop when he was seven, to all the spoonfuls of mashed potato he'd pilfered during his period of employ at the café. He sent me a birthday card; he's remarrying Barbara in the spring. To be honest, I probably won't sing at their wedding. I may turn up, get shit-faced, and eat all the crab-cakes, but that's as far as I'll go.

And what about me? Well, right now I'm bald, alone, tumescent with birthday cake, of no fixed abode and no definite plan. But I made it. I made it to my birthday, and there's no reason why I shouldn't make it way beyond that. I've done more, in the last fifteen weeks, than most people could hope to do in a lifetime. I've eaten more, drunk more, I've plumbed the depths of human sexuality and I've sung like a demon while I was at it. Who knows what's left, how many more mountains I can climb and barrels I can scrape before my number's up? I am Judy Bishop, and this is the beginning.

ACKNOWLEDGEMENTS

This was very much a team effort. There are many people who deserve a quick thank you, if not a large drink. First, my agent Caroline Wood, without whose timely intervention I would still be sitting, sans novel, in an Oxford basement vaguely wondering what to do with myself. Thank you for that, and for sticking by me even when I spent the next eight months behaving like a large, drunk toddler.

Aurea, Rebecca, Emily and Vanessa at Short Books, for taking a punt on my manuscript. Sorry I was such a pain about the second draft.

Charlie Covell – the first person ever to meet Judy B – for her friendship, support, and willingness to read draft after draft without complaint.

Sarah Teacher – editor, friend, and one-time platonic bedfellow.

Polly Findlay, Ed Behrens, Laura Power and James Copp, for getting me through the summer of 2006.

Mike Lesslie, superstar.

Sam Kenyon and Sam Brookes – two equally brilliant men – for more kindness, generosity and insight than I had any right to expect of them. Here's to many more at the British Library.

Dominic Mattos, for the gin, the tolerance, the Etons, and the undying spirit of Ethel Merman.

Chris Paling – Judy's Godfather.

Thew Jones – my reason for living.

Laura Corcoran – without whom Thew would be pointless.

Harry Lloyd – my Hungarian editor.

All those who generously read and commented on early drafts: Ben Hall, Sarah MacCormick, Mary Nighy, Hellie Atkinson-Wood, Amanda Hennedy, Harriet Pennington Legh, Anna Stothard, Rachna Suri, Kirsty Mann, Alex Fielding and Olivia Hungerford.

Many thanks all round.